WIDE OPEN

a wide awake novel

SHELLY CRANE

Cover design by Okay Creations
Cover model : Kerrigan Arnold
Photography by : K Keeton Designs
Book Interior by: E.M. Tippetts Book Designs

Printed in the USA

1 2 3 4 5 6 7 8 9 10

Available in paperback, Kindle and eBook formats through Amazon, CreateSpace, Barnes & Noble, Apple, and Kobo.

More information can be found at the author's website:
http://shellycrane.blogspot.com

ISBN-13: 978-1494765590
ISBN-10: 1494765594

The love you fight for is the love that can mend bridges, heal scars, and open closed hearts

- Maya's fortune cookie

> Life moves on, whether we act as cowards or heroes.

Milo

My MOUTH tasted like vomit. That wasn't unusual. The arm creeping over my middle wasn't unusual either, nor the way I felt completely repulsed and sick. I worked so hard drinking, doing any drug I could get my hands on, sleeping with any girl who looked in my direction and didn't slap me for my foul mouth as I told her all the things I wanted to do to her. Slurred, really.

I knew it wouldn't be long until Mason was there to pick me up. The small get-togethers he wouldn't get wind of, but the big ones, he always came and tried to save me. It had been about a month since I'd seen him. He just didn't get it. I didn't want to be saved.

At least, not at first.

I hated him. I hated him with every fiber of my being for what he did to Mom. I couldn't stand to look at him let alone live with the bastard. So I started going out all the time just to get away from him, only seeing Mom during the day when I skipped school and Mason was at work.

But she never remembered me the right way, so it was pointless to keep seeing her. I tortured myself by staying there, and I *wouldn't* feel guilty for leaving. I spent so much time gone that it felt like I didn't live there anyway, so I stopped going home.

Mason texted me so much that I eventually tossed my cell out the window of my friend's car one night. They laughed and laughed, whooping and telling me how free I was. We smoked enough dope to chill for the next day and a half. I never went back to school after that. I never went back home either. Why would I? No one understood me; no one really cared about me. They all just wanted me to "make something of myself".

How can you do that when you don't even know the parts that make you up? The parts that make you *you*? The parts that piece together and make you feel whole? I hadn't felt whole in a really long time. I felt older than I was. I may be a seventeen year old, but inside I felt like I was fifty.

The girl next to me groaned and dug her nails into my side a little. "What time is it?" her raspy voice breathed against my shoulder.

I leaned over the side of the bed and lifted my phone from my pants pocket. My new cell was dead. "Don't know. Does it matter?"

"I have to work tomorrow." She yawned and stretched.

I started to get up, but she grabbed my arm. I winced at the burn on the inside of my elbow. I looked down at it, seeing the bruising from the needles under her fingertips.

"I'm outta here." I shook off her hand.

"Wait. Why so eager to get away?" She rolled over on her stomach, her naked behind peeking out from the sheet, her feet swinging back and forth in the air. "You weren't so eager to leave earlier."

I scoffed. "Passing out and wanting to stay are not the same thing."

"Sometimes they are. Sometimes it just doesn't matter." She watched as I zipped my jeans, commando. "I'll cook you breakfast," she bribed.

I paused. I couldn't even remember the last time I'd eaten. I was so thin that I had to belt my pants to keep them up. I always crashed wherever I was or with a friend, ate whatever came my way, but sometimes it didn't come very often. For all intents and purposes, I was homeless, but had yet to sleep outside.

At her mention of food, my stomach decided to throw a fit. "What do you want for it?"

"Got any blow?"

I reached into my pocket and pulled out the little baggie. "Some."

"Split it with me," she said, biting her lip and sitting to let the sheet fall away. I stared at her chest since she was offering the view. She slithered up to me, unzipping my pants as she pressed her lips to my ear and said, "Come back to bed for a while. We'll hit the blow, and after, I'll make you some eggs."

"Why do you want me to stay?" I asked, not really caring, but wondering why she was offering me more sex and breakfast.

"Because," she pushed my pants down my hips, "my parents will be gone 'til tomorrow morning, and there's nothing better than sex after a hit."

I watched as she took the baggie from me with her fake nails. She leaned forward and kissed my cheek before dipping her pinkie nail in and sniffing the little she took up her nose. She put her finger back in the bag and I took it, rubbing what was left of the powder on my gums.

Normally, I would have bolted, but I didn't have anywhere else to go. The promise of food was almost as satisfying as the sex I was about to have.

She set up the lines and after we did them, one after the other, she pushed me down on the bed and straddled me. I rolled with the drugged ecstasy that crawled slowly through my veins as she groaned and moaned on top of me.

And that was how Mason found me.

The door opened and my head fuzzed over as I turned to look at him. His eyes locked on mine before he turned away, but not before I saw the disgust on his face. I gripped the girl's hips to make her stop, since someone coming into the room wasn't a clear enough cue for her. I pushed her onto the bed and sat up, scooting to the edge.

I stared at his back in the doorframe. "Leave. I don't need you here."

"You do, Milo," he said before turning. He looked and saw all there was left of me. I suddenly felt like I was wide open for him to see it all, for him to see all the rot and gore inside me. He shook his head, his eyes searching my face. "God, help me. You do need me."

I scowled. "No, I—"

"Milo…when's the last time you ate something?" He rubbed his hair. I noticed how good he looked. He looked like he'd gained some weight, the good kind. His arms and torso were bigger, new tattoos peeking out from his shirtsleeves. I realized it had been weeks since I'd seen him.

I stood and yanked on my jeans, spitting my words, hating how good he looked, knowing he was happy with that girl I'd seen before. "None of your fu—"

"Milo!" he scolded, just as a hand crawled around his arm. The girl—his girl—looked around him, the sympathy pouring off her in droves as she looked at me. He touched her arm, his fingers caressing, smoothing. He looked back at me. "Don't use that filthy mouth with Emma here."

She gulped as she looked at me. Her eyes lingered on my stomach before she looked up at my face. She smiled, just barely. "I've got some hot coffee in the car if you like mocha," she offered.

He looked at her again as she came to his side. They barely fit in the doorframe together. He circled her waist with his arm, looking strung out and guilty. It angered me that he felt like he deserved her or anything else that would make him happy. "Trying to lure me out with hot coffee," I mused angrily. "Wow, Mason. Getting the girl to do your dirty work for you."

"Milo," he snapped.

"It's my coffee," she smoothed over, "but you're welcome to it. I haven't drank any yet."

She rubbed his chest and he sighed. He looked at me again, renewed determination in his eyes. "Let us take you to get some food at least. Anything you want."

"No." I searched for my shirt and tugged it on roughly. I realized it was inside-out too late, but left it. I didn't care.

"Come on, Milo. You can still hate me, but do it while you're eating something." I gave him a droll look. "Milo…you look like hell, bro."

"Aw, thanks," I sneered.

"I'm serious," he said quietly. "Please, Milo."

He begged me. He had never begged before, just ordered me around, dragging me back to the house to my room, and then I'd sneak out before he woke up. He'd never tried to feed me before.

"Come with us, Milo," his girl asked. "There's an omelet place five minutes from here that's pretty amazing."

I gritted my teeth. I didn't want his charity. As if she read my mind his girl said, "I'm buying."

She smiled and tilted her head. I sighed, sticking my dirty-socked feet inside my boots without tying them. "Whatever. I eat, then I'm out." I looked over at them and glared. "Don't try to stop me from leaving."

"We won't," she insisted. She rubbed Mason's arm and looked up at him sadly. She looked as if she were about to cry. I had no idea why. It couldn't be for me. I didn't even know this chick.

I led the way from the room. The girl I'd left on the bed yelled something at us. I could tell she was mad, not understanding what was going on, but I kept walking. I was pissed, really, because she had gotten my last hit and I hadn't gotten off before Mason interrupted us.

Mason's car wasn't parked on the street. I looked for it, but Blondie passed me and went to a big truck in the driveway. He got a new truck? How the heck did he have money for that?

I didn't say a word as I climbed into the backseat. She handed me the coffee, and I snatched it from her hands, tossing the lid off, and gulping it down. It burned my tongue and lips, but my fogged brain was past the point of caring or stopping. As I finished it, I watched as she scooted all the way over to press against his side. They whispered things back and forth that I couldn't hear. The drive was short. Blondie had been right about that. We piled into a booth in the back, them on one side and me on the other, and I didn't even pick up the menu.

It pissed me off just smelling the food. My stomach growled so loud and hard that it hurt. I was cold and rubbed my neck. When the waitress came, I ordered a root beer and a western omelet with cheese and hashbrowns. Mason ordered the same and the girl got waffles.

Before an awkward silence could settle in, she started talking.

"I'm Emma, by the way." She smiled. I stared at their intertwined hands on the tabletop. Mason had never had a girlfriend before, really. He wasn't the touchy-feely type either. I was oddly fascinated at the way his thumb ran over her knuckles, over and over.

"Hi, Emma," I spouted sarcastically and let my gaze settle on her face.

She was one of those girls who was gorgeous by design and didn't even have to try. Her eyes, her nose, her cheeks. They all seemed to fit so perfectly. Her lips—they were Mason's favorite thing, other than her legs, which I knew were his absolute favorite. He'd always been a legs man. And she had some nice twigs on her, from what I'd seen. I settled my eyes lower on the barely-there sliver of cleavage that peeked from her top.

It was the first time I'd seen a girl blush in what felt like years. The girls I kept company with didn't blush. They were beyond that point, beyond the level that allowed them to feel embarrassed about sexual things. They'd done it all.

This girl… I shook my head and smirked at Mason. "Not sampled the goods yet, brother? She's mighty skittish."

"Shut your face, Milo," he stood and growled.

I was actually taken aback a little. This was as worked up as I'd ever seen him. And over a girl of all things? Holy crap. He was in love with this chick. I felt my hatred soften a little before snapping it back in place. I rubbed my neck again on that itchy, cold spot.

"Whoa, Nelly," I joked. "Calm the eff down. It was just an observation."

I laughed. It sounded strange even to my ears. It sounded like a sick person's laugh. I glanced at Emma and felt a little bad at the embarrassed way she tucked her hair behind her ears. I squinted. Was there a story there I didn't know?

"I'm Milo," I mocked. "Nice to meet you, princess."

"We've met before, and you know it," she countered easily.

"Yeah," I muttered and rubbed my cold neck. "I remember. You held my hair back as I puked." I laughed condescendingly.

"Basically." She smiled, not falling for my ploys to piss her off. "You're welcome, by the way."

I didn't respond to the beauty queen. I just pointlessly stirred my root beer. She was beautiful to the point of distraction—sweet and annoying all wrapped up in one—and I could tell she had my brother wrapped around her finger, whether she knew it or not.

And it pissed me off. Mason shouldn't be so freaking happy.

And he was, I could tell. He watched her when she wasn't looking. His entire presence shifted when she did. Thankfully, the waitress brought our food, and just as I was taking a bite, I saw the ring on Emma's finger.

"You're getting married?" I heard my gravelly voice ask.

Emma pulled her hands into her lap, as if unsure if I was supposed to know that. Mason lifted his arm around her shoulder and pulled her close, kissing her temple. It shocked the hell out of me how much I wanted to be happy for him.

"Yeah," he said low. "I asked Emma to marry me."

I didn't ask when or how. I didn't care.

"And she said yes," he continued harder.

7

"That's great," I spouted sarcastically with a mouthful of food.

"And Mom's doing fine, too, by the way."

"I didn't ask," I growled and took another bite. I could see I was going to have to get out of here so the food-shoveling kicked up a notch.

"She has a nurse who comes and helps take care of her. I work with her every day on her exercises, but she still can't walk. She and Emma get along great, too. Emma was one of my patients and lost her memory as well."

I jerked my gaze up to the beauty queen. She was watching me with parted lips, her eyes practically begging me to give in to Mason and stop the feud. I wondered if she knew what Mason had done, how Mason had—

Mason leaned forward and glared as he barked, "Don't look at her like that. And yes, I told her all about me. How I'm the devil who destroyed your life and Mamma's. How I killed my best friend." She gripped his arm, tugging on it and pleading with him to stop. "She knows it all."

They stared at each other, and I believed him that they had talked about it. It looked like they had talked about it plenty, in fact, but I could also tell she kissed his boo-boos and made him think that it was all okay.

But it wasn't.

I chugged my root beer and grabbed both pieces of toast, wrapped them in a napkin and stuck them in my pocket, scooting down the bench seat. "I'm out of here."

"Will you just eat, Milo," Mason said in exasperation. "I'm not going to make you come home. Just eat."

"You couldn't *make* me," I spat. I stood and leaned right in his face with my palms on the table. "Always trying to run my life. Good ol' Mason." I saw him flinch slightly at that. He stood, too, licking his lips angrily in an attempt to calm himself. "I hate you so much. You killed our mother."

"Our mother is alive," he replied loudly.

People in the restaurant were now privy to our conversation, but I went even louder. "What she is isn't alive! When she doesn't even remember me?"

"She remembers you," he countered.

"Not in the right way."

"She remembers you in the most important way. In the only way that truly matters."

"What could be worse than her not remembering me as I am?"

"Not remembering you at all," Emma said, barely. She looked up, her eyes dark. "When I woke up from my coma, I didn't remember anyone. Not my parents, or my friends, even the guy I had been dating. I still don't." Mason sighed, as if all of this was exhausting. "It could be worse, Milo. She could not remember you at all."

"Doesn't matter," I steamed ahead, unwilling to let them deter me. "The fact is that you ruined my mom. It's pointless to even go see her because she won't remember I've been there."

"Doesn't matter," he spouted back at me. "Doesn't negate the fact that you should come see her."

"Ooh," I mocked. "Using big words on little high school drop-out Milo. Whatever."

I turned to go, scratching my cold neck and feeling the rawness of my skin begin to set in. He grabbed my arm and before I knew it, I was looking at Mason holding his jaw as he leaned back against the table. Emma fussed over the blood coming from his lip with a napkin. I hadn't even realized I hit him until my hand started to ache. The entire diner was watching us with these looks of disgust on their faces. Well, they were watching me.

I shook out my fingers, wincing but not regretting it. I turned to go once more and heard Mason from behind me. "I love you, bro." That stopped me in my tracks. I didn't turn around. "I love you, and I know you won't ever forgive me. It took *me* a long time to forgive me. I would still hate me if Emma hadn't come along and showed me that I couldn't blame myself forever. It was an accident, nothing but. I not only lost my best friend that day because he wouldn't listen to me and drove anyway, and my mom, the way she was, but I lost you, too. I take care of Mom; I became a physical therapist to take care of her. But you, I don't know what to do for you, Milo. I don't know how to help you. If you ever need anything or want to come home, the door's always wide open. Always. I love you, even if you can't love me back."

I hated the fact that he made me want to turn around, to make-up and forget everything that happened.

I hated him. I hated all he'd done. I hated how he tried to reconcile every time I saw him. And I hated that he was getting this great, perfect little life with a wife and probably kids on day.

I didn't look back again as I weaved through the tables on my way out. He yelled my name and something about giving me some money. I should have taken it, and would have had it been anyone else, but I didn't want his money.

I walked for a long time to a friend's apartment over the Irish Mug bar. Not only would he let me crash, but more than likely he had some smoke he'd front me. After Mason's little haphazard intervention, I needed it. I crossed the street to the bar and heard the honking before seeing the bright lights. I raised my hand and saw the car screeching to a stop right in front of me. The driver cursed and honked. I flipped him off and kept walking across the road. I heard him peel away as I climbed the stairs on the side of the building to my friend's apartment. The bar was hopping; the music was so loud I couldn't even hear my footsteps on the stairs.

I knocked, but knew my friend couldn't hear me, so I tried the handle. When it turned, I pushed it open. He had called me a few times, but I never checked my messages. My phone was basically a drug ferry. I never used it except for making a drug buy or to find a friend to stay with because minutes cost too much for someone who never had money. I had odd jobs sometimes, but after you don't show up on time for a few days in a row, they can you. That was the only way I could buy minutes and buy weed on a regular basis. Usually, I floated until my next paycheck, whenever that may be, and friends would front me things if I didn't have the money.

But I was a little behind right now and owed a few people. Okay, a lot of people, and a lot of money. Even the friend I was going to see had threatened to cut me off if I didn't pay him something. I usually avoided the ones I owed money to.

I'd gotten into the other side of the business a couple times, but didn't sell much of it when I smoked it or snorted it instead. I had my foot broken once for not paying up when they realized the drugs were all gone and it was me who had used them.

I still walked with a little limp because I couldn't go to the hospital without them calling Mason or my mom. My friend put a makeshift cast on me, and I practically dragged the thing for a few weeks.

Nikko's place was dark, and I couldn't hear anything but the noise below us. I turned the corner to find him on the couch, some girl on his lap. I turned around to keep her naked behind out of my sight. I heard him curse.

"Milo! What the hell, man?"

"Sorry, uh…" I peeked back, but it was still too soon and turned back around. "I wanted to see if I could crash here."

"Damn it, Milo…" He kissed her, I heard the smacking, and told her he'd see her later, that he needed to take care of something. She walked by me and gave me a sullen look for ruining her night. I turned to find him pulling a black wife-beater on. "Dude, you can't just come in like that."

"I knocked. The music's too loud." I stuffed my hands into my pockets. "Let me crash, okay?"

"Milo." He shook his head. "You look like a heap of hell, man."

"That's because I haven't had anything all day and my nosey brother wanted to flaunt his hot girlfriend in my face."

He sighed. "There's nothing wrong with getting lit on the weekends and making a living off selling, but you...you're not just having fun anymore. You're hooked. You're hooked, messing with deals you shouldn't, and people are looking for you." He took a step forward and looked at me sadly. "I tried to help you. I knew you had it rough at home, but...you can't stay here, man. Go."

Oh. It wasn't sadness he had for me—it was pity.

"Just for the night," I begged.

"I can't." He gulped and leaned against the kitchen bar. "Mikey's looking for you. And...so is Roz. Go. Now."

The curses piled in my head. I knew I owed Roz money, but for him to start actively looking for me wasn't good for my health.

I needed a place to stay and I needed...something, anything to make me stop shaking and scratching. It felt like ants were in my veins, and Nikko needed to give me something. "Fine," I bit out. "Just...float me a J."

"You already owe me for ten joints, not to mention all the blow and nuggets I fronted you."

He looked around, nervous as all get out. My brain was in a fog. I didn't care if I slept on a bench outside. My friends usually came through for me, but lately they seemed less eager to let me stay. Fine, he could throw me out as long as he gave me something to tide me over.

"I'm good for it. My brother said he'd give me some money until I get back on my feet. I've got a job lined up starting next week," I lied. "It's just been bad lately. I'm under so much stress."

"Classic druggie line," he scoffed. "Get out, Milo. The longer you stay here, the worse you're making it for me." We heard a car door slam outside and he sucked in a breath. "Go, man, now!"

Wide Open

I went to the window and peeked past the dingy blue curtain the previous tenant had left and saw one of the guys who always set up my buys from Roz. I shook my head, backing away, and looked at Nikko to help me. "Go out the back. And don't say I never did anything for you," he growled and went to the front door. "Go!"

I ran, but as soon as I opened the back door, there was another guy there. "You got Roz's money?" he asked.

I stalled and started the typical plea. "Well, I'll have it—"

He didn't wait for anything else. His fist connected to my jaw and I heard the crunch, knowing it would hurt tomorrow, as I went down. He followed me and gripped my collar before slamming my cheek with his free fist. He beat on me for so long and hard all over that I blacked out. I came out of it a couple times, but it was so blurry and the haze of pain was thick. I could never grasp reality.

No time at all passed for me. I closed my eyes and the next time I opened them, I was in a hospital bed. No one was there with me. It was a regular room, not the ER. I lifted my head to survey the damage and immediately regretted that hasty decision. My head hurt so badly, I thought I might black out again. I pushed with my elbows and made myself sit up. I touched my head to find a bandage, my eye was swollen, my lips all busted up, and my jaw was so sore, it hurt to even touch it, let alone try to open my mouth.

I remembered being brought there, the cops, they asked questions… but I was so out of it I didn't get a word out. They said they'd be back.

I had to get out of there.

Right then, that was the only thing that truly mattered. I hadn't rolled over on Roz, that I was pretty sure, but I owed so much money to him and knew all his operations…he was still going to kill me.

I had no idea how long I'd been in the hospital, and the lack of drugs made me way more lucid than the drug-induced stages I usually resided in. There wasn't any morphine in that IV drip. I hurt all over so badly, I thought I might vomit. The fact that they hadn't given me any morphine made me realize that they knew I was a…drug addict. There, okay, yes, if I didn't get drugs every day, I felt like I'd crawl out of my own skin. So, yes, I was addicted. And they knew it because they hadn't given me anything to help with the pain.

And I knew I was in deep.

It hit me how bad things had gotten all at once as I yanked the needle out of my arm. I'd run myself into the ground. It had been way too long since I hadn't had anything in my system and my hands shook as I eased off the bed onto the floor. I tried to yank off the hospital band, but I was too weak. The name on the band read *John Doe*. So they didn't know who I was. I pulled on my jeans from the back under the bed. My body ached so bad all over, but I knew I had to get out of there.

Once all my clothes were on, I peeked out the blinds to see an officer standing by my room. I cursed under my breath. That was probably the only reason Roz hadn't come after me. But the cops wanted me for something, and I could guess it was for me to roll over on Roz. They didn't just guard anybody—only the people they wanted something from.

I pushed the food cart to slam into the bed and then jumped behind the door. When he opened it, like I knew he would, I waited until he came into the room. He cursed and moved forward, bending to look under the bed. I scooted behind him around the door and acted as normal as I could as I walked down the hall. I heard him on his radio as he said that the suspect was missing. Then he argued with them that he'd been by the door the whole time. I turned into the first stairwell I saw and took the steps as quickly as I could. I heard rushed footsteps coming from the lower floor and stopped. I could hear the crackle of a radio, so I jumped through the door with a peeling number four on it.

It led to an alcove in the hall, and I waited for them to go up as they passed. When it was quiet, I opened the door slowly and crept my way down the stairs, out of the hospital, and into the street.

I didn't know where I was going, but I knew I had to get away. It was then that I knew I'd never see Mason or my mother again.

I went to the highway, even though it was almost dark, stuck out my thumb, and waited for someone to stop and take me away—give me a ride to anywhere but there.

> Be mischievous and you will not
> be lonesome.

Two Years Later
Milo

I SAT and looked at the envelope. It had the results of my GED exam. Finally, I was going to have a piece of paper that told me I had finished high school instead of just dropping out and being a runaway.

I flipped it over and over in my fingers. It wasn't like this was an application into Harvard or anything. It was a GED, but it was *my* GED. It was all I had.

"If you don't open that already, I'm going to stab you with my fork."

I glared up at Joey playfully. "Shut it."

Joey had been my friend for a long time now. It felt like forever, but had only been a little shy of two years. Joey worked at the shelter I crawled into a few nights after I left the hospital. I hitchhiked for two days, sometimes with a ride, sometimes walking or sitting on the side of the road. I was starving, so weak I could barely walk, dehydrated except for a bottle of water a trucker gave me. Joey and her father, the pastor, pulled me into the shelter at the church in some town.

Joey was the one who made sure I got a bed in the shelter that night and for the next two months while I tried to straighten myself out. There were many bumps in the road. I still wasn't sure exactly how many days the hospital had kept me, because I hadn't known what day it was when I went in, but the detox had begun then. I struggled with it, but had already gotten through some of the hard part. They made it clear that drugs would not be allowed in the shelter and anyone on drugs after the rules had been explained would be removed.

To be completely honest, I fell hard off that wagon once or twice. I couldn't believe how difficult it was. That first pill or sip or hit after days and days of not having anything was like pure ecstasy, my body betraying me and making me believe it was what I needed and wanted.

But Joey came and got me from wherever I was, yelled and told me how I needed to get straight, snuck me back into the shelter, and made me promise never to do it again. Finally, that promise stuck. It's been more than a year since that wagon had caused any problems for me. After I moved out of the shelter and got a job, with their help, I was clean for the most part, but every now and then it would hit me out of nowhere, and I caved. Then I felt guilty as hell, called Joey, and she'd yell and carry on, come and stay at my apartment that night to make sure I was sober and the high was gone before she went back home.

Yeah, Joey's a girl. And she was my unofficial sponsor. She was also moving away to Houston for a job since she graduated and got her degree and had a position lined up to be a social worker. I'd never done Alcoholics Anonymous or any Narcotics Anonymous or any other anonymous there was. Joey always kept me in line, even as she finished up her schooling and helped her pastor father in his shelter.

She was four years older than me, but a petite little thing who looked like a teenager. She was like a sister who wouldn't stop badgering me.

And I loved the hell out of her for it.

Her hand covered mine on the envelope. She smiled, her blond hair moving on her shoulders as the wind blew through the outdoor café we always met at.

I put my finger under the tape and ripped the top off the envelope. I read the words twice before looking up. She could tell what it said just by my face.

She stood up and jumped, her heels hitting her butt as she squealed and jumped over and over again. I stood, and she wrapped her arms around my neck, so I wrapped mine around her waist. The age difference hadn't ever bothered me. I had a head and a half on her. I'd shot up in the last year a considerable amount. Eating right and sleeping for more than a few hours was probably to thank for that.

She leaned back, her face close as she grinned. "I'm so proud of you."

Joey was beautiful. Really, seriously beautiful. Her blond hair and slim body made her a prime example of what a guy would want in a girl. Add her wit, sharp mind, and a smile that blinded you, and the girl was lethal.

In truth, I even thought I had a crush on her at one point. But it didn't last long, and that was many, many months ago. I realized she was more than a girlfriend to me—she was one of those people put in your path to change your life. She changed mine until it was unrecognizable.

I'd never be able to repay her for that.

But I was a scrawny, pathetic human back then. Now, I'd put on about forty pounds, got haircuts, brushed my teeth on a regular basis, worked out in my apartment every day, and went running almost every other day. It not only kept me healthy and clear-headed, but it kept me busy.

You know, idle hands and all that.

And how true that was. The fight in me between wanting to stay clean and wanting just one more hit was a constant battle that raged more on some days than others.

She pinched my upper arms between her thumb and fingers in several spots and grimaced. "Eew. Stop working out so much. You're going to be a meat-head if you don't cool it."

I laughed and squeezed my arms around her, making her laugh and make dying noises. "Ah! Do you really want the newspaper headline to say: 'Minister's Daughter—Death by Meat-head!'?"

"Depends." I set her feet to the ground and sobered. "Would it get you to stay?"

She laughed. "Come on, Miles." I told her I hated the name Milo, so she started calling me Miles. "Don't make me cry. If there was a job for me here, I'd stay." She smoothed the front of my shirt. "But you're going to be fine."

I sighed. "I wish I could believe that, Joe."

"You will," she said harder. She took my face in her small hands. "You don't need me here to keep you clean. What you need is to call me every day and make sure to remember I'll hurt you if I find out that you cheated. Maybe do what Dad said and join one of those little groups or something."

I sighed. We had this conversation every day since we knew she was leaving. She was worried about me. I knew. I'd never been to a group, and I didn't want to start, but I…was scared, if I was being honest. I was scared the second she was gone I'd fall off that wagon harder than I ever had. And no one would be here to pick me back up.

She bit into her lip. "Miles, please. Please promise me you won't break my heart and light up the second I walk out the door. You know how disappointed I'll be."

I nodded, and I meant it. "You're going to be so great in Houston. I want you to go and not worry about me. You get settled into your new job. I'll be fine."

I gulped. She tilted her head to the side. "Call me anytime, every day. You know you can, right? I can still kick your butt over the phone."

"I know." I chuckled. "I'll call."

"You better. Promise?"

I nodded. "Of course. Thank you for…" I shrugged. I didn't know what else to say. "I love ya, Joe.

She strangled me with her grip. "I love you, Miles. Like a crazy person. I'm really proud of you."

"Thanks."

I watched her climb into her crappy yellow smart car and drive away to pack her things to go down with her parents tomorrow. She had invited me along, but they hired a company to do all the heavy moving. I figured her parents would want her all to themselves, especially since I had invaded their lives two years ago and hadn't stopped being a pain since.

I sat down and looked at the paper that said I could finally look for a real job that would pay better than the garage I worked in. If I wanted to. It was because of Joe I had this sheet of paper.

I gulped as I felt the feeling creep over me, as familiar as breathing. As I looked at the great thing I had accomplished on that table and wished the best for my best friend as she got on with her life…

All I wanted to do was get lit.

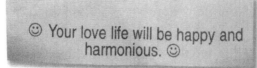

☺ Your love life will be happy and harmonious. ☺

Maya

"You need to stop and go to work."

I turned and playfully glared at my brother who sat on his couch, his grey sweats hanging loosely on his thin body.

"I'll be on time for work, Will." I continued loading the dishes into the sink. "I'm going to bring you some dinner when I'm on my break, okay?"

He shook his head, just barely. "You don't have to."

"I know that. I want to."

My older brother quirked his lips with a half-smile. "Thanks, creep."

I shut the crappy apartment fridge and brought him a bottle of the green health juice I made for him. "Here."

He wrinkled his nose. "What's in it this time?"

"Carrots, flaxseed, and kale."

He handed it back to me. "You first. Take the poison off, sis."

I put on a brave façade, putting it to my lips and sucking the juice from the built-in straw. It was like rotten…something. "Mmmm," I faked and handed it back. "It's so good. Better than donuts."

"You are such a bad liar," he laughed and took a sip. He sighed as he gulped it down. "Not bad," he lied, looking down at the floor. "I'll drink it, I promise."

I knelt down and put my fists on the top of his knees. "It'll make you better," I said and smiled, though I knew he could tell I had very few smiles left in me. "If we do all the things we're supposed to do—eat right, take all your meds—you might not be sick anymore."

He nodded and mimicked my fake smile. His words were spoken so sadly that it was hard to stop the thinly veiled grief from making an appearance. "Yeah. Thanks for doing this. It'll work." He nodded faster. "It'll work."

I leaned toward him and put my arms around his neck. He squeezed me as tight as he could, and it made my heart ache at the way his shoulder bones stuck out, digging into my own. "I love you, creep."

"Creep, I love you so much more," he answered and kissed my forehead. "Now get out of here."

"Fine," I spouted and kissed his cheek. "See you at lunch. No arguing."

He smiled in allowance. "Okay. Fine."

I saw him as he eased back down to lie on the sofa. I locked the door behind me and walked lethargically to my old '89 red Chevy truck. It wasn't really red anymore. More like a rust color, but that had more to do with the actual rust than the paint.

I didn't care. It got me from point A to point B, most of the time. The leather seats were a little cracked in a few spots, but the heater worked like nobody's business.

I pulled into the call center and slung my shoulder bag on as I hurried inside.

"Sorry," I spouted as I opened the door to find Marybeth there, her usual cup of coffee in hand. She drank coffee all day long.

"Don't worry about it, honey," she said, her sympathy jumping from her lips in a tone that told me she was far from being over with playing the I-feel-sorry-for-you card.

"Sorry I was late," I said slowly. "I know you hate that."

"I can't be mad at you for being late with all you have going on," she coddled.

"Marybeth, my brother is dying, not me," I said louder than I had intended. She looked as if I slapped her. I pushed a breath out slowly and looked at her. "I'm sorry. He's just not doing too well. And I don't want to be treated differently just because he's sick." I shook my head, knowing I wasn't explaining myself very well. "It makes me feel worse. Just…yell at me for being late, Okay?"

She cocked her head to the side and nodded once. "Okay. And you, missy, need to learn to let people help you. There is absolutely nothing wrong with me giving you a break every now and then." She placed her hand on my shoulder. "Honey, we need a break sometimes. There's nothing weak about that."

I gulped and nodded, feeling bad for snapping at her. Ever since we found out that my brother's recent sicknesses was actually lung cancer, people had treated me differently. He wasn't a smoker and neither of my parents had been. He never worked construction or around chemicals. No explanation for it. The doctors said sometimes lung cancer could come for no reason at all.

It was just my brother and me. Our parents died—Mom from breast cancer when I was fourteen and my dad two years later from an accident at his construction job. Now, three years later, Will was older than me by almost four years and I was watching him die.

We'd spent every cent of the insurance money my dad left us on Will's medical bills, trips to specialists, and medicines. Even the rent had to be paid from it sometimes because I would have to miss so much work. And now there was nothing left. But it didn't matter anyway because what he had was incurable. That's what they said after it was all said and done. That we were just fighting time, that the end would come soon.

I shook that thought away. I wasn't giving up. There had been a drug trial, an experimental thing, that people were signing up for. The credit cards were maxed out, the bank refused to give me a loan since we used the insurance money to pay for Will's medical bills instead of Dad's house payment. So they took it. I could never have afforded it anyway. But the drug trial didn't work. In the end, we lost the house and Will was still sick. But we kept trying.

I worked at the community center, which paid jack lot of nothing, but I needed to be here. After my mom died, I let teenage rebellion take me over and ruin anything that was left of the good girl my mom had raised. I was so consumed by my grief that I let everything go. I look back at my old self and shake my head. My dad and brother were hurting, too, but had managed to keep it together. They reached out to me, but I pushed them away and let the drugs and my new friends take me away.

I pretended like I was the only one in the world who had ever lost someone they loved, ever had their heart broken and grieved over someone. I wasn't. I felt so bad for being selfish and letting my dad not only have to deal with missing my mom, but worry about me, too.

A solid year of my life was wasted on my rebellion before my father found me one night at a party, threw me over his shoulder, and dared any of the boys I had befriended to try to stop him. I remember thinking how they were cowards for not even trying. He put me in his truck, carried me to the closest rehab facility, which was a town over, and dragged me inside.

I was so angry. I told them I wasn't staying, that they couldn't keep me. As soon as he left, I was out of there, I told him. It was when he got on his hands and knees and begged me, his arms on my knees as I sat in the chair, stunned, that I realized he was crying.

He told me how sad this was making my mother to see, and I spat back that she was dead. He calmly palmed my cheek and said she was still there. She was watching over us, just like she had promised us in that hospital bed before the final sleep claimed her, and that he missed me. He lost us both that day my mom died and there was nothing he could do about Mom, but he could do something for me.

He begged me to stay. He begged me to get better and come home sober. He begged me to not make him go to another funeral of another one of his girls, that he wouldn't survive it.

It broke me wide open.

I sobbed into his shoulder and let him be my father for the first time in months. He held me as long as I needed him to. I said I was sorry, and I promised him I would stay.

And I did.

I was there for two awful, beautiful months. When I came home, I expected to be met with contempt for acting out. My brother embraced me at the door and hugged me so long and hard. I broke down again and clung to them both for forgiving me and taking me back without so much as an angry look.

That year was one of healing for us all. We'd never been closer. It was a great shock to Will and me when we got the call that Dad had been in an accident at work, but I didn't crumble this time no matter how badly it hurt and I wanted to. I stuck to Will like a lifeline and we helped each other through it all. But, as life usually works, Will started feeling bad about a month after Dad died, and when a routine doctor's visit warranted a few tests, they found more than the flu.

"Maya."

I turned my head at the insistent voice. "Yeah?"

"It's a bad one," my coworker whispered and pointed to the phone.

I sighed and looked at the phone, composing myself. As much as I didn't want to be surrounded by my past all day, I needed this job. Not only did it remind me of the girl I used to be, but I was actually pretty good at it. It felt good to feel like I was helping someone who was in the same place I'd been once. I wasn't a doctor or a psychologists; I was just someone who'd been in their shoes.

And when you're scraping the bottom of the barrel for a morsel of any help you can find, sometimes someone who's been at the bottom before is the only one who can reach you.

I picked up the receiver and mustered my most vulnerable voice, letting my guts hang out there for everyone to see. It was the only way to reach them.

"Hi, I'm Maya." I took a deep breath and leaned my head on the back of my chair. "Tell me what's going on with you."

After work, our center was where a lot of the anonymous meetings were held. Every night of the week was a different one. Tonight was Narcotics Anonymous and it was by far my least favorite because that had been one of my drugs of choice. Sure, I'd get drunk with anything you handed me, smoke anything you pushed my way, snort whatever was on the table, but my go-to was the pills. To this day, it was still a toss-up between the bottle and the pill. It wasn't a craving really, it was more like a…nagging knock on the door. It was always there.

I'd only tried cocaine a couple of times. Thank God it never got to the point of addiction for that. Cocaine addicts were a lot harder to break free.

I watched the people file in as I stood with Marybeth. Most of them looked pretty normal. You'd never know they were addicts. They were doctors, delivery boys, managers, florists, and… My eyes caught and held on a boy—man—who stood in the back as he watched everyone sit. When they began, he looked contemplative as he took a seat on the outside. He looked over and his gaze collided with mine. I'd been caught staring, but couldn't find it in me to be embarrassed. I smiled a little and looked up to the front.

The first person went up and introduced himself as Pat, beginning his story. I was more of a facilitator than a participator anymore. It had been a long while since I needed the meetings and a sponsor on a regular basis. I watched Pat for a minute, but saw the guy with the dark hair and muscle-arms get up and try to creep out nonchalantly. And he had a cute little limp, too.

I felt my jaw clench. Hot guy was pulling the chicken-out and I wasn't about to let him get away with it. I eased past all the chairs full of people to intercept him in the back.

And I was going to persuade him that yes, NA sucked, but so did being an addict. And he came there, which meant he needed to be there.

> You're totally gonna blow your
> presentation today.

Milo

As soon as I saw Joey drive away, I pulled out my phone and searched for the nearest meeting. I didn't know if I was just psyching myself out or what, but I wasn't about to throw two years down the drain. I found one the next night at some center. I only had to make it until then to see what all the fuss was about.

I went to my apartment and watched MMA on the DVR while I folded some clothes, anything to keep my mind busy. That afternoon I went to work and actually looked forward to the long night. I worked for a mechanic shop. The owner knew the pastor and took me on, though I had no experience, no real job history, and a record of being a complete tool. Sometimes I worked at night instead of the daytime. It didn't matter when we worked, and most of the time I was just dunking parts into the vat to be cleaned anyway. He was slowly showing me how to do it all.

I couldn't work on anything by myself, but maybe one day. I didn't even know what I wanted to do with the rest of my life.

Wide Open

After that night and the next day of work, I went to the meeting. It was right after work, so that was perfect. I walked, leaving my doors-off Jeep at the shop. It was only about six blocks away and I exercised a lot to keep myself busy. When I got there, I looked at the different people. They were from all walks of life and looked pretty normal. I guess I looked normal, too, though I always thought people could sniff me out as an addict every time I met someone.

There were several coffee pots in the back, and I usually liked a cup at any given time, but tonight, I just wanted to look. I needed to see what these people and I had in common. Why addiction chose us, how this group was supposed to make me feel better and keep me from wanting to go snag a bottle or hit up a dark alley for something stronger.

So I watched. There were several people off to the side who I knew were officiators or moderators or whatever they were called. They talked amongst themselves and let everyone move around them. My eyes found a young girl, someone too young and dark and gorgeous to be in this place—unless she just worked there. Though her eyes stayed on the other woman she was talking to, even I could tell her mind was somewhere else. She looked entirely too vacant, too much a shell of a beautiful girl and not enough of the spunky aliveness I knew girls possessed.

But when an older guy came and touched her arm, her face lit up as she reached around his neck. It was as if her heart was waiting for any reason to be happy so it could shine. She seemed so genuinely joyful as she watched him walk to his seat. And then the light oozed out of her like spilled paint—a slow progression back into her introverted self that just existed. I'd never felt like I'd met anyone who understood me, who felt like I felt…but this girl, without even realizing it, had showed me exactly what I must seem like. I was constantly grabbing on to moments that would make me feel something other than emptiness and guilt. And as soon as it left, I was back to wondering how I was going to make it through the day.

They all started to sit in the plain white chairs in the plain white room, in rows with no podium or stage in front. All equal and on the same level. It made me uneasy for some reason. I felt anxious about this. How was listening to people tell me how much they wanted to take a pill going to make me want to even less than I did already?

But it wasn't what I expected at all. It was way worse.

When the guy started talking, I made my way to a chair on the edge so I could escape quickly. The trapped-rabbit feeling got worse with every second I stayed. I swung my gaze over to the beauty and was happily stunned to find her eyes already on me. She smiled a little and then refocused on the guy up front. I did, too. I felt like I was about to get in trouble for not paying attention in class.

I expected the man to start telling us about his daily life and how he handled it. When that man started in on how he had ruined his life, how he had pushed away his family and severed all ties because he thought he had been validated in his anger—he let one bad thing in his life control and ruin him—it hit way too close to home.

Joey had been my sponsor for all intents and purposes, and I wasn't ashamed of that. I'd gotten over the awkwardness of being an addict. It was a part of me, it always would be a part of me, and she had helped me through that. But I'd never had to sit in a room full of people and listen to them mirror their stories with mine about how they'd screwed things up so badly they didn't know if they could ever fix them.

There wasn't a day that went by that my heart didn't question every move, every decision, every puzzle piece put in place by my actions. And every day since Mamma had sent that note to my friend's house, knowing I'd eventually make my way there and receive it—the note that told me that Mason was getting married at the church in town on New Year's. I hated him, but needed to see it. I needed to see him marry her… because he was still my brother. Back then I hadn't understood it, but now I did. I had hated and loved my brother. I hated that he was happy back then, but now, it gave me hope that I could one day be happy, too.

I slipped from my chair and wondered how the hell I was going to do this. I couldn't come back here every week if they were going to have a rehash session every time.

I could feel the beauty's dark eyes on me as I made my way down the side aisle. I couldn't help but look over and get my final look of the girl I'd caught staring at me before walking out of this place and never coming back, but when I turned, she was gone.

I felt her loss like a shot through my skull.

I actually *felt something*. That hadn't happened with anything or anyone in years. Joey didn't count—this was something I hadn't felt since I was a teenager enthralled with the new girl at school. My eyes searched the room for her and came up empty. I sighed and swallowed hard; my revelation, a fresh wound that ached in both bad and good ways.

I turned and had to reach out and grip the upper arms of the girl, who had been entirely too close for proper etiquette, to keep her from falling.

The beauty.

When her mouth opened, her voice skated over my skin, making every vein and muscle perk up to attention.

"Hey, it's barely even started and you're leaving? You're new, right?" she asked, though I could tell she knew the answer already.

"I was leaving," I answered truthfully, "but honestly, I think…I've found a reason to stay." My tone and the way my eyes bore into hers left nothing to the imagination. I was absolutely flirting with her. It shocked the hell out of me that I got so much enjoyment out of it. And I enjoyed the blush that crept into her cheeks very much.

She smiled a little in allowance. "I would think you would have a better reason to stay."

I felt my lips lift. "Mmm, right now? I don't think so."

She barely licked her lip and then looked behind me. "There's an empty chair right here in the back. We call this the **safe zone**. For the commitment-phobes."

I laughed. "I think I probably qualify. And…where are you sitting?" I asked, but we both knew I knew.

She smiled and tucked her hair behind her ear. "I stand in the back. I think I'm more of a commitment-phobe than you. Besides, I've done my stint in NA already. Now I'm just here for…moral support. And to keep the phobes from escaping."

She giggled at her own joke. It was the cutest thing I'd ever seen.

My mouth said, "Want to compare phobes…over dinner tonight?" I gritted my teeth at myself. I hadn't even been at NA for five minutes and I was already asking a girl out.

Her breath released slowly. "Addicts aren't really supposed to date other addicts. Besides, are you supposed to be dating right now?" she asked.

People in AA or NA or anything else weren't supposed to date for years or something. But I wasn't really in NA, or was I? I was just hoping I could keep myself out of trouble without Joey here.

"Whoa, who said anything about a date?" I teased.

Her lips parted and she backtracked. "Uh…I thought—"

"Is that a no, then?" I grinned along with my teasing.

"So you're not officially in the program? How many days are on your coin?"

"Don't have a chip or coin or badge or any of that other stuff. I…" I smiled and felt kind of guilty for some reason. "I've never gone to meetings."

"No meetings. No coins." She took a deep breath. "You can still answer my question of how many days sober, can't you?"

"I could," I ventured and smiled. She stared at my mouth for a few long seconds before looking back up to my eyes.

"You are a compulsive question avoider, aren't you?" Again she hit the nail on the head. She smiled to ease the sting.

"Guilty as charged."

"Would saying no flat-out help or hurt your ego with the fact that you're not supposed to be dating yet anyway?"

It was as if she knew I was hiding this big, bad secret inside and wanted to take it easy on me, but still call me on my crap.

"Not really. You see, I'm just here because I promised my friend I'd come."

She nodded, her lips sucking into her mouth in between her teeth. "Who?"

"Who what?"

"Who did you promise you'd come?" She crossed her arms over her chest and tilted her head, waiting for my answer.

"A friend. She left for a job in Texas. She was my…"

"Girlfriend," she supplied, and no matter how much she tried, she couldn't stop the disappointment from seeping into her words and her face.

Good night, the little insightful, raven-haired minx was going to slay me where I stood. "No. My sponsor, of sorts. She took care of me herself. Her dad's a preacher and they watched out for me. Besides, I asked you out. I wouldn't have done that if I had a girlfriend."

"I guess not," she said. She looked infinitely sad all of a sudden. I went to speak, but she beat me to it, leaning back against the wall. "I wouldn't be a very good date even if you were supposed to be dating." She was not going to let that go, huh? Must be a strict thing around here. "I'm…" She pulled a coin from her pocket. She held it up sadly and smiled. "Mine is a three year coin. And counting." One side of her mouth lifted as she looked at it, almost lovingly. Maybe it was full-blown love for that coin, I didn't know. "You're not supposed to date for at least one year, some say two, but I've had a million and one things going on at once." She finally looked at me again. "Boys were never one of them."

I saw it, the barely-there spark that was left in her. She thought she was used up; she thought she had nothing left to give. It broke that vessel in my chest right there in the back of the NA meeting. I knew then I wanted more than just some flirting. And the tactics were going to have to change. Flirting came back so easily for some reason, but that wasn't what this girl needed. She needed someone to show her that whatever we were before wasn't who we had to be. Whatever sins of our past could stay there and not follow us into the rest of our lives.

But that somebody wasn't me.

I couldn't be somebody's light. I barely lit my own way on most days. So I looked around before looking back at her. She had a knowing smile on her face—her gorgeous little face that pleaded with me to save her and make her whole. "Well, I guess I'll see you around."

She nodded and put her coin back into her pocket. She smiled and turned to grab a pamphlet off the wall.

"My number's on the bottom." I raised a brow at that, my grin slightly returning. Her neck turned pink and she chuckled under her breath. "I mean, the hotline's number. I work here at the center. If you ever need to talk to someone or know someone who needs to talk, the number is on the bottom."

"And you would answer the phone?"

"Sometimes. There are several of us. I'm here almost every day." She pursed her lips a little at that admission. "Anyway. Good luck…uh?"

"Milo. Miles. Whatever."

"Milo." She picked the name as if she was claiming that as the name she'd call me. "Maya."

She put her hand out and I took it, pumping it gently. "It was nice to meet you, Maya."

"Same, Milo. I hope to see you again. Here, at the center for a meeting," she hurriedly corrected.

"Maybe." I started to leave, but stopped and looked over at her. "And if I had one of those chips, it would say one year, ten months, and twenty-one days on it. Not quite two years, but it's longer than I thought I'd ever get," I mused. That just didn't seem real. If she could only have seen me back then.

"That's amazing," she said in surprise.

I smirked. "What?"

"Nothing. I assumed you were a newbie, one of those one-weekers or something. Most people who don't come to meetings have a really hard time staying clean."

"Never said it wasn't hard."

"But," she continued as if I hadn't interrupted, "that's what I get for assuming, right?"

"No, tell me what you get."

She laughed, which had been my intention. Man, she sounded angelic like that. "I'll let you figure it out."

"Maybe I will, next week."

I was being stupid. I should never come back here. This girl was going to get me into a different kind of trouble that I wasn't sure I was ready for. But I needed to come…well, I kind of promised Joe I would.

"I'll be here," she said easily, shrugging one shoulder, and smiling before moving past me to stand at the back of the group. That thought made me feel somewhat easier about this whole group thing.

I walked past the body shop to my apartment. I liked walking and running. It not only kept me in shape and busy, but it kept my limp from being so noticeable. It never bothered me too much. And when I ran, I didn't notice it at all, but when I walked, especially at the end of the day, you could tell sometimes.

My apartment was the next block over from the shop, above a little Chinese restaurant that made their own fortune cookies. It actually wasn't a bad place to live, smelling cookies baking all day. My apartment was small, and the dark brick walls made it seem even smaller. It was a studio apartment, so the bedroom and living room had no real walls to separate them. I didn't have much.

But it was mine. I paid the rent, the lights, bought my own food. The fact that I paid those bills with the new last name I had to change to Sawyer to make sure that nobody ever came looking for me didn't matter.

I took a quick, hot shower and then laid on the couch and watched hot rod rebuild shows as I ate a sandwich. I texted Joey and told her I went to a meeting. She told me she got settled into her new place and started the new job on Monday.

This was my life and I wouldn't wish this nonexistent life on anyone.

But I thanked God for that nonexistence every...

Single.

Day.

> You will prosper aqueously.

Maya

I STARED at the coin that displayed for all to see that the user had made it two years without a drink or smoke or pill. I slipped it into my purse for safekeeping. I didn't know if that guy was going to come back, but if he did, I'd have a coin for him in a few weeks when he reached his two year mark. To the day.

It had been three days and I still found my mind drifting to him sometimes. He was so different from other guys. Getting clean without doing meetings was pretty impressive. Or dumb, depending on how you looked at it.

Probably a little of both.

But I knew one thing he was for certain, brave. And scarred. That's two things, but generally I've come to realize those things come hand-in-hand. My cell rang and I glanced over at it to see HOME displayed on the screen. My heart beat so hard as I grabbed it quickly and said a prayer in my head as my mouth said, "Will?"

"It's okay. Geez, you know I can call just to call and it doesn't mean I'm about to keel over."

He was irritated. I rolled my eyes. It wasn't my fault I panicked every time he called. "What's up?"

"Will you bring home some dinner? Real dinner. I'm not eating veggies and green juice tonight." I pressed my lips together. "Sis," he prompted.

"I guess one night won't kill you." I slapped my hand over my mouth in horror, my eyes stinging. "I'm sorry. I didn't mean—"

He chuckled. "Dang. For once I thought you were being funny."

"It's *not* funny, Will," I hissed.

"Sometimes, Maya…all you have left is funny. It's okay, all right? Just bring something home, please. We'll go back to blender-veggies tomorrow. Promise."

"Fine." I wiped the stray tear that escaped. "I'll be home in a couple hours."

"Last week's *Walking Dead* episode is on the DVR. Zombies make everything better."

I shook my head and groaned out a laugh. "You're such a pain in my butt."

"I believe that's the definition of 'sibling'. Not shirking my duties. Nuh-uh."

I laughed a little harder, hating that laugh and loving it, too. I didn't laugh much anymore. It felt wrong and foreign. "See you in a bit."

"Hurry up, creep."

I took a breath before getting back to work and before I knew it, the clock said it was time to go. My poor truck sputtered and kicked as I lurched from the parking lot. It needed several things, but a battery was one. I had to get it jumped off several times the past few months. It also needed a new alternator, and the speedometer had stopped working more than a year ago, so I never knew how fast I was going, but it didn't matter. I loved my truck. I just wish I had the money to fix it.

I pulled into the lot and pushed the door open, the ringing of the bell above the door signaling my entry. The small old lady behind the counter's broken English was pretty darn adorable as she smiled at me. I told her my order of one beef and broccoli and a General Tso's chicken. And I always got some of the fortune cookies. They were the best there was. They were more like dessert than a little stale cookie with a fortune in it. These cookies made me want to believe whatever was inside it.

"Should've gotten the egg foo young," I heard over my shoulder. I turned my head and almost bumped faces with the guy as he leaned down. He chuckled and stepped back. "The foo is the best."

"Never had it," I confessed and turned fully to find a grimy, dirty mess of a man with Milo's face underneath. I found myself biting into my lip.

He smiled, but realized he was still in his work clothes. He chuckled with embarrassment and rubbed his hair. "Yeah. I have one of those dirty jobs. Sorry. I was just grabbing dinner before going upstairs."

"No, it's fine. You should be proud of it," I told him and felt my smile stretch. I remembered my dad coming home so dirty, from other work obviously, but still dirty and still proudly displaying a day's work.

"Where did you go?" he asked and looked at my face closely as I daydreamed. I cleared my throat and half-smiled. He smiled back and shrugged. "You looked like you went somewhere you wanted to be."

"My dad, he…" Just saying his name made me want to cry. So much for being over it. "He always came home dirty, too. He worked construction."

He pressed his lips together in sympathy. "Sorry."

"No, it's okay. Like I said, it was a different kind of dirty." I looked him over and felt my breaths come in and out at how different it really was. His arms had spots of black grease on them, but it didn't cover up the fact that his arms were huge. That wasn't uncommon, actually.

Addicts usually found ways to keep busy, exercise being one of them… I was analyzing him. I had fallen way down if my gawking of this hot-guy turned into analyzing him like a freaking desperate caller.

I looked up to find him watching me look him over. He had this smirk on his face that showed me my gawking had been more than a couple acceptable seconds. I licked my lips and smiled coyly. "Um, your um…" I pointed at his arm. "You obviously work out. That's good. It's a good tool for recovering addicts."

He laughed under his breath, the movement shaking his chest. "Uh, thanks."

"And," I continued stupidly, "you're eating out before going home, which is good, too. It's less temptation when you're not out in the party and club nightlife of the city."

"So, do you usually bring your work home with you or do you interrogate everyone? Is this not special treatment?"

My blush burned up my neck. "Sorry. It's habit."

"It's fine. I'll totally take those suggestions under advisement." He grinned.

I realized then that he hadn't looked away from me yet. Not once. He was so attentive—even seemed…enthralled. "It's ready, miss." I looked over to see the woman placing my bag on the counter. She looked up and smiled big. "Milo, the usual is coming, yes." She looked between us. "You want a cookie? You could share, split it with pretty girl?"

He laughed at her obvious attempt at matchmaking. "Oh, thanks, Mrs. Ming, and I'll definitely take you up on it another day." He looked back at me and smiled cockily. "But I was told I'm not allowed to share a cookie with this pretty girl for forty-four more days. Two years, isn't that right, Maya?"

"It's more of a guideline," I started, but stopped. There was no point. I smiled and shook my head. I walked and took the bag from the counter before turning back to him. "I'll see you on Friday?"

"Never saw you as a rule breaker," he mused, mocking me.

"For the meeting, beefy." I laughed. "For the meeting."

He seemed to be mulling it over with a grin, or stalling, either way. "I'll be there, gorgeous."

My heartbeats physically skipped a little at that. I smiled as best as I could and made my way to my truck. He watched me from inside and I prayed it would crank. It did, but barely. It was the first time in a long time I was embarrassed about my crappy truck as I sputtered from the lot to our apartment.

On Friday, I was cornered by the only true rascal in the bunch. Most of the people there truly wanted to get better and stay that way. This guy, however, thought the sympathy card was a free ticket to every girl's underpants. He never got aggressive; it was just beyond creepy. He put his hand on the wall by my head and I sighed before weaseling my way out of the cage he'd made. "Just listen. I know the guy. He'll give us a great deal on a two-for-one lobster dinner. What do you say? You and me."

"Perry, I've told you several times that I'm not interested."

"Yeah, but you don't even pretend and use the old we-can't-date-our-patients line that they all use, which makes me think you're just playing hard to get." And cue creepy smile.

"No, I'm not going to lie to you. I think you need to find someone that the feelings are on both sides. And stop offering cheap lobster as a bargaining chip. You're just hurting yourself with that one, Perry"

I walked away and he yelled across the tiled room just as I saw Milo come through the doors. "Keep playing hard to get, sweetheart. One of these days we'll share a lobster!"

I pressed my lips together and shook my head. Milo's brow arched as he made his way to me. "Has your heart been stolen since the last time I saw you?"

I laughed and tapped his arm with my fist. "Shut up. Don't get him started."

"So…" He looked down at me sideways.

"So, beefy." He smiled at my nickname. "I think this is where we drum on about our boring lives. How was your week?"

"Oh, just fine," he played along. "I work at Tom's Garage. He's slowly teaching me the biz. Learning a lot there. How was your week?"

"Oh, just fine," I copied mockingly. "I didn't have to talk anyone from the ledge, proverbial or physical, so that's a plus."

He leaned back against the table where the coffee was set up and crossed his arms. "So you answer the phones and talk to people who call in with problems?"

"Not just any problem. We're an addiction counseling center. We're supposed to only deal with people who are calling in about their addiction and either in denial about it or wanting to come to meetings, but we get other stuff sometimes. Technically, we're supposed to field those callers somewhere else, but when a woman calls and says her husband hits her and she doesn't know what to do about it, it's hard to tell her to go call someone else instead of saying that she needs to leave that scumbag. Mostly, I tell people that though getting help is hard, it's worth it. And that old saying about how you can't go home again is crap. More often than not, their families welcome them with open arms when it's clear they're trying to do better."

He nodded. "You're braver than I am. I wouldn't know what to tell those people. I don't even have my own problems taken care of."

"You'd be surprised how easy the answer comes when you've been through it." His gaze jerked to mine and I shook my head. "No, no, no.

We are not getting into that."

"Fair," he stated. "It's a bad omen to spill your guts and bad deeds before the first date anyway." I felt my lips part. He smiled and moved a little closer, putting the knuckle of his finger under my chin to close my mouth gently. "You didn't think I was giving up, did you?"

I could smell him and I inhaled subconsciously to breathe in more of him. My words sounded more like breaths. "I don't know what I'm thinking. I've never had someone ask me out twice before. Other than creepy Perry."

His smile was slow. "Are you going to make me ask a third time?"

"You think it's a good idea…for two people with addiction in their pasts to get together?"

"Is that you or the pamphlet talking?"

I couldn't help but giggle a little at that. "Mostly the pamphlet," I confessed. "I haven't had an issue in a really long time. I'm positive I won't have a relapse anytime soon, but positive people fall off the wagon every day."

"The thought of dating me makes you want to fall off a wagon?" He quirked a wry brow.

"No." I pushed my hair behind my ear. "You're going to be one of those persistent guys, aren't you?"

He moved close again. "Why? You don't like being chased?"

I swallowed, stalling. "I've never been chased before."

"Well, Maya," he started and seemed surprised about my comment, "I'm about to remedy that."

"Okay," I breathed and then bit into my lip, closing my eyes at the fact that I just said that. "Milo?"

I opened my eyes to find him looking thoroughly pleased. "Yeah?"

"What exactly does that mean?"

He shook his head. "You'll have to wait and see." He leaned back and looked at the group before looking back to me. "I've got some things to do at the garage, so I'll see you next week."

I nodded, knowing he was shirking his addict duties, but suddenly didn't mind. "Bye."

He backed away, his adorable limp barely noticeable, smiling. "Goodbye, Maya."

After catching my breath and thinking on that for a few needed minutes, I focused on the group again and tried to forget the guy with hazel eyes who decided I was worth chasing.

The week passed in blinks of time that flew by faster than they had in a long time. Will seemed to be doing well this week, so I didn't feel so guilty that my mind wasn't constantly on him as it usually was.

When Thursday came around, I wasted no time with Milo, hoping to get him to see what the meetings were all about and stop cutting them off before they could really begin.

"Where are we sitting today?"

He smiled. "Oh, *we're* sitting?"

"I figured we may as well." I turned to him and had to look up to see his face. He seemed taller. "You see, it's cheating if you stand in the back or sit in the back row. Like I said, they're afraid to commit, so I figured we could sit today. I haven't committed in a long time. Can't hurt."

He seemed to be thinking about it. Like actually thinking, not goading me.

"So let's commit," he finally said and smiled, but it was different. I wondered what had happened to cause the change.

When we sat down in the middle aisle seats, he put one ankle over his knee and fidgeted as they got the meeting started. He followed the guy who made his way up front with his eyes the whole way. It came to me. I'd forgotten that he'd never been to a meeting. I didn't even know his story. I was being an awful counselor. I leaned over and put my hand on his arm to steady myself. His face was so close when he turned to look at me. "I'm sorry. We can stand in the back. It's not a problem. I was just joking anyway, for the most part. We can take it slow."

"Nah," he waved it away, but gulped. "This is how we're supposed to do it, right?"

"Okay," I said, but didn't feel right. He looked a little green.

We listened. The guy started his story with him dropping out of high school, him losing all his friends because no one wanted to be around a mooch, his dad getting so angry with him that he'd call the cops on him when he showed up because he stole things to sell. When the guy started to tell us about his brother and how they hadn't spoken in years, Milo cursed and got up, practically sprinting to the exit.

I followed him, gripping his arm before he could make it out of the foyer. We were out of the meeting room. No one could see us unless they came looking. He stopped in his tracks, not turning to face me, his muscles so taut my fingers felt like they were gripping stone.

"Milo," was all I could say.

"I can do this on my own." He turned slowly, his face tight and angry, but I could tell it wasn't with me. "I've done it without the meetings for almost two years. I don't need this. I don't want to listen to someone complain about their life. That's not what I signed up for."

"What did you sign up for?" I asked softly. Before I knew what I was doing, I felt my fingers in his. Gosh, he was so warm. He softened a little, swallowing as he searched my face for something.

"You don't want to know me, Maya. You don't want to be put into my world. It's not pretty. It's not some fairy tale that I can give you or anyone." He looked sad as he pulled his hand away. "I can't do this. I can't come and listen to them and know that I'll never be able to make amends like they can."

"But you can," I insisted. "I know for a fact that it's never too late."

He laughed sadly, without a trace of humor or malice, and spoke softly, "Maya...you don't know what you're talking about."

He spun around, gripping and rubbing his hair as he pushed through the doors and down the stairs in the parking lot.

It was my job to know what I was talking about, to help people when they needed someone to help them sort through things. I hadn't thought of Milo as one of those people. He obviously had issues about some things—I assumed his family. I knew it was a touchy subject, clearly, but there had to be a way to break him out of his own head and show him that generally, people were forgiving.

He just had to give them the chance to.

> Don't worry about the world coming to an
> end. It's already tomorrow in Australia.

Milo

I FELT awful the next day. Of course I hadn't said it in anger, but the fact that I walked out on her like that made me feel like crap. And all I wanted to do was get high on something. Anything.

It had been two years since I'd seen my family. I'd felt guilty about that because I knew Mason looked for me. At first, I didn't want to see him at all. As the anger ebbed away, I wanted to see my mother, but knew that going back would only bring them trouble if Roz was looking for me.

Would he still be? After all this time?

It wasn't that much money that I owed him to begin with…I couldn't even really remember. But the fact that the cops knew I had info and wanted me to give it up—Roz would want me dead for that alone.

Maybe I could sneak back for a quick visit, see Mom, and then come back on the sly. I needed to try to get some closure on this. If a guy just talking about his family gets me so worked up, then I needed to face this head-on and figure out what I needed to do.

There was still this part of me that wanted to be mad at Mason. Even though I know it wasn't his fault and I'd done some stupid things in my time that I was sorry for, he was still the cause of all the things that happened to me in some way.

Wasn't he?

I didn't even know anymore.

So I decided to go with my gut. I bought the things I needed before asking my boss if I could borrow some tools and for a few days off. I took my Jeep over to the center and spent a couple hours in the parking lot, doing what needed to be done as much as I could tell. Then I left a note and went home to get some clothes in a bag for the trip.

I couldn't believe how this trip had come out of nowhere, out of seemingly nothing. I never imagined I would go back, not just because of Roz, but because…I never thought I'd want to.

As I drove through the mountains, loving the cool air that swamped in from the open doors, I thought about what that guy had said last night. He had been selfish and stupid, thought that whatever he was mad at his family for was validation for acting out and taking one more hit of whatever he could get his hands on.

When he talked about how his older brother tried to save him all the time, and it made him hate him even more…

I didn't know how I was going to feel about Mason. I guessed I would see how I felt when I saw him. More than anything, I needed to see Mamma. And then an awful thought hit me. What if something had happened to her and they couldn't find me to tell me?

I violently pushed that thought away and turned the radio up louder to drown out all my thoughts. I drove as The Cure's "Just Like Heaven" took me home.

After a few hours, I pulled into a drive-thru and got some quick dinner. I wanted to go to the house and see Mom now, like pulling off a Band-Aid. But I knew Mason would be there, and Emma—that girl he married.

Mason was married. I couldn't even wrap my head around that. It had been two years. A million things could have happened by now. They could have a kid, they could have moved, they could have put Mom in a home, though, if I was being honest, I knew Mason would never do that.

As a little bit of love for my brother seeped out, my hatred smacked it back down. I loathed this fight in me that I didn't seem to have any control over.

I checked into a motel in town and lay in the bed, the TV on, but I wasn't really watching it. I knew by that time, Maya had to have gotten off work and found my note. I hoped I hadn't messed up things too badly. I was sure she was even more cemented in her belief that two addicts shouldn't date. It was clear I had things to work out, and she probably had plenty to deal with without adding me to things.

Either way, I barely knew the girl, but she had made me feel something—something real, something not manufactured or fabricated. I didn't know how easily I could let that go, but if she wanted me to leave her alone, I would.

I closed my eyes and tried not to think about it.

But I would be lying if I said a girl with pale white skin and hair as black as coffee didn't star in my dreams.

I sat outside my old house on the curb for over an hour. I swallowed down the last of my Big Gulp of root beer, my last attempt at stalling. I didn't know what to say to her. I didn't know why I was scared. Mason's truck wasn't there. I knew Emma most likely wasn't there either.

I didn't even know what this meant. It wasn't like I could move back here and everything would go back to the way it used to be, even if I did want to. Roz wouldn't let me come back. I just needed to see Mom. Where we went from there…we'd cross that bridge later.

The more I sat there idly, the more I wanted to turn the Jeep around and find something to put in my veins to make me forget it all.

I pulled the sleeve of my shirt up and looked at the inside of my elbow. I hadn't used the needles long enough to leave permanent scars like some people. You could barely see the marks there anymore—not like they used to look, not like they used to feel, all bruised and angry.

I couldn't think about that now.

I swung off the seat and reached for the flowers I bought for Mamma. I didn't know why I bought them. She wouldn't remember me giving them to her, but she wouldn't remember me coming to visit either. I had to get out of the mentality that it only mattered if she remembered. *I* remembered, and it was my duty to see her and make sure she was all right. It wasn't fair to leave it all to Mason.

Guilt hit me big time as I climbed the porch stairs and looked at all the new wood that took its place. The house had been painted a pale blue. There were flowers in the yard, and the front door was different.

Mason had done all that?

I stood, staring a hole in that door. What was I going to say to her? Taking a deep breath through my nose, I raised my hand and knocked hard with my knuckles. A middle-aged woman answered the door not five seconds later. I'd never seen her.

For a second I panicked that one of my fears had come to life and they had moved, but I remembered Mason telling me he had hired a nurse for Mamma. This must be her.

"Hi, can I help you?" she inquired, looking at the flowers curiously.

"I'm…" I cleared my throat. I was sure she would know I was the scumbag son who never came to see his mom, but I said it anyway. "I'm

Milo. I'm here to see my mother."

That sentence—that one sentence—brought so much guilt on me that I nearly choked.

She smiled tightly and opened the door wider. "Milo. Yes, Mrs. Wright talks about you all the time."

"She does?" I asked before it clicked. Ah, she talks about me because she still thinks I'm a sixteen year old boy living at home with her. "Yeah, uh, how is she doing?"

"In general, medically," she asked with a raised eyebrow, "or just today?"

She was subtly calling me out on not coming to see her. I deserved it. "All of the above." I gulped. "I know I haven't come to see her. I've been… away."

"I've noticed," she said and turned toward the living room. Nothing there had changed. It looked exactly like it did the day I left. "Mrs. Wright, you have a visitor."

"Who are you?" she asked the woman.

"I'm your nurse, Patti," she answered and I gathered every ounce of courage I had. "Your son Milo is here to see you."

I pushed my feet, one in front of the other, and turned the corner to see my mother. She looked older, but good. She looked healthy and well taken care of. "Hey, Mamma."

"Milo," she gasped. "Son, what happened to you?"

I went to her, pulling a chair from the dining room table over in front of her, and placed the flowers on the table next to her. The nurse took them and said she'd put them in water for her. Mom's eyes never left me as she looked me over.

I took her hand in mine. "It's been a long time, Mamma."

"Has it? Is that why you look so much older?"

I laughed. "I don't look *that* much older, do I?"

"You're different," she mused and reached out to touch my face. "It's not just your face. You're different."

I nodded. "Things change. I changed. I had to."

"Because of what happened to me?" she asked sadly.

"No, because of what happened to me," I corrected. "I made…a mess of things. I took a bad situation and made it worse, made it all about me."

She pursed her lips. "People tend to do that sometimes, son. It doesn't make you a bad person."

No, it made me an awful person. I smiled as best I could and changed the subject. "Enough about that. I missed you."

"What do you mean you missed me? Where were you? How long has it been?"

"Too long," I answered, the rest of the words getting stuck in my throat by guilt. "Too long, Mamma."

I spent the next two and a half hours there. She forgot everything several times while I was there, but I found I didn't mind that as much as I thought I would. Just being there with her at all made me feel so much better.

I asked her about sending the letter to my friend's telling me that Mason was getting married, but she didn't remember. When I went to the bathroom, I peeked inside Mason's room and saw how much that girl of his had done with the place. It was always pretty neat and clean, but the curtains matched the bed, the bed matched the pillows. There was a stack of useless and strange and fun fact books as tall as the lamp beside the bed. I wondered what that was about.

When I went into my old room, it was completely empty, save a couple of boxes and some bags of stuff that was brand new from the store.

I deserved every bit of it, but it still stung to not see my things there.

I left before lunch because I wasn't sure if Mason would come home for lunch or not. I was being a coward, I knew, but I couldn't make myself face him yet. I needed to take this one step at a time.

And frankly, Mamma was the most important step.

I drove back to the hotel and gathered my things. I'd come back another time. I knew the nurse would tell them I had come by, and that was all right with me. I'd come back later on and take another step.

I couldn't believe how much better I felt, how much lighter I was.

I paid up the room and went across the street to get some gas and snackage for the road. I went inside to pay for my full tank and grabbed an egg salad sandwich and two bottles of root beer. I snagged a bottle of juice to even the health conscience playing field and went to pay.

The blonde in front of me turned like she forgot something and almost bumped into me as she swung around.

"Oh, sorry," she muttered and hoisted her purse higher on her shoulder. Her stomach was huge and round. I smiled at her antics as she snagged a pack of powdered donuts from the shelf and got behind me in line.

I moved and got back behind her. "It's fine. Go ahead."

"Really?" she asked sweetly and finally looked up at me. She smiled. "Thank you. I'm running so…" Her face changed, her mouth fell open. She looked familiar. "Milo?"

I tensed. No one was supposed to know I was in town. Who was this chick? She was too proper to be any girl I'd ever been with. "Uh…yeah. Do I know you?"

She stalled, uncomfortable. "Um, yeah. We met a couple of times." It clicked, just like that. My heart practically stopped. She was a little plumper in the face and the belly, of course. Her hair was longer and pulled to the side across her shoulder. It was her, but she informed me before I could say it. "I'm Emma, Mason's wife."

She was still beautiful, and I could tell her personality fit and she was just as beautiful inside. Panic smacked into me. "Is Mason here?"

"No," she said quickly, as if she could tell I was about to bolt. "I'm running some errands. He's at his tattoo shop."

I watched as her hand covered her belly. I couldn't stop my sigh. I had missed so much. My niece or nephew was in there.

"It's a boy," she supplied softly. She smiled and continued. "Mason was just about heartbroken."

I laughed. "What a sap. Of course he would want a girl."

I realized that we were standing there talking about nephews and Mason like it was commonplace. I looked up to find her eyes pleading.

"Milo, please. He misses you so much. He looked for you everywhere. We had signs all over town. The police were looking, too. They told us what happened…at the hospital." I tensed and looked around. She put her hand on my arm. "Please don't run, Milo."

"I can't stay," I said truthfully. "I did too many things in this town. I ruined any kind of life I could have here."

She winced. "I know. I know you can't come back. Just please…don't run." She searched in her purse quickly and pulled out a pen. She wrote a phone number down on my palm. "It's mine, not Mason's. Just…" She shrugged.

"Okay," I agreed to our silent agreement.

"You look…so good, Milo," she said with a smile. "Really good."

"So do you," I countered and glanced at her belly. "Pregnancy looks good on you."

She laughed sadly. "Yeah, if *cow* was in style, I'd be great."

I laughed but sobered. "Listen, I'm sorry about how I acted the last time…"

She smiled and tilted her head. "Water under the bridge."

"I can't believe Mason's going to have a son…and I'm going to miss all of it."

"You don't have to." The sympathy poured off her. "I don't know where you are or what you're doing for a living or anything, but…we just want to see you—Mason just wants to see you. He thought something awful happened and it was his fault because we…came for you that night."

She barely caught the sob in her throat. I swallowed. I couldn't even tell if I still hated Mason. My brain wouldn't even process that thought.

"I had to get out. I met some great people and they helped me. I'm doing good. Tell Mason he doesn't have to worry about me anymore."

She gave me a wry look. "You know better than that. He loves you. He'll never stop trying to make up for everything, whether you're fine where you are, he'll never stop looking for you. In his own way, he'll always be looking for you."

I looked at her hands, the way they twitched and wrung like she wanted to snatch me up and drag me home with her.

"Yeah," I muttered distractedly. "I've gotta go, Emma. I can't stay in town too long."

"You went and saw Mamma, didn't you." It wasn't a question. I swung my head up at the fact that she called her *Mamma*, too.

"I did," I confessed and couldn't stop the smile. "She's doing really well it seems." I sighed and shuffled my feet. "I'll come back to see her soon."

She leaned forward slowly and put her arms around my neck as much as she could with her belly in between us. "Thank you. They miss you."

I held my sandwich in my hand, but managed to get an arm around her. I didn't say I missed them, however. I was barely hanging on. I'd done it, the first step was done, but I wasn't ready to jump back in head first. "Thanks, Emma." I pulled back and look at her. "For taking care of them for me."

She nodded and knew this was it. "Please call or text. Anytime. I won't make you talk to Mason if you don't want to. Just let us know you're okay."

"Yeah," I agreed and smiled down at her. "I definitely want to come see my nephew."

"Please," she said again and turned slowly. She paid for her things and waved to me before she walked out. I could tell she didn't want to, but she also didn't want to scare me off.

As soon as I paid for my stuff and got in the Jeep, I pulled out my cell and put her number in. Then I did something. I took another step. I texted her…knowing that by doing so she'd have my number.

Tell Mason that I'm doing all right.

The drive back was both easy and hard. I wished I could change things. I wished things could be different, but I couldn't change my past or the things I did. There was no choice but to pay for them.

I thought of that man telling an entire roomful of people about how he thought his brother had hated him all those years for the crap he'd put him through. How he knew his mother and father were so disappointed that there was no way to come back from that. But when he'd finally made the plunge and went home, they all just missed him. They just wanted him back.

I wondered if my reunion with Mom would have been different if her memories had been intact. I couldn't think about that though. I couldn't go back to being scared. It was time to take responsibility and take my life back.

If I wanted any shot at a real future, the past had to be put to rest.

I stayed busy the rest of the week, anticipating and dreading the meeting. I knew I'd see Maya and though I barely knew her, she had already made a huge impact in my life. She was an off-kilter puzzle piece and showed me a few more that weren't in place either that I needed to fix. Mamma was just the beginning.

It's funny that you know the things you need to do and that have to happen, yet it's so hard to take that first step. But once you do, even though you know it's going to be hard, you don't want to stop. The needed momentum keeps pushing you toward the prize, and you let it because you know that as hard as this hurts, you can never go back.

You can never be the person who just exists for the sake of existing anymore, you have to be that person who lives.

My boss asked me why I was so smiley all week. Other than seeing my mom, the one woman in the world who loved me no matter what, I didn't know. Except for the fact that I knew and simultaneously hoped that things were about to change.

My smiley demeanor took a nosedive, however, when the time came for the meeting. I wanted Maya to do what she felt was best for her. If she didn't want to see me at all, honestly, I would leave her be, though that was the furthest thing from what I wanted.

I told her I'd chase her, but that was before she saw how pathetic and sad I was—a guy who couldn't even sit in on a meeting where people talk about their feelings without getting up and leaving. Twice.

I rubbed my head as I made my way inside. I had worked out a lot more than usual, trying to keep myself busy, and my arms ached in a good way from it.

Even as I made steps in the right direction, I still felt like I was falling behind.

I held my breath as I opened the door, and there she was. She was turned with her back to me as she looked out at the roomful of people. She was wearing a blue dress, short and sleeveless. She must have been wearing heels the last few times because with her little black flat ballet looking shoes on, she was a lot shorter than usual. And then I scolded myself for missing what those legs must have looked like with heels on.

I knew then that the chase was back on. The feeling of being alive—she gave that to me, and there was no way in hell that I was letting that go. Not now when I was on the edge of something epic changing for me.

I stuffed my hands into my pockets to contain them and tried to look normal, natural, as I made my way to her. Someone was wrapping their coat around herself as she exited and bumped into me with her elbow.

"Sorry," we spouted at the same time.

I knew Maya heard my voice because at the sound of it, her entire body straightened. She turned quickly, her shiny lips parted, her eyes wide and rimmed with sparkly make-up.

"Milo," she breathed, and her little hand made a fist. "Where have you been? I went by your place."

"I had some things I had to do—back home." I took another step closer, bringing us about five feet apart. "How, uh…how's the truck? Everything running—"

I barely saw her move as she pushed my stomach, forcing me to retreat against the alcove in the foyer that led to somewhere I didn't know. I felt her hand on the back of my neck as she pulled me down and her warm breath on my lips before she touched me. It took a second to respond because I was caught so off guard. What the hell was she kissing me for? I had acted like such an ass.

The suction her mouth made had me swaying as reality crashed back into me. *Good night,* she was kissing me. And she was being thorough.

The hand on my neck loosened, and I knew I'd waited too long to respond. When her hand slipped down to my shoulder, I stopped her and put it back on my neck where it belonged. I wrapped my arm around her waist, my hand coming up to hold her face. Her skin was softer than I imagined it would be. When I kissed her back, she made this long drawn-out moan under our breaths and went back down flat on her feet. She'd been on her tiptoes the whole time. I tugged her back up with my arm around her waist and held her there. Our breaths panted against each other's, and for a second I had a flash of another time when I'd been with a girl. It had been so long ago. I never kissed them. It felt like I was taking something from them when I kissed them. Their body was one thing, but their lips were sacred. In truth, I'd only ever kissed two girls my entire life.

And one of them was kissing me now.

The other was the very first girl, my first everything. She was my girlfriend in high school, when we both were so young. She tried so hard to help me, fix me, be the one to save me. But when it all slid downhill for me, she bailed. With good reason.

She was too sweet, too innocent, not ready to deal with the emotional bags that I brought with me everywhere I went. I didn't blame her. In fact, I looked back at her and that whole relationship—my only relationship— with fondness. She was there for me when the accident happened. She helped me through that in some ways. I would always be grateful to her for trying.

I changed things up, turning us so that Maya was pressed to the wall instead. I let my elbow rest on the wall by her head and didn't mind that I had to bend to reach. That mouth was worth any kink I'd have in the morning.

She let her hand slide from my neck, but she fisted the fabric of the front of my shirt. She broke away with a breath and looked up at me. It looked like she was on the verge of tears, but she was smiling.

And heaven help me, it was absolutely beautiful.

She spoke softly. "You have no idea what you've done for me. You just have no idea."

I chuckled. "It's just a few truck parts. No biggie."

"It was a huge biggie," she insisted in a whisper and put her arms around my waist. I felt her exhale, like a thousand pounds had been lifted from her. "You saved my brother's life."

My brow creased as I rubbed my hands down her back. "What was that, sweetheart?"

"Maya," someone called. We looked over to see an older woman holding a cup of coffee and looking perturbed yet irritated. "It's time. It's starting."

Maya looked up at me and licked only her bottom lip. I felt a small rumble go through me. What the hell was wrong with me?

"I have to go," she said and smiled beautifully. "Please come and listen?"

I nodded. "That's why I'm here. To stay."

In truth, I had decided I needed to be the one up at that podium one day, but for now, I needed to make myself commit. No more back row for me.

I was done with being a coward.

She smiled small as she walked away with the other woman. I went and sat right smack in the middle of the room—addicts surrounding me at three hundred sixty degrees. I took a deep breath, preparing myself for whatever I was about to hear. I felt this little push to go up there, for me to be the one to tell all today, but I wasn't ready. Not quite.

I looked up to find Maya at the podium. She was twirling a coin in her fingers, that loving, possessive look in her eyes like before. It was a coin. I lifted my eyes to find her gaze on me. She smiled and licked her bottom lip before closing her eyes and opening just as she began to speak.

"When I look at this coin, I see a completely different life, the one I could have lived, the one I was saved from by someone who loved me enough to come and find me, be the bad guy that I needed him to be." She lifted it, though it was too small to see the numbers. "I got my four-year coin today." The room around me erupted with applause and she tried to hide her tears, but finally just smiled through them. I couldn't even clap I was so in awe of her. This seemingly simple thing was so indescribably beautiful as I watched her be embarrassed and try to finish her story. The way she tugged at her earrings while looking at the floor, the light in her eyes as she spoke of her brother and father, the sadness that overcame her as she talked about her father dying and how much she wanted to get high, but her brother watched over her, and she somehow made it through without breaking her clean streak. All of it played out across her face and movements, and I'd never been so enthralled, never seen anything so beautiful.

She told us everything. When she was done, the hour was up and everyone clapped and went up to congratulate her.

But I held back. I wanted her to have this time to be the center, to soak up the much-deserved congratulations. I went to the front steps and sat. So many things weighed on me. I knew by then that Mason knew I had stopped by and Emma had told him I saw her at the store.

I watched several people go and even more come for another meeting. My peace was weird. I hadn't felt peace of any kind in so long that it almost felt uncomfortable.

"Are you waiting for a cab or for me?" I heard.

I turned to Maya and let my grin show. "Definitely not a cab." I stood and brushed off the back of my jeans. "You see, I'm a mechanic, ma'am," I said in my best Southern gentleman voice. She giggled. "I know how to fix things. My Jeep runs just fine."

"Good to know. You know, this guy fixed my truck for me," she took slow steps toward me, "and left me a note to explain before going incognito for six whole days."

"Pfft. That guy," I shook my head, "is obviously a tool."

"He's a crafty, sweet, son of a gun, and a pain in the butt."

I laughed. "All that?"

"All that," she confirmed and made the last step. She looked up at me.

"Thank you. You didn't have to."

"I wanted to." My fingers reached out and barely gripped and grazed the ends of hers. "I was being a coward. I took it out on you."

"You're not the first person to take it out on me and you won't be the last. I'm a counselor, remember?"

"But I'm not one of your callers," I corrected. "And you're the girl I'm chasing."

She smiled wider. "You're not going to let that go, are you?"

I chuckled. "After that kiss?" She blushed a little, her neck turning pink. "No, I won't be letting go after that."

"I sort of attacked you, huh?" she laughed out breathily.

"Sort of?" I stepped half a step closer, barely a sliver between us. "That was…"

"Scary?" she supplied with a little laugh under her breath.

"Awesome," I countered and lifted her fingers in mine, toying with them between us.

"You deserved it," she said breathlessly, looking at our fingers together. "I would never have been able to get it fixed otherwise. And my brother—we had an emergency this week, and if you hadn't fixed my truck—"

"What happened?" The words jumped from me, concern etching my forehead. "Did something happen to you?"

"Everything's fine. It was him, not me. But he's fine now, so thank you. Your timing was amazing."

"Don't worry about it. I wanted to. You *can* make it up to me though." I smirked. "What time should I pick you up tomorrow?"

"For…a date?" She may have been trying to look serious, but a smile sat in the corner of her mouth.

I didn't answer. She knew exactly what I meant. I grinned down at her, making her squirm. She wasn't getting off easy. She tilted her head to the side and then said, "Okay. You can pick me up at six."

"Great." I felt her closed fist in my hand. "Will you show it to me?"

She squinted in confusion, but I gently squeezed her hand to tell her. She slowly opened her hand to reveal the coin. I lifted it reverently in my fingers, and prayed and hoped and begged that one day I would have one with that many years on it, too.

"It's beautiful, isn't it?" she whispered, a tear running from the corner of her eye like it was finally free. "That stupid, ugly coin is really beautiful."

I wiped it from her cheek with my thumb. Holding her face, I moved and put my lips to her forehead. The way she gripped me around my waist so tight made me think she hadn't had someone hold her in a long time. Maybe ever. And this girl needed to be held. She deserved to be absolutely adored.

When the door opened behind us, it had been so quiet and still that we both jumped at the sudden noise. She giggled and leaned back. "Thanks. Um…"

She smiled and seemed as unsure about all this as I was. "Yeah, um," I joked.

She licked her bottom lip as she smiled. "I better go. I'll see you tomorrow?"

My eyebrow rose. "You think I'm going to stand you up?"

"No," she shook her head and walked backward to the doors, "just checking."

"Nothing could stop me," I heard myself say. I scoffed at how easily I turned into mush around her.

Her smile was gorgeous as she went back inside. I turned and raised my fist in the air in triumph, closing my eyes. That girl was going to be mine. I know I didn't deserve her, but I couldn't stop chasing her.

I opened my eyes, the smile a mile wide on my face, and quickly put my arm down at the sight of her friend—the one with the coffee cup still attached to her hand. She gave me a solid glare. "If you hurt her, I'll end you, hotshot."

Hotshot? "Yes, ma'am." I nodded and cleared my throat. "I won't."

"Good." She smacked my chest with the back of her hand when she passed me. She stopped. "Holy cow." She gripped my arm. "What do you have in here? Rocks?"

I chuckled. "No, ma'am. It's a good way to keep idle hands busy."

She looked at me closely, her eyes squinting a little. "You're going to be good for her. I can tell."

"Well…thanks?"

She laughed and started to walk through the doors. She turned back and smiled. "Hotshot?"

"That's me," I joked.

"She's going to be good for you, too."

I nodded and watched her leave. Of that I had no doubt.

The next day at work was the only day it seemed to drag on. Most of the time I was perfectly content to stay busy and do what needed to be done, but that day was brutal as it crept smugly by. It must have wanted to torture me.

My boss knew it was about a girl. He said I was mopey, whatever that meant. I wasn't mopey. I was anxious and excited and couldn't wait to have my mouth on hers again. That wasn't mopey, but I'm not sure what you would call it.

When I finally was able to go home and get a shower, I put on some dark jeans and threw on my black leather jacket. The nights were cold. It was almost time for the snow again and the top would have to go back on my Jeep.

I rubbed my hands together when I went outside. It was colder than I thought. I had called the center that morning and gotten Maya on the first ring. She gave me her address and her cell number, since we'd forgotten to do all that the night before.

When I pulled up, I parked on the street because the driveway to the duplex apartment was full. I got out and saw Maya in the doorway as I was coming up.

I stopped.

Maya was standing in the doorway, looking absolutely gorgeous in black tights and a dress with a flowy jacket thing. But she wasn't alone, and her arms were wrapped tightly around some other guy's neck.

Ignore previous cookie.

Maya

"I'll be fine. I always am," he insisted.

"Will, I know, okay, but it's been so long since you've been alone this long. And what the doctors said, it's getting more aggressive."

He sighed and put his palms on my shoulders. "Babe, you are an over-worrier. I know how to use a phone."

"But you had a bad episode this week, and I don't feel right—"

"This is the guy who fixed the truck, isn't it?" he guessed.

I hadn't told Will about it because I didn't know what it meant, really. I didn't want to tell him a guy I'd only known for a month or so surprised me with fixing my truck as an apology for something he didn't even need to apologize for. Therapy and recovery are hard. We tend to rebel. It's not a big deal. We lash out. It happens. The guy didn't need to go to extremes to say he was sorry. But then Will got sick a couple days later. My phone was dead and I couldn't find Will's anywhere. If I had gone to take him to the hospital and it wouldn't have started...I don't know what would have happened.

I don't know why these things happen. I don't know why Milo would have picked that week to lash out and then fix my truck. I don't know why Will had an episode that week when it had been months since he'd had a bad one like that. I don't know these things, but I couldn't help but be grateful to Milo for that chain of events.

I had been cautious about dating him. Dating anyone, really, but him because he hadn't been clean that long. But two years to an addict was a lifetime. He had been a number to me, a statistic, a project. A very sweet and charming project, but one nonetheless. But now, he was more than that. He was no longer someone who was cute and tried to charm me as I pushed him away; he was someone I wanted to pull closer.

I'd never felt that. That was pathetic on so many levels, but I was so young when my mom died, and I was never interested in real relationships. I just wanted to be numb, get high, and forget everything for the hour the drugs provided me. And when I got clean and started working, my work consumed me. When Dad died, my grief consumed me. Now my sick brother consumed me.

I'd never been at a point in my life where a relationship was even on my radar. And if Milo hadn't come and smashed my pretty fake plastered smile, replacing it with a real one, I still wouldn't be interested.

Was that wrong? Should I tell Milo the timing was off? Was I just grateful and that's why I felt so strongly about him? I didn't want to hurt him, and I didn't want to be hurt.

"Earth to smitten girl," Will said, waving his hand in front of me.

"Whatever." I rolled my eyes. "Yes, he's the one who fixed my truck. I owed him, okay? But after this, I think I'm going to…just tell him we should be friends." He gave me a dull look. "What? I am in no position in life to be falling all over some guy."

"What position do you think you need to be in? Everyone has things going on in their life, Maya. You just have to make room for the things that are important."

"You're important," I said, almost angrily. Taking care of him wasn't some pointless existence.

"And I'm right here," he soothed. He squeezed my shoulders. "Sis, you can't tell everything else in your life to take a hike just because I got sick."

"I want to take care of you."

"And you do." He sighed and hung his head. "I'm older. I'm supposed to be taking care of you."

"I like the job," I joked, but didn't smile.

"I'm just one little piece of the picture. You do an amazing job taking care of me. You sacrifice a lot. There's nothing wrong with taking a night for yourself. Hell, take twenty. Go out every night if that's what you want." He smiled crookedly and it reminded me of when we were kids. "I want you to be happy. I'm fine here." He laughed.

"You're not fine," I whispered.

"In fact, it's better when you're gone because no one makes me watch *Seinfeld* re-runs over and over and over..."

"You love it," I shot back wryly.

He shrugged. "Maybe. The Soup Nazi, at least."

I pushed my arms around his neck. "You're all I've got, Will. I'll always put you before any dumb guy."

"And I love you for it, but tonight I want you to go and have fun with this guy who is so smitten with my sister that he fixed her truck to surprise her." He looked at me closely. "That's huge, Maya. What guy does that?" he asked in awe.

"Milo," I answered and smiled. "Milo does that."

"Milo sounds like a keeper."

"Yeah," I said slowly, "but he's an addict, too."

"I hate that word, you know. There should be a new word for someone who was an addict but isn't anymore."

I smiled. He meant well, but someone who wasn't an addict would never understand. "Once an addict, always an addict, Will."

"But he's clean, yeah?"

I nodded. "Two years."

"So you're both…rehabilitation enthusiast. There, new word."

I laughed hard. "And what does that mean?"

"It means you're addicts, but you want to be clean *more*."

I smiled, feeling my eyes beg to water. "I love that."

"I love *you*," he insisted and then raised his head. "And I think Milo has arrived."

I turned to find Milo in the driveway. He was stopped about half way, looking at Will and me with a strange expression. He nodded when he saw us looking and I realized what this must look like. I pulled back and gave Will a look. I wasn't going to introduce them yet. Not yet. Will was a part of my life that was mine and sacred. He was all I had left in the world and I wasn't mixing that with first dates.

Will waved to Milo and went back inside. I had asked him to please call me even if he felt a little bad. I knew he was already because I could see it in the way he creased his brow.

I didn't want to leave, to be honest. As much as I liked Milo, and Will wanted me to have a life, with the week Will had, I didn't want to leave him.

I made my way down to him. He smiled, but it was a little strange. Strained. "Hey."

"Hey," he said gruffly and cleared his throat. "You look seriously gorgeous."

He looked back up to the house before back at me. "That was my brother Will. We live together."

"Ah," he said, and it was almost comical how much he relaxed. "The one I saved this week by fixing the truck. Care to explain that statement?"

I struggled with my scarf. I hated them honestly, but they were warm and I was always cold. They were functional, not fashion, but I grabbed one of the pretty ones for a night out with him. "Maybe later, if that's okay."

"Whatever you want." He helped me with my scarf, wrapping it around my neck a couple of times, which I was sure was some fashion faux pas. "It's freezing tonight. Ready to go?"

"Um…" I sighed. I felt awful, but I just couldn't. "Listen, um…I don't think we should…"

He stuck his hands in his pocket, a breath puffing from his lips. "Are we back to you thinking it's a bad idea?"

"No, I don't think that. I just… My brother's sick."

He squinted in sympathy. "Oh. The flu or something? That sucks."

"No. I, uh…" I swallowed.

"If you need to stay with him, you can," he said and bent down to be in my line of sight when I wouldn't look up. "Maya, what's going on? This seems like something bigger than your brother getting the sniffles. Are you okay?"

"He's *sick*." I gasped a little at the fact that I told him like that. I covered my mouth with my hand and stared up at him. Just a few people even knew about it. I didn't tell anyone unless I had to.

His entire demeanor changed. He softened and put his arms around me, letting me bury my freezing nose in his chest. "You don't have to tell me anything, but you know that my shoulders are always warm, right? *I'm* always here if you ever need anything, or just want to talk. You're always helping people with their problems, but does anybody ever help you with yours?"

"A guy wanting to talk," I mused. "A true sign of the apocalypse."

He chuckled and leaned back. "That invitation is only for you, by the way. Your bossy, coffee mug friend is not invited."

I felt my smile. The twinge of guilt that came with that smile was present, but not as potent as usual. "Did she say something?"

"Only threatened my life. Nothing major."

"Aww," I crooned. "She's the sweetest boss ever." I felt his fingers on mine, but kept my eyes on his face. "And you're the sweetest guy. That's why I hate to do this to you. In fact," I closed my eyes, "you should probably just run now. I'm a basket case. My life is my job and my brother. I don't know…" I looked him right in the eye so he could see that I was serious. "I don't know how much I have left over after all that. I feel empty and drained, and the thought of dragging you into this makes me so sad. You're off the hook. You don't have to chase—"

He swooped down, capturing my face with his palms and kissing me softly. His mouth breathed hot life into me as I felt that kiss in every pore, every molecule. His hands were freezing, but I couldn't have cared if my life depended on it.

He licked my lips and I opened my mouth just enough to taste him. Hanging on to his arms, kissing him back, I heard his response loud and clear. He wasn't giving up the chase. And I didn't want him to. As selfish as that was, I didn't wanted him to stop.

He stopped slowly, stalling and slowing our movements to a snail's pace. He made an angry little chuckle under his breath. "This is ridiculous." He lifted his head just barely. "I can't stop kissing you. It's all I've thought about all day."

"You don't have to."

The smile sat crookedly on his lips. "Come on." He tugged my hand for me to follow him. "Let's go."

He was headed toward my apartment. I sighed. He was letting me stay and trying to not make me feel bad about it. And walking me to my door to boot. But when we got to the door, he opened it and started to scuff off his boots on the rug. "What…" I stopped my rude question just in time.

"I thought it was obvious." He grinned, daring me to say something. "I'm inviting myself in."

"Um, you don't have to—"

"Look." He gave me that look. The one that said he was serious, the one that said he was about to be so sweet, it made me ache. "You want to stay with your brother because he's sick, you're worried about him. Okay, I get that. It's not a problem. Stay. But I'm not ready to say goodnight yet. So," he continued, taking my hand and playing with the tips of my fingers, "we'll order some take-out, you can watch over your brother and I get to hang out with you. We can watch a movie or something."

I just stared. I didn't know that the male species even had the capacity to dream up a sweet plan like that. Apparently, I didn't give him enough credit. He winced when I didn't say anything. "If that's okay, of course. I wasn't trying to overstep." He nodded his head once, like he understood something. "You don't want me to meet him yet, do you? Yeah, I was moving things pretty fast, I guess." I tried to speak, but he backed up a bit and rubbed his hair. "I'll see you next week. I hope he feels better-"

"Milo, shut up," I scolded and laughed a breath. "A girl can't get a word in."

He stood silent, watching me. He was such a strange combination of cocky and insecure. One minute he was spouting how he was chasing me, no matter what, and then the next he was trying to skirt away with his tail between his legs.

"I don't want you to go; I'm just surprised you want to stay."

His jaw twitched. "This is where you are."

I didn't know my heart could hurt so good.

He took the end of my scarf and unraveled it from my neck gently as he continued, his face so close. "I've never met someone who made me feel..."

I wasn't sure if he trailed off or if that was his whole thought. I made him feel. That thought made my insides giddy, because he made me feel, too. It was always drugs. No boy or man had ever made me feel before.

It scared the hell out of me, yet made me feel like I was the only girl

72

who mattered. How could someone you barely knew alter your life and perception so much? He made me question everything. I had been just surviving, taking care of my brother because I loved him and had to, but after he was gone, I didn't know what would become of me.

I was just existing, but he made me want to live.

"Stay," I commanded softly.

His lip lifted just a bit. "I like this bossy side of you. A lot."

I laughed under my breath. "I'll remember that. Come on, hotshot."

He barked a laugh as I grinned, walking backward. "She told you about that?"

"What, about her threatening your life? Yeah." I stopped at the door and loved how he took my fingers in his and toyed with them. I watched them, fascinated. "My brother—just don't say anything about him being sick or whatever. I don't really bring anyone here."

"It's okay." He lifted my chin. "Maya, it's okay."

"By the way, thanks for not jumping to conclusions and getting all mad about seeing me in the doorway with another guy. I saw your face. I'm sorry I forgot to tell you about my brother living here. Another guy probably would've been upset before I could explain," I assumed anyway.

"Well, a lot of arguments are based on assumptions. A lot of assumptions are made about me because I'm a guy, because I'm an addict, because I'm only twenty. You get my drift." I nodded. "So I try really hard not to assumption-jump as a way to hopefully send that karma back around to me."

"That's a very good way of looking at things. A very *mature* way of looking at things."

He shrugged. "I had to grow up fast."

I nodded, swinging around to find Will on the couch. I hoped he wouldn't be angry for bringing Milo here. "Will."

He looked back over his shoulder and did a small double take. "Hey."

"Will, this is Milo. Uh, Miles."

"Hey, Will. You can call me Miles if you want," he reminded me. "Milo sounds like a cat." Somehow I knew that Will would be calling him Milo, too, though. Milo came around me to the sofa and shook Will's hand. "Nice to meet you. We decided to stay in and get some take-out, if that's all right with you."

Will scoffed and gave me a sideways glance. "She wouldn't leave, would she?"

I crossed my arms behind my back and looked at the floor, but Milo came to my rescue. "Actually, I'm beat. I work over at the mechanic shop on the main drag. I figured we could just eat here, maybe watch a movie or something."

Will laughed. "Wow, she has got you whipped like butter, you liar."

My mouth fell open, but Milo busted out laughing. "Guilty," he confessed and looked over at me with a smile that said it was the truth. "Whatever makes her happy."

Will was looking at me, but I couldn't remove my eyes from Milo. Where did this boy come from? Where had guys like him been all my life? Granted, I'd been preoccupied. I didn't realize guys like that existed.

Will coughed his words. "Cough, smitten girl, cough."

I glared at him playfully. "What?"

He procured some caveman voice. "Men. Need. Food." He pointed to the kitchen. "Woman. Make. Sustenance." I raised my eyebrow. Will hadn't been like this in months. He never saw his friends anymore. They came around for a little while, but once Will couldn't keep up with all their fun at college, most of them stopped coming around altogether. All he ever saw was me. "Or just order some take-out, whatever."

I shook my head and rolled my eyes as the boys laughed and started talking about some movie they wanted to see. I was sure it was blood and guts. I yelled, asking what they wanted to eat as I took out all the menus, spreading them on the counter.

A head appeared above my shoulder and one hand on my side.

"What do we have here?"

"Um…" I breathed and swallowed. I could feel how warm he was behind me. "Take-out menus. What do you want? A few places deliver."

"That's fine with me." He pointed at the Chinese place under his apartment. "I'm fond of this one for obvious reasons."

I smiled. "I was going to pick that one anyway. I'm in the mood for cookies."

He leaned on the counter with his elbows, his jacket gone, and said, "So, I didn't really have a say? You just made me think I did."

"Basically," I spouted playfully as the Chinese place answered on the first ring.

I got it all ordered and we sat in the living room talking about the new Bond movie. I folded my legs under me, keeping the skirt of my dress to my knees. Milo had taken off his boots and jacket. He sat with me on the couch opposite as my brother, our legs touching, and every now and then he would reach down and rub the tips of my fingers against each other.

Will was still in his sweatpants and t-shirt, but didn't seem to care. His blanket was thrown off, but he was at least leaning back and resting.

When the doorbell rang, Milo jumped up to get it, insisting he would get this one. I twisted my lips, but let it go. We divvied up the right orders and dug in while I bought their blood-and-guts movie from On Demand. When my food was done, I pushed my box aside and turned to face the TV, my back to Miles. One of my knees was up to my chest and I was about to find another spot because it was pretty uncomfortable when I felt his hands on my shoulders, pulling me back to lean against his side. In return, he slung his arm over my lifted knee and my shoulder.

I found myself sighing, wondering when the other shoe would drop. There was no way he was this awesome all the time.

When the movie was over, Will was fast asleep. I laughed. Poor guy. "He's such an amateur."

Milo laughed quietly. "Hey, we didn't eat our cookies."

I leaned over, snatched one up, and turned to face him, poised with the fortune cookie in between my fingers. "Ready?"

"Ready," he confirmed and we broke them open at the same time. He opened it, but didn't read it. He popped the whole cookie in his mouth.

I pulled the paper out and read out loud, "You only need to look to your own reflection for inspiration. For you are beautiful." I made a *how about that* face.

"That's true," he agreed and brushed some cookie crumbs off my dress from my knees. "Didn't I say you were gorgeous?"

"You did." I licked my bottom lip. "What does yours say?"

He sighed, grimacing like he didn't want to read it. Then he said slowly, "Conquer your fears, or they will conquer you."

"Oooh, I like that one."

He stared at it for a few long seconds before crumpling it between his fingers. "Just a stupid piece of paper, right?"

I took it from him and tossed it along with mine into the empty box on the table as if I could take the frown that had suddenly appeared on his face and do the same thing. "So," I began and leaned back, thumping my fist on his knee, "what now, hotshot?"

He scoffed. "You're going to call me that forever, aren't you?"

Forever... "It's a big possibility."

He laughed, rubbing his chin. "You have work in the morning."

I nodded. "So do you."

"Yeah, but I don't care."

"Me neither," I whispered back.

"Then let's play a game." He grinned. "Would you rather eat a fox's tail or a rattlesnake?"

"Eew. Neither!" He gave me a stern look that was more cute than anything else. "Fine. Fox tail." He waited, looking amused. "Okay, would you rather live on a deserted island with one person of your choosing or…win a million dollars?"

"Easy. Deserted island."

"Really?"

"Yeah. An island, back to basics, no traffic or jobs or bills. No stress. Just us." My gaze swung to his. His lips twitched. "Or whoever it was I took with me."

I let that slide, barely. "But think of what you could do with a million dollars." There wouldn't be any more worrying about Will's medical stuff with that kind of money.

He shook his head. "Ah, money does things to people. Plus, an addict with all that money at their disposal isn't a very good idea." My lips pursed. He did have a point there. "All right, would you rather kiss a total stranger or lie to your preacher?"

"Kiss a stranger," I answered quickly. "I despise lying, no matter what it's for."

He shifted a little, leaning toward me. "Not even a white lie, not even a lie that was meant to keep someone safe."

"Safe? Like, from emotional hurt?"

"Sure," he said, unconvincingly.

"Even then. I know I'm a hypocrite because I used to lie all the time to my dad, sneaking out and not coming home, lying about where I'd been. Maybe that's why I hate it so much."

"I have a brother," he said suddenly. "In the interest of being honest." He looked up and captured my gaze, holding it hostage. "I got into some trouble back home and had to leave. I haven't been home to see my brother or mom in years. I went to check on my mom the other day, when I was gone. My brother's wife is about to have a baby."

"You're going to be an uncle."

"Yeah, but I won't be there. I can't be. I screwed up. And this is one of those things that can't be fixed. One of those things…that I have to lie about sometimes."

I nodded, not pushing. "Okay, I guess I can understand that. Will you tell me one day?"

"I'll tell you," he promised. "And you'll tell me yours."

I nodded. "One day."

Will's snore was loud and startled me. Milo and I stared at each other in some kind of silent agreement. He stood and held his hand out for me, pulling me up. "I guess I better go, let you get some sleep."

I followed him to the door and watched him slip on his boots and jacket. "Thank you. For dinner and for staying. I worry about him too much, he says, but it's my job, you know. He's my only brother."

I tried not to notice his wince, but I knew I'd hit a nerve. "Not a problem. We should do it again. Soon."

"Are you asking me out again?" I crossed my arms behind my back and looked at him coyly.

"Are you saying yes?"

"Yeah," I answered, not even waiting the customary pause for etiquette. He had to know I was interested by this point. Why hide it?

His smile was gorgeous. "Good. I'll call you. And when I say I'll call you, I mean I'll actually call you."

I nodded and took the end of his shirt in my fingers, too chicken to touch more of him. "Thanks for not pushing me about Will. I feel like I'm responsible for him and I don't know how to react sometimes. I don't like to talk about it, really. It makes it...real."

"I don't know what's going on and I don't want to push you. I'm so out of practice," he said with a sad chuckle. "I don't know how to do this anymore, so if I push too far, if you aren't comfortable with me, if I'm moving too fast, just say it."

"I think the fact you care about that at all is a good sign," I whispered, awe-filled.

He leaned toward me and stopped with very little room between us. I waited. "How far do you want me to chase you, Maya?"

I breathed, "As far as it takes."

He pressed the slowest, sweetest kiss to the corner of my mouth, letting the backs of his fingers rub my cheek. "Bye, sweetheart."

I nodded. "Bye."

I watched him go and finally felt like I could breathe. He climbed in his Jeep and waved as he drove off. I turned and felt like mush as I leaned on the door with my back.

"If you break out in song, I'm gonna gag."

I glared at Will's head, poking out from behind the couch. "Go back to sleep, sloth."

"Creep's got a boyfriend," he sang. "Creep's got a boyfriend."

I gathered the trash from our dinner and tossed a napkin at him. "Shut up."

I smiled as I turned and felt that smile in my very bones. I had this strange feeling like I'd just gone on my very last first date.

> Your troubles will cease and
> fortune will smile upon you.

Milo

MY PHONE dinged with a text as soon as I opened my front door. I grinned, shaking my head and locking the door as I reached for my phone. She was adorable. I wondered what kind of sass remark she had for me.

When I pulled out my phone, the number was unknown.

I'm glad you came to see her.

Mason. I knew it.

I put the phone on the coffee table and sat back looking at it. I got up and took a long shower—stalling—and put on the pajama pants that Joey had gotten me for Christmas that year. I never slept in a shirt now that I lived alone. Waste of clean clothes if you asked me.

I didn't know if I could answer Mason. I didn't know if I was ready to take that step. I knew there would be no going back after that. The one person I wanted to talk to about it, I couldn't. I didn't want to tell Maya all my sins. I didn't want her to know that side of me, ever, even though her job was talking to people about the crap in their lives. Was that realistic? I knew it wasn't, but it didn't stop me from hoping I could somehow keep it from her.

So I did the second best thing. I called Joey.

Even though it was past midnight, she answered and we talked for over an hour. She knew most of the things in my past. I had no choice back when they first helped me but to spill it all. They wouldn't have helped me change my name and get set up there without the truth.

Joey and I had only spoken a couple times since she left, but we fell right back into our routine. She told me I should do what I felt was right. If I never wanted to talk to Mason again, then don't. She scolded me for going back and seeing my mother. She said my safety was more important than seeing her, especially since she didn't remember the visit anyway.

I had always agreed with that, but this was the first time I wanted to hear something different. I wanted to hear it was amazing I got to see my mom and sometimes being stupidly brave was the only way to get over things. I didn't want the stigma of my past to cling to me forever. Eventually, I wanted to forget it all and move on.

Now I didn't know what to think. Maybe Joey was right. But for the first time since I met Joey, I wanted to keep something from her. Maya was mine and I wanted to keep her that way. I didn't want to tell her all about her. I wanted to keep to all to myself. Not because I was ashamed or didn't want her to know, but because…I just wanted something that was mine. Something that I didn't have to share or explain or analyze. I didn't know what that meant.

I woke the next morning, freezing, with a kink in my neck. I pushed off the couch, cursing myself for falling asleep, and hurried to get dressed.

I was late.

I got to work almost forty minutes after I was supposed to be there

"You're late, buster."

"I know. Sorry," I muttered and quickly got busy. "I fell asleep on my couch. Don't worry, I'm paying for it big time."

I rubbed my neck and winced. I grabbed the bottle of Tylenol from his desk and downed a few at the water fountain.

"Good," he mumbled playfully. "The public caning will be postponed then."

I shook my head and got to work to make up for the time I'd lost.

I called Maya on my lunch break. She made some joke about a three-day rule or something and said I was breaking guy code. I spent my whole break laughing at her and didn't even get to eat before it was time to go back.

She asked if I wanted to have dinner at her house again the next night. I agreed.

When I showed up, she answered the door with a hand towel thrown over her shoulder. Her smile hid nothing as she grabbed my hand and pulled me inside. She took me straight to the kitchen. I didn't see Will anywhere as we went through the house. The table was set for three though, and I could tell she went all out. It made me extra smug, if I was honest, that she would go to all the trouble for me.

She hadn't seen the box in my hand so as she peeked over a tall pot and stirred, I went up behind her, put my chin on her shoulder, my arm around her waist, and brought the plain white box around in front of her. She turned her head and her nose touched mine. She didn't lean away. I could feel her heartbeat pick up as it pulsed through her body, along with her breaths.

"You got me fortune cookies."

I nodded, my nose rubbing the end of hers. Her eyes fluttered, and the ecstasy of that look would haunt and be the star of my dreams for the rest of my life. "Mmhmm."

She took the box.

"Open one," I commanded.

She opened the wrapping and broke a cookie in half, my face waiting right there over her shoulder. She licked the crumbs off her thumb and held the paper between her fingers. "The love you fight for is the love that can mend bridges, heal scars, and open closed hearts."

She made a small gasp and looked over her shoulder at me again. We waited. It was like a dance and we weren't sure who was supposed to take the lead. I didn't want to move too fast with her, but she did kiss me first at that meeting. We both held back this part of us that no one was allowed to touch. But if I didn't kiss her right now, I was going to bust wide open.

I eased into her space and smiled to myself when her eyes closed. She *had* been waiting on me. When my lips touched hers, she relaxed her entire body, leaning on me and turning toward me. She blindly set the cookies on the counter and I wrapped my arms around her. My palm found the small of her back and she gasped just a little when I used that spot to pull her all the way to me.

She fisted the front of my shirt and dragged me with her as she leaned against the counter, never breaking our kiss. I lifted her easily to sit on the counter, and only barely moved between her knees. I needed to leave some space between us. I wanted her to feel safe with me, in every way. As much as I wanted her, as much as she set me on fire, more than anything else, I wanted her to open up her soul and let me into that part of her she didn't let anyone see.

Her hand pushed through my hair and tugged. I almost lost it. I groaned into her mouth before pulling away. She looked so stunned, her mouth and eyes wide—I cursed myself for going too far. "I'm sorry," I said gruffly.

"Why?" she said, her face looking truly puzzled.

"I don't know how to act with you, Maya." I sighed. "I can't feel out the line I'm not supposed to cross."

She smiled, bemused. "Okay. Here's the line," her hand held at her head, "and here you are now," she finished, her hand at her waist. "I'm perfectly capable of saying 'no' or 'slow down' if I think we're going too far or too fast."

"I just…don't want to scare you."

How the hell did I tell the girl I wanted to be with more than anything else that I'd only ever slept with girls who used me for that purpose or drugs and I had no clue of how regular girls handled their sexual situations?

"You're not scaring me. You couldn't scare me." She pressed her lips together, uncomfortable. She closed her eyes, her throat worked through a gulp. "I'm not a virgin. Far from it." I didn't know why that surprised me, but it did. "I spent a long time being a girl that would do…" She looked at my shirt, her lip quivering.

I lifted her chin. I needed to hear this. "Tell me." She stared into my eyes and I knew. I was knocking on the door of the things that were closed, the things she didn't want me to see. "Please, let me in," I whispered against her cheek.

She steeled herself and sat up, speaking softly but firmly. "Okay, the line is here and you're here now, all right? Let's just cool it."

Her hands were on the same level. So the sex stuff she was fine with, it was just talking about it that wasn't what she wanted. I leaned back, letting her hop down.

"Whatever you need."

"I need to eat," she said, a fake smile on as she continued cheerfully and went to turn off the stove. "I'm starving and I made all this food. Let's eat. Will!"

Will came in, ashen and pale. "Dude, you all right? You look like death warmed over."

He stopped. Maya dropped a plate full of food. He looked at her and her wide eyes told me there was something I didn't know. "What?"

"You didn't tell him?" he asked. He looked hurt more than anything. "Why, Maya? Didn't think he'd come over if he knew?"

She shook her head angrily. "Because I don't want to talk about it."

"You need to talk about it," he spouted, glaring at her as he sat at the end of the table. "You need to freaking open the vault."

"Shut up, Will," she said back and looked at me in apology. "Sorry. Brothers and sisters fight, right?"

"Right," I heard myself mutter. This was way more than that. They knew that I knew it, but no one was handing over details.

I bent down and helped her pick up the sliced squash that had fallen. I stared at her face as she picked up the pieces, slamming them into the bowl with every toss so hard that half of them ricocheted back out. I gripped her hand. She looked at me with an *I dare you* look. She wanted me to ask, to get in their business when it was obvious she didn't want me to know whatever it was. I wasn't going to do it though, no matter how badly I wanted to know what the hell was going on.

"I got it, sweetheart," was all I said and picked up the squash one piece at a time, so she'd have enough time to straighten her glare and realize I was here to stay. She thought I was going to bolt, but I wasn't.

I shook my head at myself for being such a hypocrite. I had things I never wanted her to know about. How many times had I thought that if she knew the kind of person I was before, she would run for the nearest hill to get away.

We sat and had one of the most awkward dinners I've ever participated in. The honey glaze chicken she baked was amazing. There was also wheat and oat rolls and sweet corn on the cob so tender.

Neither of them seemed to be enjoying it. I sucked down the last of my sweet tea and she got up to get the pitcher.

"I could have gotten it, but thanks."

"Welcome," she muttered sadly. I didn't get it. She was the one who got angry, and now, it seemed as if she was pouting.

Women.

"Hey, Will, did you see on the news that the Broncos might be firing their general manager?"

He looked up, barely having touched his food, and smiled to show his gratitude for my attempt to make table conversation. "They won't. It's all bull."

"You sure? They sound peeved."

Maya took my plate before I could say anything and went to the sink with them. She scraped them and filled the sink with water. I looked and saw no dishwasher. I heard a cleared throat and saw Will giving me a look. He ticked his head toward his sister and mouthed, 'Go on.'

I smiled, caught. 'Thanks,' I mouthed back.

"Thanks for dinner, creep!" he called before shuffling out of the room to somewhere into the dark hallway.

I heard his door close. She didn't turn, just kept washing. I grabbed the dishtowel and scooted beside her, taking the plate from her when she would have put it in the sink. She watched my hands as I rinsed the plate. She did that for a few heavy seconds before beginning her washing again.

It took us all of ten minutes to do them all. I dried my last plate and stuck it in the cupboard before laying the towel across the sink edge. Her eyes, so full of sadness and responsibility that didn't belong there, searched me. I let her, not saying a word until her eyes met mine.

She licked her lips. "You're still here."

"Yep."

"You don't want to run screaming from the basket case?"

"I don't see a basket case." I inched toward her, back to not knowing my place or boundaries. "I see a girl who has a lot of things to take care of. A girl with a lot on her mind. A girl who's struggling to see how this strange guy fits in her life."

"You would fit," she corrected and made a fist with her fingers. "I just don't know how to…" Her lip quivered, and I knew my heart was about to take a hit. "I don't how to let you in and keep you out at the same time."

Breathe, man. "Why do you have to keep me out?"

Her face was tight, like the cry-face was about to make an appearance. "Because you can't come in. I don't want you there." She sniffed. "There are certain things in my life I don't want you to know, that I don't want you to ask about."

I took a deep breath. It seemed as if my body had forgotten how. She was cutting us off before we could even get started. "You don't have to do this, Maya. We can take things slow. Really slow."

"A snail would be too fast, Milo."

"I won't ever ask about that part of you. If you want to talk about it, okay, but I won't push you. I told you that. You said where the line was, and I stopped. I'll always stop."

"I can't. I have so much going on right now. I can barely think straight with what's already on my plate."

She turned, but not before I saw her face crumple. Her shoulders shook once. "Just go, okay? I'll talk to you later."

I couldn't stop myself. I knew she was sending me away because she was scared. She wouldn't be so upset if she didn't want me to stay. I put my hands on her arms and pressed my lips to the back of her neck. She sighed, but that was it. She didn't cave, and I knew I'd lost her. At least for the night. "I wish you could find me in the depths and pull me out, but you can't," she whispered. "I'm too far away."

When she said for me to chase her, she meant it. I could see it now. She knew this day would come. The day when the wrong question was asked and she'd shut down, unable to do anything but. But I knew it in my gut that she wanted me to chase her to the depths and pull her free.

"I'm gonna go, but not forever." I kissed the cool skin on the back of her neck. "I told you I'd chase you, and I intend to." She tensed and shuddered. "Bye, sweetheart. For now."

I turned to go and heard her sob, but I didn't stop. She needed to do this. It hurt to hear that and not snatch her up and hold her, but I knew if I didn't leave now, I really would lose her forever.

She needed the chase. She needed me to show her that I wasn't going to leave her for good, that I wanted to save her, and I wasn't afraid of the demons that followed a person. I had my own.

Just as I was about to pull into my driveway, I got a call. It was pretty late, so I answered cautiously. The preacher said the boiler had stopped working at the shelter and wanted to see if my mechanical hands could try to fix it.

I headed to the church feeling pretty crappy about the night. It certainly hadn't gone as I planned, and even though I knew the journey wasn't over, I felt like we were walking on a frozen pond and spring was coming.

I would tiptoe all the way to her if that's what it took.

I would chase her *as far as it took*.

☺ I cannot help you, for I am just a cookie.
☺

Maya

I SOBBED hard on the kitchen floor, his box of cookies in my lap. I sobbed so hard that my eyes wouldn't stay open any longer.

I never wanted anyone before, never wanted the hassle of having another person try to pry his way into a heart that was broken long ago.

I thought I was a lost cause, an empty shell, a vacant body wandering around, waiting for the next person to be taken from me. When he showed up, he made me *want* to be pried open like a fortune cookie.

And at the first sign of him trying to dig a little deeper, I sent him away and basically told him I wanted nothing more to do with him.

I shook my head. I was such a coward. And Will. He knows me. He's called my cowardice 'the vault' since I got back from rehab. I don't like to talk about things. I don't want to rehash. I just want to forget.

I wiped a tear angrily. I was going to have no one in my life if I kept doing this. It hurt so bad in my chest, to talk about the way I used to be. About the way Mom's death made me a weak, pathetic version of myself that I despised. It wasn't her fault, and she would be ashamed to see how I handled it.

No more.

I stood and wiped my nose and eyes before making my way to Will's room. I knocked and he answered immediately. I went and sat on his bed edge gently. He stared. He was a lot like Milo in that way; he waited for me to be ready and didn't push. I crawled up the covers and laid my head on his shoulder. I took his fingers in mine, trying not to feel how cold they were, trying to push away what the doctor said last week, and let it all spill out.

All of it. I'd never told him that piece of me before, and if I was going to tell anyone, it was going to be Will.

I told him how little I valued myself or my body. How I did anything anyone wanted if they'd let me stay there and give me something, anything to make me numb. How I only passed my classes at school because I paid for the test answers. About how even though I was better, I thought about how much I wanted to get high every single day. I told him how I didn't know what I was going to do when he was gone. How he was everything, and I had told Milo he was sick, but not how sick, because it was my job, my burden. Will was mine and I didn't want to share his last days with anyone else. I didn't want their sympathy or pity. I just wanted to get through each day, because that in itself was hard enough.

He squeezed my hand the best he could and listened, not saying a word. I sat there forever it seemed and told him all there was to tell. At some point, I fell asleep and woke right where I'd fallen asleep. His color looked better today. I eased off the bed and ran to grab a shower.

I had somewhere I had to go before work.

But when I drove by his apartment, his Jeep wasn't there. His Jeep wasn't at the mechanic's shop either.

I felt doubly awful. I still had a half hour before I had to be at work, so I figured I'd go get some muffins and coffee for everybody. As I drove through town, I did see his Jeep at the church in town, the one with the shelter we worked with a lot. They helped people and sent some of them our way.

My breath caught. I hoped yesterday didn't make Milo do something…but then I realized how arrogant that statement was and rolled my eyes at myself. I pulled in and wondered if it was too stalkery to go and see him in there.

Should I wait it out and talk to him after work and hope everything was okay. Joey, the preacher's daughter, pulled up beside me, her music blaring, her blond hair blowing in the wind. She hopped out, her jaw dropping at the sight of Milo's Jeep. She turned positively giddy as she bounced her way inside.

It was then that I had my first taste of jealousy. It sucked majorly. He had never mentioned her before, but if this was where he got help from, he knew her, probably very well.

Then there they were—she was hanging on his arm and he was smiling as they climbed into his Jeep. I stared, my heart hurting so badly. Then I remembered what Milo had said about assuming. I closed my eyes and took a deep breath. He wouldn't do that to me or to her. He wasn't *that guy*. They were probably just good friends and he hadn't mentioned her yet. I opened my eyes, begging them not to betray me, and looked over to see her scruffing his hair.

He laughed and pushed her hand off, but then he saw me. His whole face changed from one of carefree happiness to one of fallen upset. I felt that like a bullet through my chest. She made him laugh and smile. All I had done was make him work for my attention. Made him *chase me*. What guy wants to work that hard for a girl? Especially a good looking guy who could have a lot of other girls.

I saw him move to get out, but she stopped him, putting her hand on his arm. He looked at her and back to me. That was it for me. I put the car in reverse, looking at him the entire time, and backed out. He shook off her arm and got out, holding his arms out in a *Don't do this* motion.

Joey basically glared at the whole scene, not understanding anything, which made it clear that she had no idea who I was either. I didn't peel away in anger; I pressed the gas slowly, and honestly in my heart and soul just wanted him to be happy and find some peace. If it was with her, then so be it.

She was a beach and I was a storm. It was a no-brainer who the choice would be.

All that morning, I secretly hoped Milo would come and set me straight. I took extra calls and didn't take a break because I needed to keep my head busy. Listening to the caller's problems and telling them what steps to take was easier than dealing with my own.

When lunch rolled around and he still hadn't come, I waved off everyone who invited me to go eat with them. I wasn't hungry. It appeared sulking was on the menu.

I sat on the front steps, closing my eyes, getting some air, and trying to pretend I wasn't falling apart. Though, one good thing did come of this. Will told me last night after I spilled my guts all over the place that me to trusting him was all he ever wanted. I hadn't realized that he thought that me not telling him things translated to me not trusting him. That wasn't it at all.

I just didn't want him to know all the ways I was capable of being so weak. I didn't want him to worry about me when he was gone. I wanted him to know I was going to be fine.

I didn't have much faith in him, it turned out. He said that by knowing I'd gone through all that and still came back, fought it with everything in me, that he knew without a shadow of doubt I was going to be okay.

But I didn't. I doubted it every day.

I opened my eyes to find Milo knelt down in front of me. I hadn't heard him come up and had no idea how long he'd been there. "Milo," I said, my voice shaking.

"You know, I kinda like that name when *you* say it."

"I wasn't spying," I insisted. "I was just driving by. I went by your place and your work, and you weren't there. I wanted to come and tell you I was sorry."

"Joey's just a friend," he said and lifted his hand to rub my cheek. "There's absolutely nothing going on. She was my sponsor or…whatever. She's the one who helped me stay clean. I lived at the shelter for a while, and she and her father helped me find a place to live and a job. I wasn't hiding her from you. We just hadn't gotten that far yet."

I barely contained my gasp. He supplied more information in that one plea than he had the entire time I'd known him.

"It's not uncommon to develop feelings for your sponsor. It's why it's recommended that sponsors be the same sex. It's called 'hero worship' or something."

He chuckled a little, clearly annoyed. "You think I have hero worship for Joey?"

"I don't know." His shoes were suddenly very fascinating to me. "You were laughing and smiling with her." I sighed forcefully. "Look, I'm not being jealous." One of his brows rose. "Maybe a little, but I'm talking big picture. I'll just bring you down. It won't be easy with me like it could be with her or someone else." I looked him right in the eye. "Someone not an addict. Someone who hasn't lost almost everything. Someone who can tell you about her past without wanting to scream." I swallowed painfully. "When you said you were going to chase me, you didn't realize what a chore that would be." I smiled sadly. "Someone like you…I know you've been through a lot, too. And I hoped one day you'd tell me about it, but I was a hypocrite because I never wanted to actually tell you about mine. Someone like you shouldn't have to work so hard for something that should be so simple. Love should be simple." It hurt to say those words.

I couldn't even be embarrassed that I'd said "love" to him. I was in too deep.

I felt his hands on my cheeks, forcing me to keep my gaze on him. "Love isn't simple, Maya."

"But shouldn't it be? Shouldn't it be easy?" My voice cracked and I knew I was barely hanging on.

"You don't appreciate the things that come easy. The things we fight for are the things that we keep with us for forever."

I thought about how my dad fought for me. How he bailed me out of jail so many times and kept believing I would come back to him one day.

I felt him wipe a tear with his thumb. "Whatever it is that you're thinking about right now, that—that will be with you forever."

If he was asking me if I thought what was between us was worth fighting for, then yes, I believed that. I just wanted to believe I was worth it.

I nodded, finally, so he'd know I was listening.

"I was late to work yesterday, so I couldn't be late today, too. Otherwise, I would have come after you sooner. And this wasn't something I was about to try to do over the phone."

"It's okay," I assured him and covered his hand on my cheek with mine. "I'm glad you came at all."

His lips twisted. "Did you honestly think that after the speech I gave you last night, I was going to be done with you so quickly? And that I'd go out you if I really wanted to be seeing someone else?"

"I thought you realized your error and figured out I was a lost cause."

He smiled. "Someone said that about me once. Not too long ago."

"They were wrong."

"So are you, about this."

"I thought I was the counselor and you were the newbie," I joked.

"Role-playing," he mused and grinned. "I like it." His grin faded away and he looked completely serious in his mission as he leaned forward while also tugging me closer. My hands gripped his shirt at his sides to balance me as he took my lips.

I didn't think. I just felt.

I let everything I felt in that moment, just this moment, roll over me and take control. When my mouth opened under his, it wasn't careful like before, it was an invitation. I could tell when he knew this time was different. He dove deep, and the groan that rattled from him made me flush. He let one of his arms wind around my waist and press me to him as his tongue plundered. I felt my fingers wrap in something soft and tugged. Tugging on his hair made him produce all sorts of noises that had me smiling from the inside out.

His thumb smoothed my cheekbone, such a contrast to the scruff from his chin. His hand rubbed across the bottom of my back, over and over.

He pulled back and looked at me. For once, I didn't squirm. I figured he deserved it for putting up with me. "Can I see you later?"

I nodded emphatically. He smiled wide at that. I swung my arms around his neck and pulled him back to me. His palms moved to my sides, and it was amazing how warm they were. It was like he was on fire.

I nibbled and bit into his bottom lip.

"Good night, woman." He chuckled against my mouth. "You're torturing me."

"Are you on your lunch break?" He nodded and looked at my watch, lifting my wrist. "And you're late," I guessed.

"I'm not going to have a job anymore if I keep this up, bt would be worth it."

He leaned up and kissed my forehead before standing. He smirked, walking backward away from me a few steps before turning. I wasn't ashamed to say I watched his behind as he left. He turned quickly and his smirk grew into a burning smile that had me struggling for normal breaths. "I saw that," he said smugly. He chuckled, probably seeing the way my neck turned pink from where he was. "Bye, sweetheart."

"Bye, Milo," I said loudly, letting him know that Milo was indeed the final name I had decided to call him. A man should be called by the name his mother gave him.

You will make change for the better.

Milo

I KNEW I was pushing my luck, but I asked to be let off work an hour early. Tom was such a sap—a sap that brought in his wife's cookies and homemade sweet bread almost every day. I'd been to their house once and never, ever saw two people who loved each other the way those two did.

So I knew the big softy would understand.

I told him a basic rundown of everything that had happened and how I needed to beat Maya home, to get a few things ready. That I needed to take the chasing up a notch if I wanted this girl to trust me and let me into every single part of her. That she put up a very convincing front, but inside she was a girl screaming for someone to love her unconditionally, to promise to never leave her as everyone before had done, even if they hadn't meant to.

I may not have embellished that much, but he got the gist.

He laughed and cheesy-smiled as he said I could take off early, especially when I told him what I had planned. So I went to my apartment, took the quickest shower of my life, and then high-tailed it downstairs to pick up the order I had called in at the Chinese place.

I knocked on Will's door and hoped the guy wasn't sleeping or at work. I hadn't even thought about that. I didn't know if he'd gone back to work or not. He answered, looking crummier than before, if that was possible, but immediately brightened at what he saw in my arms. He laughed. "Wow. Whipped like butter."

I grinned. "They are revoking my man-card as we speak."

He laughed his words. "Come on in."

I felt a little bit of embarrassment, but there was no backing out at this point. Extreme measures were called for with this girl. "Thanks, man."

"I take it you made up?"

I dumped everything on the table. "Why? This wouldn't be a good apology?"

"It totally would be." He grinned, enjoying my squirming. He was a tall guy, his hair dark like hers, his skin pale but different—where she was fair, he looked pale in the sick way. "However, from the stupid grin on your face, I'd say this wasn't an apology. You're trying to drive your point home. Am I right?"

"Your sister is a beautiful pain in my rear."

He laughed hard, leaning on the counter with his elbow. "That's the best description I've ever heard."

"I have some things I have to do tonight, so I figured I'd…" I looked at the pile. "Make sure she was thinking about me."

"Mission accomplished, brother." He laughed, but that turned into a cough. A deep cough.

"You all right? Still sick?"

He looked up. His head shook just barely, not in answer, but in disappointment. "She's going to come around one day. She'll bust wide open and everything she's kept locked away will come spilling out. Just tell me that you'll be there to pick up the pieces and she won't be alone.

Tell me that you won't be the guy who likes the chase and then bails when things get hard." His throat worked. "Tell me she'll have one person in her life who won't leave her."

This was way more than some big brother talk. God, no... "Will, what's wrong...with you? What kind of sickness do you have?"

He chuckled a little sullenly. "Strangely...in this case, it's not mine to tell." He sobered and shuffled his bare feet to stand in front of me. He was taller than me by a mere inch. "If you're not up to the task, then leave now. I love her, but I know her. She won't survive anything else."

"This isn't some fling, if that's what you mean. I don't know what's going on with you, man, but Maya and me... She's safe with me. I promise you."

He nodded. "That's all I needed to hear."

He patted me on the shoulder as he passed. I watched him go. You couldn't miss how thin he was, how miserable he was, but tried to pretend he wasn't. I leaned against the counter and thought. I wondered when she was going to tell me everything—about her brother most of all.

I had to figure out a way to show her she could trust me with this.

I looked at the pile I'd brought and smiled as I imagined her coming home to find it. And then I got to work.

I hopped out of the Jeep at my apartment and jingled my keys in my hand, smiling to myself smugly as I thought about her coming home. I changed before taking off to the farewell dinner for Joey. Her parents were throwing her a *Congratulations on your new job* party at the church.

She seemed a little different though. She didn't seem as happy about the decision to leave as she had been before, like maybe things hadn't turned out as perfect and rosy as she thought they'd be. After I saw Maya at the church the other day and knew that she had gotten the wrong idea about Joey and me, Joey had acted a little strange about her. She said that any girl that stalked me all over town wasn't worth my time, but she didn't understand anything about Maya and me.

I knew Maya hadn't 'stalked' me all over town. I believed her when she said she happened to see my Jeep when she drove by, but Joey had always been that way. She didn't give people many chances, she didn't waste her time on guys who didn't call her after a date. She was respectful of her parents, but pretty much did whatever she wanted to. She was a definitional free spirit, and I had always wondered why, since all of those things made up Joey, she had given me chance after chance, helping me come back to the land of the living.

That girl was a conundrum.

I pulled into the preacher's driveway and accepted all their hugs and answered their questions on how I was doing as I made my way inside. Joey's mom cooked a meatloaf dinner, enough to feed the whole town. After it was over, Joey and a couple of her friends wanted to go out her last night in town before she went back to Texas and begged me to tag along.

I caved and followed them out to a bonfire some people were throwing at the lake. We roasted marshmallows, or burned them really, and then they started dancing to some Taylor Swift CD. I was done at that point, happy to retreat and listen to some of the guys tell their high school football stories and about how college sucked, nothing like everyone made it out to be.

Since I might attend college next year, somehow, I asked some questions of my own. When the beer was brought out, I told Joey I was gone. She was a little miffed at them, saying she didn't know that they'd be drinking or she wouldn't have invited me. I told her it was all right, though her not knowing a bunch of college kids at a lake party would be getting drunk was a little naïve of her.

She pulled me aside and asked how I was doing. Were the "meeting thingies" still working out for me? As much as I loved her and owed her a huge debt of gratitude,

she was pretty clueless sometimes.

I assured her they were and that I was fine. It didn't take much convincing and she was bouncing off again to enjoy her farewell party. I rolled my eyes at her and laughed when my phone dinged as soon as I walked into my apartment.

I pulled it out, expecting it to be her asking for a ride or something, but it was that same unknown number as before.

Your nephew is due in a few days.

I took a deep breath as I plopped down on the couch, my elbows on my knees. If I expected Maya to face her past, then I had to stop running from mine.

So I heard. What you naming him?

The response was slow. I knew he hadn't expected me to answer.

Jackson

Emma doing OK?

She's great. Hasn't been too rough on her. I think she kinda likes it.

She looked really great. Mamma did too.

You can come back anytime.

I left it with that.

I spent the next hour running around the neighborhood and doing weights. Running at night or early in the morning was my favorite time. It wasn't hot and there was hardly anyone around. I could listen to my music and not worry about traffic, go shirtless and not feel weird.

I was just getting back when I saw a dark-haired beauty on my stairs, headed back down toward the lot. "Hey!"

She turned, looking relieved. I picked up the pace and rushed over to her, running a backward circle around her, grinning. "Well, what do I owe the honor of this visit?"

"I'm glad you're home," she said and smiled, but it wasn't the happy, giddy smile I had been hoping for.

"Yeah. Joey and her friends dragged me out for a while, but I was done pretty quick. I came home early. You all right?"

She moved to hug me, but I stopped her. "Don't. I'm disgusting. You'll get—"

She pushed my hands out of the way and pressed herself to my chest, her arms gripping around my neck. I sighed into her hair and clamped onto her hips.

"Thank you," she murmured into my neck and reached onto her tiptoes to kiss the skin there. My hands tightened on her hips. "You have to be the sweetest man I've ever met. Did you buy every cookie Mrs. Ming had?"

I leaned back a little and lifted her chin. I brushed my thumb over her skin there a couple of times and I'd be lying if the shiver that went through her didn't thrill me to my core. "I wanted you to be thinking about me."

"I'm always thinking about you," she said, almost distractedly, almost as if she didn't even have to of about the answer.

"I know how much you love those cookies," I said, completely off my game. She wasn't being the cute, giddy girl I had expected. I didn't know what was going on, really, but something had happened. Something had clicked.

In the streetlights, I saw her barely shudder, I saw her eyes barely sheen over. I took her face in my hands. "Sweetheart, what's going on?"

Her hands pulled me down while she lifted up to kiss me. Once, twice, again, she kept coming back for more. I couldn't have stopped the moan that bellowed from me when her hands coasted from my shoulders all the way down to my behind. But she didn't stop there. She stuck her freezing hands inside the back of my sweatpants.

I reached back and took her hands gently away, replacing them to my neck. I was in sweatpants, it wasn't leaving much to the imagination, and she was making it infinitely worse. She sighed into my mouth, thinking I was fighting her and pulling back. I wasn't. If anything, I was about to make things so much worse for myself. "Hold on to me, Maya."

With my hands behind her thighs, I lifted her petite frame as if she weighed nothing at all. She didn't wrap her legs around my waist but instead clamped her knees as I turned and sprinted up my stairs with her. She gasped with shock that I could do that and hung on tighter. When I opened the door, I knew she'd been inside. There was a box of cookies with a note on the counter that said in big letters: YOU GET ME LIKE NO ONE ELSE.

I set her on the countertop, but before I could say anything, she was back to making me forget my name, let alone what the hell a cookie was.

It was strange in the weirdest, best way.

It was slow and unhurried. She wasn't pulling and grabbing at me in passion; she was smoothing and coaxing me in reverent fervor. It was so totally contradictory that my head spun as she leaned back and tugged me to bend on my arms on either side of her. Her mouth said thank you and never spoke a word. Her tongue licked at my own as her fingers seemed to count my ribs deliciously.

She smelled amazing. I had no idea what it was, but something good and sweet. Her lips were sweet, too. Cookies, I realized. Her jeans were tight. I let all my weight bear down on one arm so I could push one of my palms down her thigh. Gah, I totally got why Mason was into legs now. The right set of twigs could make you absolutely insane.

I stuck my hands inside her tiny little jacket to grip her sides. She pulled back a smidge. "I can't believe you went running with no shirt. It's freezing out there."

"It's not freezing when you're running." I covered her mouth again so she'd stop talking about it.

She pulled back and put her hand on my chest, her fingers caressing and begging me to make all that pain in her eyes go away. "You'll get sick," she whispered. She stared at my chest, her eyes suddenly vacant, like she wasn't there. "You'll get sick and you'll leave me, too."

That sounded like something that Will had said. I waited, my breaths panting in the space between us. I stayed right there, silent, ready, strong as I could, knowing this was it. What Will had said would happen was happening. My girl was about to break wide open, and I had to be there to make sure she didn't fall apart, even if this was the first small step.

After a long time, I bent as I lifted her chin with my finger. "Maya, I'm not going anywhere." Her lip quivered, something I was beginning to recognize as her last defense of keeping herself together. "I've done so many bad things. I was...not a good guy. I don't deserve you, but there's nothing you can tell me that will make me leave. I am so stuck on you."

"Sometimes things happen," she whispered, tortured.

I covered her lips with my thumb. "I'd fight hell to come back if that's what it took."

One tear made the long journey from the corner of her eye to her jaw. I leaned in and kissed it away, not knowing what else to do. I had to find a way to make her see that she could trust me.

"That night," she began, and I knew this was it. She looked at my eyes and begged me not to disappoint her, begged me to forgive her for things I hadn't even heard yet. I gazed back, letting everything show on my face, and pulled the stool over, turning it around to sit on it backward. "That night in my kitchen when I told you I wasn't a virgin." I nodded. "I used to do things...sex...for drugs."

I nodded again. I wasn't going to confirm my own past. This was her time. She waited, looking more shocked by the second. Her mouth fell open finally and she shook her head. "Why aren't you disgusted? I am!"

she shrieked.

I wrapped my arms around her middle, keeping her from escaping, and whispered into the skin under her ear. "Because the girl you're telling me about was a different girl than the one sitting here now. The one who's sitting here now is strong and courageous and knows she's an addict; she deals with it. The one you're talking about was having a hard time dealing with things, she let the drugs carry her away for a while, and got so desperate that she'd do anything to get them before she got help."

Her chest began to quake softly. "Why?"

"Why what, sweetheart?" I said gently.

"Why do you want me?"

I didn't even have to think. "Because anyone who's been through what you have and can still come out in one piece on the other side is a beautiful creature that I want to know."

"I'm not in one piece," she argued.

"Oh, yes, you are, Maya. It's hard. It's always going to be hard to some degree, but you're here, you're not giving in. You're taking care of Will, whatever he has wrong with him, taking care of others, always helping and giving them your time, and you don't give up." She couldn't hold the sob in any longer, but I kept going. "Why *wouldn't* I want you?"

Her eyes were as wide as half dollars. She swallowed and smoothed her hair, looking around the room. No… I thought I had her this time. I thought she had finally opened up to me. I thought she was finally going to let me in.

"Milo?" she asked and took the box of cookies in her hands.

"Yeah," I said, defeated.

"Put on a shirt, all right? And will you grab a blanket? There's somewhere I want to show you."

My heart hurt it leapt so hard. I grinned without saying a word and ran to do what she asked as she took the box of cookies from the counter and cradled it to her chest. I drove her truck, a little smile on my lips as she told me where to go and sat smashed up against my side. She had me pull into a little gas station that was open twenty-four hours. We went inside and got hot chocolate and then I followed her, bemused, as she led the way out to a row of big satellite dishes that lined a hill behind a fence.

"They don't use these anymore," she explained and looked at me a little sheepish. "I used to come here a lot. I stopped when I got messed up. It was like I didn't want to…taint this place. I found it with Will. In his rebellious days, he used to try to find all sorts of odd jobs so he didn't have to get an actual after-school job. The store owner told him if Will cleaned up all the trash from around the store, he'd pay him a hundred bucks. Will used to have to drag me everywhere with him. When I started driving, I came back here. I…love it here."

She looked up at the sky. It was clear. I hoisted her up and she took the blanket from me before I climbed up myself. We laid there under the covers for a long time in the pitch black of the night before she spoke. Again, I just waited, knowing she would start when she was ready. She lay on my arm as a pillow, and my other arm was draped over her hip.

When she spoke, she dug her nails into my arm without realizing it, but it was okay. If that's what she needed to do, then I would take any pain to help her through it.

With her butt nestled to my front, she told me about all the "awful" things she had done for drugs, how she wound up having to get her GED because she got kicked out of school, not for her grades—she paid for test answers and cheated on homework—but because of her behavior and missed days. Her dad was always rescuing her from parties and strangers' houses. All of it sounded eerily familiar. She told me she couldn't even remember how many guys it had been, their names, where, when, how, what drugs she had done.

Then she told me about how her dad saved her, how she hated him so much for embarrassing her like that, how she was ungrateful, and it took a long time for her to see what he had actually done for her—it wasn't about interrupting a party, it was so much more than that. Then she told me how he died.

And she bawled.

I held her so tightly, so afraid that she was going to fly apart as she sobbed and told me that as soon as she felt like she might be okay, as soon as she felt like she might survive the fact that her dad was dead, she found out her brother was dying, too.

She told me everything. All the things she had been too scared to put words to. She said giving them words gave them life and made it too real. It wasn't that she didn't trust me; she didn't want them to be any more real than they were already.

I turned her toward me and kissed her face all over, her eyes softly. I knew it would be bad, but how did people survive things like that? This tiny girl with such a big heart and spirit with a little spark that was dim, but still there inside her? Will was right. She wasn't going to survive if anything else happened.

She was strong, but there's only so much a person can take until they break, until that person's spirit is chased down the rabbit hole, too scared to come out for fear of being smashed. I held her to me tight and silently promised her and myself that I was never going to let go. No matter what I had to do, I was going to keep that promise.

Maya

I woke with his warm chest on my cheek. It was still partially dark outside, but right then I couldn't find it in me to care.

At some point last night, Milo had carried me back to the truck and we had snuggled up in the seat. Last night we had laid in the dish for hours. I couldn't believe it was all out in the open. It didn't seem real.

And he was still here.

Obviously, he could he faking. He could be acting as if it didn't bother him when in fact it did—

I felt warm fingers smooth the lines between my brows. "Hey," he scolded, his voice roughly sexy from sleep. "No regrets."

"I don't have regrets," I challenged and lifted my chin a little on his chest. "Do you?"

He lifted my chin farther, kissing my closed lips, but still kissing me. Morning breath forgotten, he still wanted to kiss me even though I was clearly a rotten apple? He pulled back and licked his lip. "I'm going to keep on kissing you until you stop making that self-deprecating face."

"There's no such thing."

He leaned in and pulled my torso up this time for a full body experience of licks and bites and nibbles. I gasped when he let me go. "Are you finished?" he asked. "I can go all day."

I smiled, couldn't help it. "Is that supposed to deter me or..."

"Oooooh," he mocked with a grin and settled in closer. "She shoots, she scores."

I giggled. "You're pretty cute."

He looked at me funny and then grimaced. "Oh, my... No."

"What?"

"You're a morning person." He wrinkled his nose. "Look at you. All smiley and sassy at whatever the hell time it is before the sun comes up."

I giggled and then covered it. "Um...sorry?"

"*Good night*, I need coffee." He pulled me into his lap before scooting under me and sliding over in the driver's seat. He gripped my thigh and tugged me closer. "Let's go get breakfast."

"My favorite meal of the day," I gushed happily and slipped my arm through his.

He chuckled and rubbed my leg during the short drive. In no time at all, I was scarfing bacon and eggs. He watched as he ate his own, his eyes lit with fascination.

"What?" I laughed, mumbling around my eggs.

"I've never seen a girl eat like that."

I glared and cocked my head. "Like what exactly?"

His lips twitched as he pushed his plate aside and leaned across the table. "I am going to sound like a total chick right now, but God, I just... God, I am so glad I met you." I bit into my smiling lip. "A girl who's beautiful, humble, eats real food, has completely real boobs." My brows rose. "I assume," he recanted and grinned devilishly. "Is short, but still manages to have legs for days, wickedly smart, genuine, loving, and knows what's important." He shook his head.

I laid my fork down gently and pushed my plate over near his. "Is that really how you see me?"

"Yes. I think your boobs are totally real." I chuckled under my breath, but my eyes never left his. His never left mine. He reached over the short Formica table and cupped my cheek. "Yes. That's you, sweetheart."

My breath eased out slowly. "I really love it when you call me 'sweetheart', Milo."

"I love it when you call me 'Milo', sweetheart."

I was absolutely falling for him. There was no turning back now. But could something I wanted so much last? Could something that seemed so easy really be that easy?

He paid the check, and I didn't protest. I could tell he was the type that was raised to pay, and that fighting about it was futile. Besides, it was nice. I hadn't had anyone take care of me before. It felt odd to let someone look after me for once.

"Hey now," he scolded like he'd done this morning, rubbing between my brows. "Don't do that. No waiting for the worst to happen."

I smiled as best I could. "It's hard for me to accept it when good things come my way. And before you make some smart remark, yes, I'm talking about you."

He smiled, but didn't crack any jokes. He leaned in, taking me in his arms and pressing his lips to my ear. "Fall, sweetheart. I'll catch you."

When one door closes, another opens.

Milo

THE NEXT four weeks were amazing ones.

Maya and I had become that gross, disgusting couple people didn't want to invite out to dinner because they couldn't keep their hands off each other long enough to make it through a course.

Man, did I love that.

Just about every night I was at Maya and Will's, she was at mine, or we went out for dinner and a movie or something. We went to an NA meeting every week and sat through every one of them together. Will seemed to perk up the past week, too. He seemed relieved that I knew about his illness. He was strange that way. Most people with an illness didn't want you to know, but him—he wanted you to know and just get everything out in the open. We wound up becoming pretty good friends, and I even took him to the doctor once for Maya, who had run out of sick days.

Of course she was going to take it off anyway, but I insisted, and Will insisted even more than I did. It was a long drive into the city to the Cancer Treatment Center—about three hours. He said, and I quote, that riding with his nail-biting sister was like pulling out his hair one by one because she was just so worried the whole time. Will and me? We got greasy burgers, and we jammed to The Black Keys the whole way. I didn't go into the doctor's office or caner wing of the hospital with him, but I sat in the waiting room. It was pretty uncomfortable, and it made me feel bad for Mason having done this for Mamma so many times and I hadn't been there for any of it.

Will and I didn't talk about what the doctor said. I figured if he wanted me to know, he would have said. He didn't, so I didn't. He fell asleep halfway home, and I was forced to think about my own brother. I felt guilt pile on me in a way I hadn't in weeks. I was doing something like this for someone else's brother and not my own.

When we got home that night, I don't know how she knew about the junk food and loud music and the pit stop to the smoke-filled arcade, but she knew. It was the first time I got chewed out Maya style. Will took it like a champ because obviously he was no mere novice of the inner workings of his sister's psyche.

I, on the other hand, saw the tirade as a ticket to the crazy train and used that term to describe the fight. Yeah, I said "crazy". That only escalated things to nuclear levels, to which I was saved by Will, who hugged his sister to him and with three words reduced her to a sobbing mess.

I'm still here.

It hit me, like a ton of idiotic bricks. But before I could apologize, she was apologizing to me, and before I knew it, when we were doing more than that.

The make up make out was worth the fight, believe me.

A few days after that, I was getting ready for dinner out with Maya and her brother. He said he felt like the squeaky third wheel, but I knew she worried about him. He rarely ever left the house, so we were taking him to a new restaurant in town that boasted *the best breakfast for dinner food you can find*. So we were going to sample to whole-grain pancakes. Maya said it was the best of both worlds. She still felt like Will was eating well and healthy but eating bad at the same time. He just shook his head and didn't argue.

I had just gotten out of the shower when I heard Maya talking to someone in my living room. I didn't even know she'd gotten there yet. With my towel wrapped around my hips, I peeked out my door and gave her a small wave. She was on the phone, but she gave me an uneasy look.

She was on *my* phone.

"Sorry. Here he is. He just got out." She handed it to me and looked at the floor. "I'm really sorry. It rang and it's habit to answer Will's all the time. I'm…sorry."

I gave her a funny look. "It's all right." She looked at my chest and I realized I was only in a towel. Her eyes drifted lower and closed.

I took the phone. "Hello?"

"Milo?"

"Mason?" I said in surprise. I hadn't heard his voice in so long…it sounded so foreign yet so familiar.

"You said to call when she was having the baby, and she's having the baby. She went into labor about an hour ago. I don't know where you are, but…if you left now, you might make it before he's born."

I looked into Maya's eyes that were now open and searching mine. I didn't know why I did. I hadn't even told her about my family or anything and she hadn't pushed me to. I thought she might make me feel guilty about her spilling all her guts and me having yet to spill mine, but she didn't. And now, she searched for clues as to whether or not I was going to slam the door closed. Now that the opportunity was knocking, was I going to slam it in her face like I'd done before, or face it?

"Milo?" he asked again, defeat in his voice. He thought I was bailing, too.

"We're on our way," I told him, my eyes on hers—always on hers.

"I don't know who she is," he said quietly, "but, man, I like her."

"Yeah, I kinda like her, too." I hung up and took a step closer to her. "Call Will and tell him our date is cancelled. You and I are going to meet my nephew."

"You're not angry with me?"

"Why would I be?"

"For answering your phone," she whispered. "I know you don't want…"

"No," I whispered back. "I'm not angry."

"I thought you didn't want me to know them," she confessed.

"I didn't want you to know the old me."

She swallowed and put her hand on my chest. "You really want to take me with you? To meet your family?" She looked up, her eyes burning into mine. "You can do it alone if you have to."

"You don't want to come?" My heart ached at the thought of that.

"I do. A lot. I just don't want you to feel like I'll hate you if you don't bring me. It's a big step. It's been years, right?" I nodded. Long, hurtful, stupid years. "I won't. I'll be right here for you either way."

"I want you to come with me," I insisted and pulled her to me, my arm hooked around her hip. "Can I ask one thing, though?"

"Anything."

"Can we wait until this is over before I explain anything to you? Because I want you to fall in love with them before I tell you and you hate me. That way you won't leave me."

She palmed my cheek, taking a deep breath before blowing her peppermint breath against my lips. "I won't leave."

"Please. Don't ask me anything until we get back, okay?"

"I won't push either."

"I know," I said, and knew it for truth. I pressed my lips against her cheek. "And I love that about you."

She sucked in a quick breath. I moved, searching for her lips until I found them. Her cool hands on my warm-from-the-shower bare skin had my own hands gripping her to me tighter with the amazing feel of it. Her mouth opened under mine as I pushed her against the back of the couch. One of her legs lifted a little as her butt took the hit. "I would love to let you violate me as long as you wanted to," I said against her lips, "but I think babies probably don't wait."

"I think you have this backward, mister." She giggled at her joke. Good night, it was adorable. "You're going to meet your nephew!" she squealed happily. "You're an uncle. Oh, my gosh. That's the hottest thing," she breathed.

"Really?" I asked, really, really intrigued.

"Babies make a man…" She shook her head. "That's it. Babies make a man a *man*."

I chuckled. "Uncles aren't really classified as men. We're supposed to be silly and throw the kids around, get them in trouble, and pump them with sugar before we take them home."

"Yep," she agreed with a small smile.

"You are pretty confusing right now, woman."

She laughed and pushed my chest, turned me, and slapped my butt. "I'll call Will and get Marybeth to babysit him. Get dressed, uncle."

I was more nervous now than I had been on the ride over to see Mom weeks ago. I was irritated, agitated, anxious, and though I knew I was being a jerk, Maya trying to make me feel better every five minutes was making me feel worse.

I knew when all this was over and we were on the other side of this thing that I wasn't going to have Maya any longer. I just knew it. It almost felt like I should just piss her off now so it would be easier to walk away when she left me later.

The more we drove, the more nervous I got. The farther we got, the harder I gripped the steering wheel.

"Milo, it'll be okay."

I gritted my teeth. "Just stop, Maya."

"I don't understand. You seemed so excited before and now…"

"Now, what?" I looked at her in the dark of the car and back to the dark road. "Now I'm just understanding better that I was naïve to think that a baby was going to make everything better. I can't just walk in there after all this time and expect them to just open their arms."

"They want you there," she insisted harder. "He called you." She covered my angry thumping fingers on the steering wheel. "Let me drive."

"I can drive. I'm fine."

"Milo, you're not fine. Just let me drive so you can relax and think."

"*Good night, Maya,*" I growled angrily. She sat back, her face tight. "I said I'm fine. Just stop already." I sighed and looked back at the road. "It's been a long time, and you have no idea what I've done. I don't think it's too much of a stretch to be a little apprehensive about seeing my brother that I haven't seen in years!" I was yelling. Yelling, like a freaking ass. "I was awful to him. He tried to save me over and over and over and all I did was spit in his face and yet, he still tried to save me. He took care of me when we were kids when my dad left. He takes care of my mom and his wife, and now he's having a baby. A *baby.*" I shook my head, my hands gripping the steering wheel so tight it hurt. "So don't make out like I have no right to be upset."

I was doing it again. I was letting my bubbling anger at myself turn me into the person who turned and ran when he faced down his past. I couldn't seem to stop.

"Milo, I know it's hard—"

"This isn't some boo-boo to kiss better."

"I'm not saying it is. I've been there." I felt her hand on my arm. "It's hard to believe they'll forgive you."

"Maybe I don't want him to," I yelled. My voice bounced against the glass so hard it hurt my ears. I felt bad. I felt so bad, but I *couldn't* stop. "I certainly don't deserve it."

"That's not for you to decide. You do what needs to be done, try your best to make up for what you've done, move on, and work hard every day to go forward, not fall back."

"That all sounds a little easier said than done."

"It is."

I scoffed. "Do you hear yourself? This is an awful pep talk."

"I'm not going to sugarcoat things for you because that's not going to help you in the end. I'm not going to tell you things are going to be easy when they aren't. You need to know that things are always going to be hard," she said loudly to the side of my face. I hadn't looked over at her in a long time. I was being such a coward. Her fingers dug into my arm harder. "But family can make it easier."

I scoffed again. "Wow. No, they don't."

She yelled as she continued. "And the fact that you have family, and are considering not reconciling with them at all because you're a coward makes my sympathy for you plummet." I gulped, understanding her anger coming at me from all sides. She had one family member left to her name, and he was about to taken from her, too. But…how did family make addiction and crap like that easier? How did they make me not want to get high? That made no sense.

"Just stop, okay? Just stop. I don't want to talk about it anymore. Maya, I'm sorry you think I'm being selfish. Or childish, or naïve, whatever it is that you think about me right now, but every person is different and handles things differently. I'm not sure I'm ready to…ready to…" What the hell was the matter with me? "Ready to stop hating him. Ready to stop hating myself."

I took a courageous breath and turned to look at her. She was staring patiently at me, not smiling, not frowning, just being there, just like she said she would be. She'd been here herself, done this, walked people through this. I gently knocked my fist on the wheel a few times.

I would not do this to her right now. And more importantly, I was not going to do this to myself again.

I was done running.

I looked behind me and pulled off the highway into a gas station. Under the awning, I put the car in park and sighed, leaving the Jeep running as I leaned my head back on the seat. "Damn it," I growled, "why does this have to be so hard?"

She leaned over and put her hand on my cheek, pulling my face to look at her as she leaned over. The black hair fell across her shoulder, and she looked like my own personal raven-haired angel right then.

"Milo, I wish I could tell you that it wasn't and that it was all going to be okay. That you'd never want to get buzzed or drink again, that you'd never want to run, scream, or... But that's just not true. It's painful and it's our burden to bear, but we don't have to do it alone."

I looked at her. Just looked at her. She was still there, and I couldn't believe it. Why? After all the awful, stupid things I said. Why would she even want to be there?

I met her in the middle of the console and took her face in my hands, pressing my forehead to hers. She closed her eyes and I got so much happiness that she could still feel safe with me after the ass I was. "Maya," I whispered and kissed her lips once, "I'm so sorry."

"Aren't we all," she whispered back.

"No, Maya," I started, but she stopped me, putting her thumb over my lips. Both of our hands were on each other's faces, our breaths collided between us.

"Everyone, but especially people like us, just want to be forgiven. We want to be welcomed back in with wide open arms and told that people make mistakes." I caught a tear that raced down her cheek with my finger. "I'll always be here, baby, with arms wide open."

Baby. She called me baby. "That goes double for you," I said, my voice gruff. "Sweetheart, I'm so sorry for talking to you that way."

"It's forgotten," she promised.

I had to tell her. I just had to. I hurt with whiplash from the way this whole conversation was going from one end to the other, but I had to say it. "Maya, remember when I said I'll catch you if you fall?"

She sucked in a breath so hard that I felt the cool of it against my lips. "Yes."

"Well, I hope you'll do the same for me." Her breaths were rapid against my chin. "Because even though we just had that stupid fight and this may be the most idiotic time to say it, I'm falling so hard for you."

She pulled back to see my face full on. I kept going. "You bring me back from the ledge. You make me feel like I'm not just…existing." She gasped and covered her mouth with her fingers. I didn't know what that meant, but I kept going. "You give me a reason to see a future for myself. I never saw anything there except a blank space. I don't know if it was blank because I was scared or I was just vacant, but…you make me feel alive."

She let her hands fall from her mouth and stared at me. I couldn't go any further. If she was disgusted, then I had to stop. I scoffed and shook my head. Gah, I was such an idiot. Of course she was disgusted. I had just been yelling at her not five minutes ago and now I was spouting my love for her? She was probably looking for the nearest exit.

Her hand on my face brought me back to her. "I'm sorry," I said immediately. "I shouldn't have."

"Shouldn't have what?" she asked. She laughed and I was more confused than before. "Wow, Milo. You're really working yourself into

119

frenzy, huh?"

"Uh…What?"

"You are the most cocky…self-conscious boy I've ever met."

"Is there such a thing?"

"Yes. I'm looking at him."

"I don't know what that means."

"It means that you are comfortable enough to come out of the shower with nothing on but a towel, then ask me to come meet your family which you haven't seen in years, yell at me with no mercy, then tell me you almost love me, and then backtrack with an apology, assuming that I *will assume* that you're crazy or something, like I'm not just as crazy about you as you are about me."

All the air left my brain. "Maya," I whispered.

She leaned in and pressed her lips against mine. "Milo."

This time when I took her face in between my hands, I kept them there for a good long while. This wasn't a make out session; this was a love on session. This kissing was deep and slow and all consuming breaths and hands and fingers and tongues, moans, groans, aches, and so achingly slow.

I know, I know. There was a baby coming, but that baby was coming either way. And either way, I was going to meet him, and either way, I was going to reconcile with my brother.

Right then, I had to do this.

I had to love on Maya the only way I could and thank her for bringing me back to life.

I did let her drive the rest of the way and I was glad because by the time we reached the hospital, I was a wreck. She gripped my hand so tight as we went inside. I felt like such a little pansy for being so scared. I mean, this was Mason. My brother, Mason. I didn't even know how I was going to feel about him yet. What if I saw him and still hated him? What if I saw him and wanted to do nothing but run the other way?

I hated this so much.

Maya asked the lady at the desk for Emma's room number, but she didn't need to. Mason stood at the end of the hall, pacing. He looked up and saw me, almost as if he could sense me in that moment. The second his eyes locked on mine, I knew I was going to be okay—everything was.

Maya rubbed my arm soothingly, noticing the way I'd stiffened.

All I wanted to do was hug him and tell him how sorry I was, how I was such an idiot, how I was sorry for leaving Mom like that. Before I knew it, my feet were moving. He seemed surprised, even more so than I did.

When I reached him, I bear-hugged him and felt his arms wrap around me. I felt years of hate crumble around me—an avalanche of pain and hatefulness and stupidity and doubt. It was awful and wonderful. It was beautiful and painful. I hated it and loved it. I felt Mason shaking and realized he was crying.

That added more guilt for all the pain I'd caused him. I could hold it in no more. I put my mouth to his ear and told him quietly. "Mason… you have no idea how sorry I am. Forgive me for…" I couldn't finish. I was going to lose it.

"Don't," he said, his voice gruff. He pulled back and looked at me. "Don't. You don't have to say anything. I'm just happy to have you back. That's all I ever wanted. You look so good." He laughed and wiped at his eye embarrassingly. "Emma told me you looked really good, but I didn't believe her."

"Yeah," I said. What else could you say? "Uh, Mason. This," I gripped Maya's hand and pulled her to my side gently, "is Maya."

"Hi, Maya," he said happily and shook her hand. "Really good to meet you."

"Nice to meet you, too."

"So, where's Emma?" I asked, wondering why he was standing in the hall.

"You just caught me coming out to give her parents a second to go in. They only let a couple people in at a time so. It's almost time." He sat hard in the chair and gulped, but looked deliriously happy. "I'm about to be a father."

> There is only one happiness in
> life: to love and be loved.

Maya

"Where's Mamma?" Milo asked.

Oh, my gosh. He really did call her Mamma.

"She's home with the nurse," Mason told him and stood when a prim and proper man and woman came out. "How's Emma?"

"She's asking for you, Mason. Go," the man ordered.

Mason started to go, but turned quickly back. "Uh, Rhett, this is my brother, Milo, and his…friend, Maya."

"Brother?" the man breathed in awe, and I knew they had to know about Mason and Milo's estrangement. Of course they did if Mason was married.

"I've got it, Mason. Go on," Milo said and waved his brother ahead as he turned to Rhett—coolest name ever—and smiled his charming smile. "Hi. I'm afraid I'm the problem son, Milo." He stuck out his hand. "Nice to finally meet you."

They didn't laugh at his joke. Not a snicker.

I felt awful and frankly, a little peeved with the mister and misses for not trying to help the obviously nervous wayward son find his way back. "And I'm Maya," I injected, way too happily. "Wow, a baby. If he looks anything like these two Sawyer boys, he'll be a heartbreaker one day, right?"

"Sawyer?" the woman asked, her perfectly manicured brow raised.

"My name was Wright," Milo leaned in and corrected, his lips touching my ear—as if that itself were the apology. "I had to change it. I promise I'll explain that later, too."

I looked up at him and I knew he would. I felt a smile line my lips. Though, honestly, there wasn't much to smile about in that second. There was currently two very pompous looking adults who didn't look very happy with, and Milo had changed his last name, which could mean a multitude of things, but the fact that instead of letting me guess and be confused and over-think all night, he rushed to let me know that he would explain. That there was a valid explanation and he wasn't going to shortchange me in that.

That itself seemed like an almost-explanation.

And for now, that was enough for me.

He leaned in close and spoke low. "Wow, I don't know what the hell I did to put that look on your face, but you need to write it down so I can commit it to memory."

I bit into my lip to stop from kissing him. His smirk was adorable as he turned back to the couple still looking at us. He took my hand as we faced them again. With his hand in between both of mine, I felt whole, even for just a minute.

Milo asked politely, "I'm sorry. I didn't get your names, but I assume you're Emma's parents."

"Oh, my goodness. Yes, of course," the woman said, flustered and embarrassed. "Silly. Excuse us. Yes, this is Rhett and I'm Isabella. I didn't know that you'd met Emma."

"A couple of times. Yes ma'am," he informed her. He rubbed his head and looked back at me a few times. "It wasn't always under the best terms, but I'm doing a lot better now."

"That's good to hear, son," the man said, but you could still hear it. The tone. They always wondered if you were just telling them what they wanted to hear. "Do you have a place to stay?"

"Oh, we've got to get back—"

"Babies take a long time," Isabella told us and flashed white teeth. "A really long time. You didn't think you'd just run down here and run right back, did you?"

We looked at each other and shrugged. Hadn't really thought it through, to be honest. I hadn't even grabbed any clothes. "Well, let's wait a while and see how it goes."

She said it as if her word was bond and that was that.

We didn't say anything; we just smiled and went to sit a little farther down in the corner. I asked Milo if he wanted to go walk around his old town and he quickly said no. I was hungry and he was, too, I knew, but I wanted to wait until he heard something from Mason before I said anything to him. He seemed calm enough, but I knew it was a matter of time before he started to get nervous again.

And I could guess when we went to see his mother is when it would happen.

And why wasn't his mother up there? They said she needed to stay with the nurse, so maybe she was sick. That was another one of those things I wasn't going to ask. I wanted to know, of course I did, but I promised him I'd wait. And I would.

When Mason came out again, he was jumped by Emma's parents, so he quickly shooed them back to her. He seemed relieved but so exhausted as he came over to us. I tried to stay quiet and let them have as much privacy and "them" time as possible.

"So, how are you?" Mason asked quietly.

"I'm good." Mason's eyebrows rose in question. "Really good, I promise. I live a few hours from here."

Mason shuffled on the wall they were leaning on. "You know you can come back, right?" Milo sighed. "Milo," Mason argued.

I was so lost, but tried to pretend I wasn't.

"I don't know, Mason. I'm finally okay. I was so not okay there for a while. I know you know, but I'm…" He looked at me and his eyes pleaded for something, but I don't think even Milo knew what. "I'm really okay," he finally said.

I got it then. His brother was asking him to move back home, and he was saying that he didn't want to. I had to agree. It may have been selfish, but if Milo left, I'd be devastated to go back to the way things were before.

"We just got you back," Mason said, completely oblivious to anything else.

"I'm not going anywhere," Milo told him, but his eyes hadn't left mine. Finally, he looked over and they did some brotherly half-hug thing. "I'll come to see you. I promise I will. Besides, I'm going to have a nephew to spoil, right?"

"Speaking of…" Mason looked around. "Where are her parents?"

"We'll be fine here. Go."

After about an hour, Mason came back and said that she was only three centimeters dilated, whatever that meant, but apparently in regards to babies, it wasn't good. Mason said we should go and crash at his house with his mom and come back in the afternoon after we got some sleep— kill two birds with one stone, or three, depending on how you looked at it. He said to sleep in his and Emma's room.

It took some arm-twisting, but Milo finally agreed to leave the hospital, and I saw the nervousness come over him in the drive over. "It's really late. Or early. Will your mom still be up?" I asked, trying to make him see that there wasn't any reason to start freaking out.

"Uh." He glanced at the clock on the dash to see it was almost five a.m. and sighed. "No, I don't think so." His hand in mine relaxed a little.

"Probably not. You're right."

"This isn't a question about your past," I began, and his recently calmed skin hardened under mine, "I just want to know one thing." I didn't wait. "Are you more scared about her reaction or mine?" He stayed silent. "I mean, you were here the other day to see her, so I can't imagine she'd be too surprised to see you. I can only imagine it's me you're freaking out about."

His thumb rubbed over my knuckles so softly it made my chest ache. He waited a long time before he said softly, "I just don't want to lose you now."

"You won't," I promised.

"You can't say that when you don't know everything."

I leaned over the console and kissed his cheek. "Milo, I don't know why you have it in your head that you need me so much and I'm just enjoying the ride, but I need you, too." He looked over, our noses almost bumping. "I was scared to tell you about my past. So scared that you weren't going to want anything to do with me anymore. But you did, and so will I. Stop ending us before we've even begun." I kissed his cheek once more. "And find us some food before we go to your mom's or else you are going to have one cranky female on your hands."

I relaxed into my seat, his hand firmly clasped into mine. His chuckle told me this conversation was effectively ended for now. "All right, you win. If it's still open, I know the best greasy burger in town."

One drive-thru, two stoplights, and one left turn later, we pulled into a small, cute house's driveway. He finished off his fries and drink and threw all the trash in the back. "I didn't realize I hadn't fed you all night. I'm sorry. I was too preoccupied and wasn't doing a very good job of taking care of you."

"I can feed myself. I just wanted to stay with you."

His eyes stayed on my face for a long time. "Come on. I'm beat. I know you are, too."

When we got inside, there was a woman wearing scrubs asleep on the couch. He took me straight to a bedroom and began kicking off his shoes. The bed was slept in, and you could tell they left in a rush. I went into the hall and looked for a change of sheets. When I came back with some, he seemed grateful. "Good. I was a little grossed out by the thought of that."

I smiled. After we made the bed, he began to rummage through the drawers. He pulled one of Mason's shirts out and handed it to me. I shook my head. "That's too weird. I can't wear his clothes."

He looked down. "Okay. Here." He pulled off his shirt. "Put this on. I'll borrow one of his tomorrow."

He left and I knew he was giving me privacy to change. Then I heard his voice by the door. "Here. These, too."

He tossed in his loose plaid boxers. I gawked at them. "Um, what are you wearing, then?"

"I'll borrow some flannels from Mason. It'll be fine," I heard through the door.

I hurried and put the clothes on, doing the cliché sniffing of the collar as I pulled on his plain blue shirt. Good Lord, it smelled so good, like him. His boxers were way too big, but stayed on my hips. I gulped as I looked at that bed.

He came in wearing nothing but a pair of red flannel sleep pants he must have found somewhere else in the house. He rubbed his hands together and looked at my legs and kept looking, his lips parted. "I turned up the heat. It's a little cold in here." His eyes lifted up my body to my face. "I'm going to make a pallet on the floor, so go ahead and—"

"What?"

"Maya, I'm not going to make you sleep with me just because there's nowhere else to sleep."

"We're adults, Milo."

He scoffed. "With those legs? You think I can be an adult with those legs next to me?"

I grinned; I couldn't help it. "Stop it. I trust you."

There was that word. It must have meant something more than that, because he sobered up quickly. "If you're sure. I don't want you to feel like you have to."

"I've already slept with you once."

"Satellite dishes and truck front seats don't count."

"Oh, they count," I argued and grabbed his hand, dragging him with me. "Come on. I trust you completely to be the gentleman I know you are."

"It's not just that." He sat next to me on the bed. The lamp on the bedside table was the only light left on in the room. My legs were folded under me, and one of his knees was bent as he slid next to me. "It's not just about trust. I know you know I won't do anything you don't want me to, but I want you to feel safe with me, too."

My brow dipped. "Isn't that the same thing?"

He smiled sadly. "No, it's not." His hand lifted from his lap to cup my cheek. "When a guy tries to pull a move and a girl says no, that's being a gentleman. That's trust. But sometimes girls let guys go further than they really want to because they feel like they should. Being safe is knowing that no matter what happens between us, how far we go, how hot things get, I won't be pulling any moves at all."

I wasn't sure what to say to that. He was a guy, so I knew he wanted to, but I wasn't sure when I would be ready for that. I knew he was trying to protect me because he knew about my past.

"Baby." He pulled at my attention and I sighed all the way to my toes. He'd never called me that before. "Tell me the truth. Do you feel safe with me? Do you know that no matter how much I kiss you and touch you and want you that I won't take it further than that until we both know you're ready? And you can tell me to stop at any time and I won't get angry with you like those guys used to?"

"I know, Milo," I told him, my voice soft and sincere. I leaned in and kissed him, my lips barely whispering across his skin. "I've never felt so safe."

He gripped my hips and pulled me into his lap. Our faces were the same height this way, and with his hand buried in my hair, he studied me once again. "Thank you for being there for me today."

"There's nowhere else I want to be."

He chewed on his lip a little. "I promised we would talk tonight."

"We can wait 'til we get home. It's been a long day. And you've barely even gotten to see your brother. Just wait. I'm not going anywhere."

His head shook as he looked into my eyes. "Where did you come from?" he muttered under his breath. He linked our fingers, pressing and locking them together, releasing them and locking them again right before they could be free.

"What are those?" I nodded toward the stacks of books everywhere. "They have tons of them."

"I don't know. Let's see." He reached back, but kept me on his lap. I had to put a hand on his stomach to keep from toppling over. He came back with a book and cracked it open to the middle. He read aloud. "A duck has three eyelids." His eyes lifted. "Hmm." He went back to reading. "It's impossible to sneeze with your eyes open. A man's beard grows faster when he anticipates sex." He lifted his head and looked at me, his smirk in full-swing.

I giggled. "Oh, I like that one."

"I think that last one needs to be tested out." He set the book away and clicked off the lamp. "Maybe one day we'll see if that one works, yeah?"

"Yeah."

"But not today," he reminded.

"Yeah. Not today."

His arms wrapped around my waist and his mouth closed over mine gently before pulling away. "Come on, baby." He pulled me with his arm behind my back. "I'm beat."

We lay facing each other, and I couldn't believe I was in the house Milo grew up in. I couldn't believe his mother was in the other room. I couldn't believe I'd met his brother, and he was as sweet and adorable as Milo was. Then a thought hit me. "Why aren't we sleeping in your room?"

"It's not my room anymore," he said simply.

There was a bizarre peace in that statement. An understanding of one's new place in the world he created for himself.

His fingers skated across my cheek. "Even in the dark, I can see your brain working a mile a minute." His nimble fingers turned me, putting my back to his front, and he nuzzled into my neck, pulling my bottom to be snug with his hips. He put his lips to my ear and whispered, "Turn it all off." His hand swept down my hair and scalp.

"Don't worry. Even if I can't sleep, I'll still be on my game tomorrow." He gave a short snort of a laugh. "I'll still be here for you no matter what. It's why I came."

"You didn't come to learn all my secrets?" he asked in a joking, conspiratorial whisper.

"Maybe a little," I stage whispered back. "But mostly I came for the free food."

He laughed softly into my ear, my back shaking with his chest. "I knew it." He kissed my hair. "Just don't think. Sleep."

"You're so good at that," I confessed, even as my eyelids obeyed his command.

"At what?"

I turned my head to rub my cheek against his nose. "Making me feel like no matter where I am, I'm right where I belong."

"You *are* where you belong," he growled and tugged me closer.

I heard his name sighed from my lips before his hand reached for my chin. He pulled my face around and his mouth latched on mine. His fingers were so gentle, even as his mouth commanded and demanded, almost as if he was taking what was already his.

He stayed where he was behind me on his side and kept me on my side as well, knowing that the awkward position would be a barrier in and of itself.

He urged me to open for him. I knew that our night was just beginning and it was going to be torturous in the best way.

After my lips ached and my breathing was so hard, it beat against his lips, he pulled back just enough to pant his words. "I can see you in my life so clearly, just like this. Us, after a hard day, just wanting to be together, wanting to get lost in each other in the dark."

I couldn't breathe. I couldn't imagine anything better. "I've never been able to imagine my future before. Never could see what that would look like because I knew Will…" I caught the sob right on the edge. He put his forehead to mine and smoothed my cheek with his thumb. "But right now? I could totally see this," I whispered.

"This would be so easy to fall into and never want to come back out of."

I nodded. He was right. I had never even wandered near the L word, let alone thought about saying it. It was scary territory, but I knew he wouldn't leave me alone there. I knew he wouldn't take me for a ride and then dump me off somewhere with a broken heart.

This all seemed to happen so fast, even though it had been months, it seemed like minutes. I guess in the grand scheme of my life, it had been.

"Get some sleep, sweetheart," he ordered against my neck and nuzzled in for the night.

You have a charming way with words. Write a letter this week.

Milo

HEAVEN.

I was in it.

Surrounded by it.

Smelling it.

Feeling it.

Touching it.

Her behind was still so snugly fastened in the crook of my hips when I woke I thought I had woken in hell and this was my torture device for the rest of my life—the thing always out of grasp to taunt me and tease me…but there she was, under my hands.

I breathed in her neck and groaned at the smell of us mixed together—her in my shirt that was too big, her in my *boxers* that were too big. *Good night.* She was a walking, talking heap of adorable sexiness. I could have stayed in that bed all day, but I gently picked up her arm up to find on her watch it was already a little after one in the afternoon. I was sure she wanted to get home to her brother. If this baby didn't come soon, we

133

were going to miss it.

I nuzzled my way into her neck, kissing and nibbling. "We've got to get up, beautiful."

The giggle. Oh, my good Lord, help me. "Why? It's warm under here."

"You want to see a baby, don't you?"

"Did they call?" she asked, sitting up excitedly. Her hair was swept over half her face.

I smirked. "No. Not yet."

"Then that baby apparently doesn't want to see us." She plopped back down on her side, away from me.

"You're forcing me to use extreme measures."

"Don't do anything you'll regret."

"Last chance."

"Milo!"

"Here goes." I pulled her over to face me, her giggling the whole time, and started kissing her neck and sucking dramatically. When she started squealing, I knew I'd won.

"Um, excuse me, Milo?" we heard at the door.

We looked at each other and laughed like we'd been caught. "Uh, yes?"

"Your mamma says to bring out that giggling girl she can hear you done brought home with you right now and come have some dinner with her."

"Ohp!" Maya said and pressed her lips together. "It feels like high school all over again."

I smiled but knew our little fun morning-slash-afternoon was coming to a halt. She was about to meet my mom; my mom who wouldn't remember her twenty minutes later. I'm sure she would love that. And to know I had completely left my family when they needed me most—spazzed and did nothing but care about myself and ran away—that was really going to make her just fall head over heels for me.

"Hey," she said softly, her cool hand pulling me from my memories. "I'm not going anywhere, remember?"

"Yeah," I said, but didn't know if I meant it.

"Come on." She tugged on my arm. "I want to meet your mom."

I didn't know if I should warn her or not. A part of me wanted to let her be ambushed with it, that way she'd be angry about it. That way she'd have something to want to leave me over, but I had already seen what the future looked like with her in it, and I was done with pushing her away and running from my past. "Okay, but, uh, one thing."

"Okay."

"Without going into too much family history, my mom was in an accident a few years ago."

"Okay," she said softer, more sympathy seeping through.

"Her…short-term memory doesn't work anymore. She remembers me and her life and everything, but she can't remember anything after the accident." Maya looked confused, but took my hand in between hers. She had no pity in her eyes though. That was a first. Usually, the few people I had told—because I had to tell—they looked at me like I was a kicked puppy. "So she'll remember you when she meets you, but only for a few minutes. And she only remembers me from when I was a teenager."

"I'm so sorry."

"She's doing well. Mason takes good care of her."

I waited for it, for her to break her promise and bombard me with a million questions. At this point, I wouldn't blame her, but she didn't. I could tell she wanted to, but she didn't.

"Okay. Let me get my clothes on and my hair finger-combed, all right? Thanks for letting me wear these." She fingered the collar of my shirt she was wearing.

"Of course. I'll borrow some clothes from Mason."

She leaned up and kissed my forehead as she stood. "Don't peek," she whispered as she went behind me and I heard the rustling of her clothes.

Good. Night.

"Mamma?"

She turned and smiled, but it quickly changed. It was practically a carbon copy of the reaction I had gotten last time - so happy to see me and then so confused at what she saw.

"Milo…"

"It's okay, Mamma." I bent down on my haunches in front of her and took her hand in mine. "It was an accident. It messed with your memory. I'm a little older; you just don't remember." I looked back at Maya and she knelt on the floor next to me. "This is Maya. She wanted to meet you."

"Oh, my gosh," Maya whispered under her breath. "The fact that you *actually* call her Mamma makes me fall in love with you a little bit."

I stared, slack-jawed and amazed. She straightened and smiled at my mother as she proceeded to charm the smiles right out of her and the nurse, too. Before I knew it, they were all drinking hot tea and eating cookies. Maya had explained who she was several times with the patience of someone way beyond her years and I was falling in love more than a little bit.

That should have scared me, but I got a freeing sensation from it. I'd never seen binding yourself to someone as being freeing before, but that's what it felt like. With her, just us, together, it felt like we might could take on the hard road of addiction and not knowing what the future held for us.

After lunch, I asked if I should take Mom to the hospital, but the nurse thought she should stay and see the baby at home. Maya and I headed back. We hadn't heard from Mason, so I didn't think we'd missed anything.

And we hadn't. When we arrived, Mason looked like hell warmed over. The bags under his eyes were dark and he was so tired. The doctor had told him the first babies sometimes fought hard, and this one was taking his sweet time, but at least Emma was almost ready now. She had almost fully "dilated" overnight, whatever that meant.

Emma's parents weren't there yet since they went home to get some things and showers, so Mason wanted us to go in and see Emma while we could. I didn't really want to, to be honest. Emma was this angel that had been stuck between Mason and me while he had rescued me. She had seen me at my absolute worst, literally seen me with track marks in my arms and a girl having her way with me, called me on my crap, brought my brother back from his self-loathing that I inflicted on him, and was now giving him the only thing that he really ever wanted. And she was this weird copy of our mom, too, with her memories gone.

She was too good for the likes of me.

So was Maya for that matter.

This whole thing was bringing up all this stuff that I knew it would, but it physically hurt to feel. It hurt to know that Maya was better off without me. That I didn't deserve to be within twenty feet of her, let alone be *with* her. And Mason. God…how did he forgive me so easily? Maybe he hadn't. Maybe he hadn't had time to think about it yet. Maybe he didn't want to fight at the hospital. Maybe he didn't want to fight at all, but would always hold a grudge. Could I blame him? Of course not.

"Milo?"

I looked up to find Mason and Maya looking at me. Both looked pretty worried. "Yeah?" I said, not surprised by how gruff my voice was.

"What's up, man?" Mason tried.

I shook my head. "Nothing."

He stopped me with a hand on my shoulder. "I've been trying to get your attention for over a minute."

"Nothing." I pushed, but he pushed harder. I was kind of shocked by how strong he had gotten the past couple of years. Apparently, I wasn't the only one. "Mason, I'm fine."

"Milo," he pleaded. He looked back at Maya who seemed to know there was something going on and wasn't going to let me get out of it.

She had inched back a good bit and hooked her finger over her shoulder. "I'm going to go get sodas. Be back in a few minutes."

I looked back at Mason's face and knew there was no getting out of it. He didn't say anything else, so I didn't beat around the bush any longer. "Why, Mase?"

He knew exactly what I was talking about. Why did he forgive me so easily without so much as a fight or discussion? He just hugged me when I walked through that door after more than two years and that was it.

He smiled a half-smile, the way he used to do when we were teenagers when he was about to tell me something he had learned about life that Mom would never tell me that should have been my father's job. "Because you're my brother, Milo. I love you, and all I ever wanted was to be there for you. I screwed everything up, and then all I wanted to do was make everything up to you."

"Mason, you didn't screw anything up. It wasn't your fault," I said and realized I believed it. I actually, for the first time in my life, believed it wasn't Mason's fault Mom was in that accident.

His face confirmed his shock. "What?"

"I was a stupid kid, Mase. I wanted to blame someone and you were the only one there. And then, like a coward, I ran. There's..." I gulped. "There's so much more I want to say to you, but right now, I just can't. I hope that's okay for now. There are a few things I still need to work on first, but I'm trying."

"Milo, you're here," he said happily and hugged me to him, patting my back hard. "For now, that's all that matters." He leaned back. "It's pretty daggum obvious you're working your butt off to get your life together. I can't ask for any more than that right now. Thank you for coming. To be honest, I didn't think you would. Even after you said you would."

"I know. I deserve that."

"But you look pretty good, bro."

"Thanks." I rubbed my head. "Working out and working a full-time job helps…keep busy and not want and think about…things."

He nodded, like he knew exactly what I was talking about. He could never know what being an addict was like, but I appreciate that he tried. "And this girl…" He shook his head. "Wow, dude." He whistled.

"Well, thanks, Wright boys."

We both turned at the sound of her voice to find her adorably biting her smiling bottom lip. She held three cans of soda between her hands as she walked toward us. She handed one to each of us. I thought my brother would be red-faced embarrassed, but he wasn't.

He smiled down at my girl, who was even shorter than him. "So, Maya, got any tattoos?"

"No," I scoffed.

"Yes," she corrected and smirked at me.

"You do?" I heard the growly tone of it.

"Easy, bro," Mason laughed and reached a hand out to me. He looked back at her. "Well, I own a shop here. If either of you ever want some new ink, come see me."

He looked at me. "Did you ever get any?"

I shook my head. "Nah." I couldn't admit that it felt like I was betraying him to get it done by someone else. "Not yet."

He nodded once. "Where's yours?" he asked Maya with a jut of his chin. "Or can only Milo see?" He cut his eyes to the side at me and winked.

Her neck turned a little pink as she laughed, bumping his arm with her elbow.

"Here." Her eyes met mine as she pulled the shoulder of her shirt down to reveal the yellow and black butterfly on her shoulder. Her gaze sizzled into mine. "This is what teenage rebellion looks like."

Mason leaned close and took her arm in his hand. "Huh, really clean lines. Nice shading, too."

"Okay, Mase," I tried.

He brushed his thumb over the wing. "Good symmetry."

"All right." I pushed his hand away, putting myself between them, and pulled up her sleeve. She smiled up at me coyly from under her lashes. I took her hand in mine and turned to Mason. "Let's go see Emma."

He smiled. "Great." He ticked his head toward the hall. "She missed you."

I scoff-laughed. "She doesn't really know me."

"She knows you enough to miss you."

We followed him up floors and elevators. He stopped at the door and turned to us. "She's been pregnant and doing great, but also miserable for over nine months. She says she's totally fine, but she really just wants to hit you."

I snorted and Maya may have, too. "Okay, we got it," I assured him.

"She'll burst into tears at some point during the visit, too. It is inevitable. Don't take it personally."

"Okay. No problem."

He eased the door open. "Baby," he called and the old me, the pre-hate-Mason me would have ragged on him to no end for being so whipped. He sounded so incredibly in love with the girl in that bed. When he went in and bent down to kiss her forehead, speaking softly to tell her we were there, there was no doubt that he absolutely was.

I had always known that he was, from the first time I saw them together, but this, with her being so fragile and needing him like this, it was different than before. Before, he was the one who needed her so much because when he came to find me at those parties, he was more wrecked than I was.

It was strangely beautiful to see the tables turned.

"I finally dragged his sorry behind here for you, sweetheart."

"I told you he would come."

He kissed her on the mouth and her pale fingers gripped his hair. He leaned back and shielded her eyes as he turned on the overhead lights. I was awed at how not just whipped or sweet but just…thoughtful he was. I looked over at Maya and swallowed down anything that might have come up at that moment. This wasn't about us.

I rubbed her fingers with my thumb and she looked over at me. Her smile was easy. She didn't seem uncomfortable or uneasy. It was another thing I loved about her. She could be in any situation, whether or not it was about her, it didn't have to be, and she was still comfortable with that. She didn't need to be the center of attention, and she didn't need to be the wallflower. She was a go-with-the-flow kind of girl. *My* kind of girl.

"Milo," Emma breathed.

Maya let my hand go and I went, not sure what to expect from the girl who, for whatever reason, seemed to think I was worth her affection. "Hey, Mrs. Wright."

She smiled so big. "Hey."

I reached back, beckoning Maya to me. Within seconds, her hand was in mine. "Maya, this is Mason's wife, Emma. She's about to make me an uncle."

They both laughed. Emma leaned up a little to shake her hand, but you could tell she was beat. The kind of beat like you'd run a marathon with low blood sugar. It seemed like such a strange thing for something that was supposed to make you so happy to be making you so miserable.

Mason shifted down to Emma's legs, pushing up the blanket, and pulled one of her legs up to rest her heel on his stomach as her massaged her calf. She groaned in thanks, and as they looked at each other, I was once again feeling as though I was basking the glow of something I wasn't worthy of. Emma and Mason were the only love that I was ever really privy to, except the mechanic shop owner and his wife, but they didn't really count. Even back when I was a punk runaway and wanted nothing to do with Mason, I still saw it then.

And now it was still there, wrapped around them like pretty tissue paper for all to see.

We talked about nothing for a few minutes while Mason continued with everything in him to make his wife feel better. That was Mason—always trying to take care of everyone. But as much as he tried, it wasn't helping. She kept shifting, and the doctor came in and said she was close, but no cigar. It was almost time; just keep waiting.

I thought Emma was going to actually hit him, just like Mason had said. Instead she pushed a fake smile and then burst into tears as soon as he left, just as Mason predicted.

I looked at Maya and wondered if this was something she would ever want. Good night. This made me want to vow never, ever to impregnate her.

This was female torture at its finest.

Emma calmed and apologized, and Mason went back to his rubbing. She was laughing about how one side of her body would go numb if she stayed on that side too long.

"Maya, when you have a baby one day and that handsome doctor comes in and says he's going to give you something that will make you feel no pain and you'll be dilating all day in peace?" She smirked, maybe a little evilly. "He's a big fat liar! Don't listen to him. His perfect little coif of chestnut hair may have gotten him through medical school, but it cannot charm a baby from a womb and certainly doesn't make the pain go away."

As we laughed, Maya went to stand by Mason. "My brother is…

well, he's sick. I know this thing. Well, I saw it on YouTube." Everyone chuckled. I watched in absolute wonder as she pushed her fear away and told my family about her brother. I knew that was hard for her. It had taken her a long time to tell even me about it. "May I?" she asked. Mason looked at Emma and she nodded. He looked at Maya gratefully and scooted over a bit to give her room. She took Emma's socked foot in her hand and started to gently dig her thumb into spots on the sole.

Emma groaned and grabbed the rail of the bed. "Oh, my gosh."

"What, babe?" Mason rushed.

"Ah!" she groaned again. "Oh, my gosh."

"Babe?"

"Dump this guy. Marry me, Maya!"

I laughed in a snort and slapped Mason on the back. "Dude, we're cooked."

Maya kept working, a little pleased smile on her face as she looked at Emma's feet.

Emma groaned again, and though I knew it was because she was in so much pain and it was helping and all, it started to sound a little...

Emma moaned again. "Where did you learn this?"

"YouTube."

"They need a medal."

Maya laughed. "It's reflexology."

"Oh...my gosh," Emma groaned.

Mason leaned down near her face. "Baby, you gotta stop that."

She looked over to see him close. "What?" She must have seen something. She giggled, embarrassed. "Oh. I'm sorry, baby." She snapped her face back to Maya and pointed at her foot, groaning again. "There. Oh, my gosh. Baby."

"Yeah?" Mason answered.

"No, no." She pointed to her stomach. "Baby. Contractions. Finally! Contractions! Baby!"

We were shooed from the room and within thirty-five minutes, were passing around a sleeping baby boy. Emma was in and out of sleep from the medicines they'd given her. I hated to go, but I knew Maya needed to get home to her brother.

I'd never held such a small living thing before in my arms. His little breaths were so tiny, but his grip was so strong, like he trusted me without a doubt. I looked up from his face to find Mason watching me with his son.

I knew the exact same thought was running through his head that was running through mine.

The men in this little guy's life were not running out on him like our father had. No, we were going to be there. We were all we had left. I handed him to Maya because I knew leaving Mason was going to be hard. Even though I'd be back, this was hard. We really hadn't gotten to talk about anything. I still felt guilty as hell. So many things felt unresolved, yet I knew things were headed in the right direction.

As soon as she had the baby, Mason snatched me into a tight hug. "You better come back, you hear? You better come visit, and you better bring that girl with you again because I think Emma fell in love with her a little bit."

"Yeah," I whispered and patted his back. "I did, too."

"God, I love you, bro."

"I love you, too, Mase. I missed you."

He leaned back, his hand on my shoulder. "We'll…talk, okay. Don't worry about it. One thing at a time."

I nodded. "Yeah. Definitely."

He and Maya handed off the baby for a hug, and we were on our way with a promise to come back soon.

On the ride out of town though, it wasn't long before blue flashing lights were in my rearview mirror.

"I wasn't speeding," I mused as I pulled over.

Maya stayed quiet and watched as I got my insurance card and everything pulled out. I had already given Maya my jacket because it was colder than the day before, especially with no doors, and now this guy was making the trip even longer.

He came to stand at my door and gave a small smirk when he saw me. "License. Registration."

"Sure," I said and handed it over. "Can I ask what I was doing wrong? I didn't think I was speeding."

"Milo Sawyer." I nodded. "Milo, huh? That's not a very common name."

I looked over. The way he said that was like he was goading me. Like he wanted me to *get something*.

"I guess not. Sir, can you tell me what I was doing wrong?"

"Are you from around here?"

"I live a couple hours from here."

"That's not what I asked."

"Well, sir, no disrespect, but we're kind of playing the avoid-the-question game."

He chuckled. "You've got a taillight out."

That was a lie. I knew for a fact I didn't. This was one of Roz's front pocket police.

I smiled like I was guilty. "I do? Dang. Well, my girl and I were taking a drive to see my parents up in the mountains. Sorry. I didn't know the light was out or I would've gotten my dad to look at it."

"Your dad," he said slowly.

Maya stayed quiet, but I could tell in her face she was confused. And a little scared. I looked over at her and tried to tell her it would be okay. I put my hand on her leg, my thumb rubbing over the top of her thigh, as my eyes begged her to trust me. When I looked back to the officer, I eyed his book and grimaced.

"Do you have to write me a ticket for it?"

"Nah." He flipped his book and smiled. "Just get it taken care of when you get home, all right?"

"Will do."

"And get that pretty thing out of the cold." He jutted his chin toward Maya. "Wouldn't want anything to happen to her."

Maya gasped as he walked away. As soon as I shifted the gears into high so my hand could be free, I reached for her as I sped away. I prayed she wouldn't push me away, but I had to try. I knew this day would come. I knew the day would come for me to lay all my transgressions on the table and she would have to choose to run screaming or accept them as me.

That day was today.

I didn't look at her, just drove. When my fingers touched her, I expected her to flinch, but she did the total opposite. She wrapped both of her hands around mine and pulled herself close to press against my arm. "Milo, are you okay? What's going on? Who was that?"

"Can you call Will and check on him?" I asked her.

She nodded. "Of course."

"Would that be okay? If I don't take you home for a while? I need to tell you everything, and you need to hear it before we go any further."

"Yes, I do," she answered. It was like a knife through my skull. "Because I want to know you, not because I'm looking for a reason to leave."

"Let's hope you still feel that way when the night is through."

Maya

Two cups of hot chocolate later, we were both sitting on his kitchen counter, and he was spilling his guts. It hurt to hear it, see it, watch it. He honestly thought the entire world hated him and wanted him ejected for bad behavior. At one point, he threw his full cup in the sink and it splashed and spilled everywhere as he ranted and continued to tell me how "evil" he was.

Milo hated himself so much for leaving his family that it made it impossible for him to even speak of the time when he was a teenager without his hands shaking.

His words ran together, he mumbled, he yelled, he whispered, he begged, his eyes were closed at one point. He wanted to tell me so badly and wanted to run away at the same time. His entire world was tearing him apart with this. I remembered this feeling well.

I had to let him finish. I had to let him get it all out.

It was the only way to get all the rot out so the healing could begin.

Mason was at a party…drunk, left phone…Mother went to get him… accident…Milo rebelled, partying, running away…hated Mason… Mason tried to save him over and over…kept falling further…Emma and Mason…Milo crashed their wedding because he had to see…him getting beaten to a pulp for the money he owed…the hospital…the cops wanted to ask him questions…Roz would kill him…left town…found pastor and Joey…she took night classes at college…helped him stay clean…pastor found him an apartment and a job…him and Joey never were more than friends…he knew in his heart once he told me, I would leave him because why would someone like me settle for someone like him…he was so scared to see Mason because he didn't know if he was still going to hate him…he couldn't get to him fast enough…he never felt so guilty than when he visited his Mom for the first time…all he wanted was to work hard, stay clean, be with his family, be normal…

"Maya, I'm sorry that I can't be some squeaky clean man who makes a nice living. I'm sorry my past is filled with things that are nothing to be proud of. I'm sorry I can't be a rock for you. I'm sorry I was a coward who ran and kept running. But I'm not running anymore and I'm not sorry that I fell for you." Fell, not falling. My heart sighed. "Even if it's just in my heart, I'll always be chasing you. It's up to you now, Maya."

His hands gripped the countertop as he faced away from me. I set the empty cup down and slid to the my feet. His hard shoulders tensed, but he didn't turn around. I realized he thought I was leaving.

I jumped up on the counter right beside him and pulled him over to fit between my knees, his back to my front. I put my cheek against his head and my arms around his neck and hoped he understood this meant I wasn't going anywhere.

Some mistakes were bigger than others, but we all made them. I didn't want my mistakes to be held against me any more than anyone else did. I squeezed my arms and knees around him and kissed his cheek. "Thank you for trusting me," I whispered.

"You're not leaving?" was his tortured response.

"I have to at some point," I joked. "Will can't even boil water. He'll starve."

He sighed a small laugh and put his hands over mine on his chest, leaning back like exhaustion hit him. "Just know that you changed me and helped me more than anyone I know."

"Joey did pretty good," I countered, though I didn't want to. She really had kind of hindered him by not getting him into a program. She made him depend solely on her for him to stay clean. He needed to learn to depend on himself for that and healing. Forgiveness was a huge part of that. He was just now taking the first step.

"No," he said and shook his head. He turned just his head and looked up at me. "I know what Joey did. She thought she was doing right, but it was selfish. She wanted to be some hero so she could say she saved me all by herself." I pressed my lips together. I wasn't about to start Joey-bashing. She may not have pushed him through, but she at least brought him to the door. She did save him. I would always be grateful and envious of her for that. I would be thankful to her for that and be jealous that she'll always be in his heart for being the one.

He reached up and tucked my hair behind my ear. "Wow, even now you can't say one bad word about her."

"She *did* save you, Milo. She may not have done all the right things, but she took you into the shelter and got you clean. I'll always, always," I choked and looked away. He pulled my face back by my chin. He looked confused and in complete wonder that these tears were for him. I finished; I had to. "I'll always be grateful that she was your friend when you needed one the most. It's the reason you're here now. How could I not be thankful to her for that?"

He inched me down toward him, even though he was twisted at an odd angle. "You aren't real, Maya."

His lips surrounded mine reverently, like they didn't deserve to be here. I pulled him closer, my hands going to his cheeks, forcing him to open his mouth and let me in. He seemed surprised by my force, but I was over the way he acted as though hope was lost on his redemption. That my forgiveness of him was all a whim, that it was almost…unfounded.

"I got you something." I pulled the coin from my pocket, the coin I'd brought on the trip with me, and showed it to him. "I bought this for the second day I knew you." I smiled and laughed. "I said to myself that if I still knew you and you were still sober on your two-year mark, I was going to give it to you."

He took it and looked at it as if it was made of gold. "I've never had one of these before."

"It's not just a stupid coin, is it?"

"No." He gripped it in his palm tightly and looked at me like he didn't know what to say. "No, it's not. Thank you for this."

I spoke against his lips, clinging to him, needing him to listen. "I'm not forgiving you or letting it go because I just don't want the drama, Milo, or because I went through a lot of the same and feel sorry for you."

He huffed a breath against my lips. "I know."

"Do you?"

"Yes."

"Why?"

"Because…"

I put my mouth to his ear. "Because those who work as hard as you have to turn your life around deserve it. It doesn't have to given, Milo— your brother didn't have to forgive you. Of course not. But he did, and so do I. You have to forgive yourself if you're ever going to move on."

He panted and turned to look at me, his face so close as he nodded. He looked so wracked, but it was a good wracked. It was the face of someone who had been through it all and there was nothing left. I pulled him into the cave my body made with my arms and legs and let him nuzzle in close. We stayed there forever it seemed.

Finally, his lips began to move instead of resting against my skin. He pressed closer to me and kissed the column of my neck and behind my ear. I gripped his head tighter and I leaned my neck to the side to give him more room just before my phone rang. It could only be one person that late at night.

I yanked it from my pocket and put it to my ear. "Will?"

"I'm okay, Maya, but I need to go. I'm dizzy and my heart's slow."

"I'll be there in five minutes."

I slammed the phone shut and went to jump down. "I've got to go."

He nodded. "What's the matter?"

"Will's sick. Needs to go to hospital."

"I'll take you," he insisted and jammed his feet into some shoes.

"Uh…" I watched him grab his keys and go for our coats by the door. "You have work tomorrow. You don't have to—"

"You shouldn't be driving upset. Besides, he's a big guy. I can help you carry him." He grabbed my hand and towed me out the door. "Come on, sweetheart. Fight me on it later."

Nine hours later, Milo was helping Will up the stairs. Oh, my gosh, he was like a walking, talking saint. He wouldn't go home, wouldn't take coffee money, wouldn't let me drive there or back. And now Will was yakking it up with him like they were BFFs from first grade, and I was stuck worrying about them both—Will for obvious reasons, and Milo because he missed another day of work. If he got fired over this, I would…well, after I finished swooning, I'd bawl my eyes out and be so mad at him for doing it.

Milo put Will on the couch easily and went about giving him the remotes and other things guys would think to do. It was pretty sweet.

I took off Will's shoes and tossed a blanket over him before pulling Milo onto the porch. With my back to him, I began to lay into him for being so careless with his life. "You can't just buy me truck parts with your own money. You can't just miss work to take my brother to the hospital. You can't just—"

He turned me and took my face in his hands before kissing all the good sense out of me. I clung to his shirt as his arms pulled around me, hauling me into the arms that seemed to always be there lately, always ready to catch me. My arms moved on their own up around his head until all of me and all of him were touching as he kissed me gently. He leaned back just enough to speak, shaking his head. "This is what *the long haul* looks like." He kissed the end of my nose. "I'm not going anywhere. Get used to it, sweetheart."

My chest shook with a silent sob. He pulled my chin up and kissed my trembling mouth just as the door swung open.

"You don't have to do that outside like a couple of teenage delinquents. I am not Mom and Dad."

I looked over at Will and let my glare loose. "What the hell are you doing off the couch?"

"I'm older than you, warden. I'm the boss." He slapped Milo's upper arm. "Now come on. Bring my sister inside and make out in the house like a real man. Wait." He made a gagging noise. "That sounded weird."

Milo chuckled and I turned to him. "Um…I've got to go. I'll…" He looked at Will over my shoulder. "Make out with you in the house…like a real man…" Will nodded, "later."

"Yep!" Will called and went to go lie down again.

I laughed at them. Boys. "Okay. Will you tell me at least if you get fired or something? I mean…geez."

"I called work already. He was fine with it."

"You did?"

"You were busy." He shrugged. "It's fine."

"Thank you." He nodded. "No, really. Thank you."

"Maya," he sighed. "It's not a burden to be here. If you need me, call me. Anytime, okay? I meant what I said. I'm not going anywhere."

"I promise," I said and meant it, too.

He lifted my chin to kiss my lips once more before hopping off my porch. I watched him go the entire way. For once, I felt a little lighter. To not have to worry about Will all by myself felt amazing. I'd never had that before. I didn't know whether I should trust that or not, but Milo had trusted me with everything last night. He had laid it all out there for me to see.

So I would trust this. I would trust that when Milo said he wasn't going anywhere, he wasn't.

I didn't go into work that day, but Milo went to work and did some extra stuff to catch up. Will and I watched movies all day. He was acting fine. His attitude and demeanor were great, but his energy was way down. He wasn't quite right, but he had just been in the hospital, so I tried not to push him.

I hated to go to work the next day, but I had to. I hated to leave Will, but he said he was fine and seemed to be. Or at least acted like he was. He was good at that. That night, Milo came over and had dinner with us. Before I knew it, a week had passed.

Joey was coming back into town for her dad's birthday party and wanted to do dinner with Milo. So he wanted to do dinner with Will and me, with them. He said that he and she didn't speak all that often anymore. I believed him. I believed that he would tell me the truth about it, but I would be lying if I said it didn't irk me a little that she was this huge, important part of his life that I wasn't a part of.

Will said he was feeling well enough to go out, so Milo took us to this place that made whole wheat wraps with organic vegetables and chicken. The pita chips and hummus were amazing.

Milo sat next to me and across from Joey, who sulked as if she were being set up with Will or something. Neither one of us was being the way we usually were with each other. I think we both knew why, but was it also because he was trying not to make Joey uncomfortable? Did he know that she had feelings for him? Every now and then he'd reach over and rub his pinkie against mine on the table and wait for me to look at him. Then he would smile like he'd been told he'd won the lottery. I was a little confused, but understood this was territory that needed to be breached gently. This was not a guns-a-blazing kind of fight.

"I thought we were eating Chinese?" Joey asked about halfway through dinner. "We always eat Chinese."

Milo glanced at me. I knew he was doing it for me. For Will. "Figured it wouldn't hurt to eat healthy once in a while. It's pretty good, huh?"

"Eh," she said, noncommittally.

See, that was the thing with her. It was like she was never mean, but never really nice either. She was never on board with either thing and it drove me crazy that I was never justified in my anger with her.

"Want to go get smoothies?" I suggested.

"Oooh! Some of my friends are throwing a party tonight, I think. I'll text them."

Milo sat silent. A party? "Uh, I don't think that's a good idea," I tried.

"What? Why?" She looked around. "Why not?"

"Well, besides the fact that Will isn't feeling well, addicts really shouldn't be around drinking and things."

She kinda laughed. "Oh, Miles is fine. He's all better now. He wouldn't smoke a joint or drink a drop. He knows I would kick his behind."

I looked over at him and he was watching me, his eyes flicking from her to me.

I continued. "I'm an addict, too, but-"

"Oh," she said sadly. "If *you* can't handle it, then-"

"It's not really that, Joey. It's that you shouldn't put addicts in that position." She looked confused, her iPhone poised in her hand, texting finger at the ready. "It's like putting raw meat in front of a hungry dog and telling him he can't have it."

"Are you saying Miles is a dog?" she asked angrily.

I stood. "What?" What the hell? How did this happen? "No." I looked at him. Did he want me to defend him? Did he want me to fight her over him and do this? What if he was forced to choose over this? Is that what he wanted? Would he choose me? Would he be angry about that? Why was he just sitting there?

"All I was saying is that it's never a good idea to take an addict somewhere where they'll be tempted. They may say no and have no problem at all a million times, and then a million times and one is the time that they can't take it."

"No. I've worked with Miles and he is perfectly fine," she said proudly. "He would never do that to me." She hinged his whole being-clean-thing on his loyalty to *her*. Their friendship.

I spoke slow and soft. "No offense, Joey, but that's setting him up to fail. He needs to do it for himself, not because he'll disappoint someone else if he fails." She frowned and looked a little angry.

"At the meetings we teach that, yes, a sponsor is someone who helps keep us straight, gives us tough love, but the whole point of that is that the sponsor will do what needs to be done and not care about the addict getting angry with them. The addict needs to learn that disappointing people is going to happen in their life. They can't be afraid of that. What they need to figure out is how to not disappoint themselves. How to live with themselves and the fact that they wake up every day and *still* want to drink, *still* want to snort and get high and any other thing that comes their way to escape. They have to forgive themselves and move on; rely on themselves. Learn to be themselves again. Deal with their past. A sponsor is supposed to be an addict who has been through it all and knows exactly what a newbie would need, when they would need it, and what it would take to reach them. A sponsor isn't a crutch or a superhero. A sponsor is a kick in the butt every once in a while."

She looked like I'd grown two heads. She looked at Milo. He looked at her. I waited. She waited, too, seeing if he'd tell her I was wrong. She looked back at me. "But…"

"You did good, Joey," I soothed. Then I did something I thought I'd never do. I moved around the table and hugged her to me. I'd never hugged such a stiff board before. "Thank you for doing what you did. It doesn't even matter the whats and whys. You saved him." I leaned back and saw she had softened an incredible amount. "If you hadn't kept bringing him back to the shelter and making him stay clean…he wouldn't be here," I whispered the last part, because I was about to lose it just thinking about it.

She stared into my eyes. It was the first time she really looked at me since we got there. "So, you both will always battle this?"

"Once an addict, always an addict," I explained softly.

"Oh." She seemed sad and confused. "I didn't really realize that. I thought once you were over it, you were…over it." She looked at him. "Why did you go to those parties with me if you were having trouble with your addiction?"

"I wasn't really having *trouble*," he confirmed. "But like she said, once an addict, always an addict. I could control it, but it never really goes away, Jo."

She stood and gawked at him. "But you said you were fine and I assumed you were."

"Define 'fine'. What does that even mean?" He smiled, but his eyes found me with that smile. I smiled back, proud of him. He knew exactly what was going to go down tonight. He needed this, wanted this. His lips twitched before his gaze swung back to Joey. "If it means that I can control myself and that I function like a normal person from day to day, then yes, I'm fine. Does it mean that I don't wake up every single day and think about wanting something, anything, just to take the edge off... then I'm not fine, and I never will be again. No addict ever is."

She plopped back down in her seat ungracefully. "Well...I wish you had said something."

"I felt like I owed it to you to try to be normal."

She sent him a sulky look. Then she looked at Will. "Are you an addict, too?"

"Do whole grains count?" he asked with a completely straight face.

She frowned, her face ticking to the side. "Is that some new thing you smoke?"

Will snorted. Milo bellowed and leaned his head back. Joey was so mad she was red, but it was funny. Eventually the boys stopped laughing at her and we all starting acting like we normally did, mostly.

By the time they brought dessert, I was missing Milo's touch like a physical ache. I sat up with my revelation. I was an addict with him. Was I? No. If it was a normal night, it would be fine. The fact that he didn't want to touch me because Joey was here was what was bugging me.

I heard him. "What's the matter? You don't like gluten-free pudding?" I turned to find Milo's face right next to mine. I stared at him, trying to find an answer to my question there.

"The pudding's fine. It's good."

"You're awfully quiet," he said softly.

"Am I?"

He nodded. "You okay?"

"Yeah. You're awfully far away," I remarked pointedly. "You okay?"

His eyes changed as if he were thinking. He looked between me and the wicker couch we were sitting on the veranda. Will and Joey were having a conversation across from us on their own couch about none of us having any family pets and how it was a travesty.

His eyes met mine again and a small fire could have started right there in my chest. His hand snapped up and wrapped around my neck, but he pulled me slowly and gently to him. His mouth met mine with pressure before pulling back. He looked almost…angry. "You thought I didn't want this?" he whispered. "You thought I wouldn't want you in front of Joey because…why?"

"I don't know," I said truthfully. I didn't know why he was so angry about it. "I believe you when you said you didn't feel anything for her that way."

"Then what?"

"I don't know, Milo. You're just different."

"You think she has a thing for me?" His voice was high and incredulous.

"Why is that so hard to believe?"

He scoffed. "Because she's *Joey*."

I felt a scowl. "What? She's too beautiful for you? Is that it?"

He rolled his eyes. "*Good night*, Maya." He grabbed my hand and pulled me up a little roughly. Will and Joey looked up to see where we were going, but one wave from Milo silenced them both and they went right back to talking like none of it mattered.

I huffed when I saw he was taking me to the stairwell. "Milo."

He slammed the back door and yanked me behind it. Before I could think or register what he was doing, my back was against the bricks of the warm hall and his hands were on my face as his fingers inched into my hair.

He didn't beg for entry or ask sweetly to let him in as he had done before. No, his thumb reached over and tugged my chin down to give him access to my mouth and he plunged. His entire body undulated with that plunge and I found myself gripping his wrists near my face to hold on.

I opened my eyes for just a second. I had to see him. I had to see what feral Milo looked like. I slammed them shut immediately because feral Milo was mind-blowing and even then, I couldn't stop the moan against his mouth.

He reached deeper as if he couldn't get enough of it. And then he confirmed. "That noise haunts my dreams," he growled against the corner of my lips.

His knees moved in between mine a split second before he lifted me with ease, his hands finding a new home on my legs and hips as he pinned me there with his body. I could feel the coarse bricks snagging my sweater, but couldn't find it in me to care.

My hands were glad for the change-up because that meant they could go north. His breaths picked up, pants and noises got louder as I pulled and tugged on his soft, dark hair.

His lips never stopped working, never stopped their attention. His kisses were so deep that I eventually broke free and leaned my head back against the wall to breathe. I felt his lips and tongue on my neck. Apparently, all I had done was set up another kind of torture for myself. His arm circled my waist while one stayed on my leg behind my knee.

His teeth grazed my collarbone and I took his face in my hands and brought it back up to mine, keeping my hands there, feeling his stubble and the hard muscles of his jaw as his lips slid and pressed onto mine while his chest and body did the same.

I'd never been handled this way—that I could remember at least. Milo had never been this way with me either, and it was so hot and angry, and yet so sweet that he would get mad about something like that. Still, Milo was the sweetest guy I'd ever known.

As our tongues fought, they slowed. As our breaths collided and panted, they calmed. As his hard grip pulled, he began to loosen them. He took one last long hard pull from my mouth before opening his eyes and looking at me. He was barely a breath away, still holding me captive in more ways than one.

"Now. What the hell was it that you couldn't understand out there?"

I took a breath. "If we're a couple, we're a couple, right? So why hide it from her? Why make it seem like it's not a big deal?"

He seemed surprised. "I didn't want you to think I was trying to make her jealous." I squinted in confusion. "I didn't think you'd want me to kiss you in front of her, to show off or claim you," he answered, his eyes on mine, not moving for a second.

"I just think…maybe Joey has a thing for you and maybe you know it. Maybe you were protecting her by not—"

"Joey is my friend. That's all. Joey…" He licked his lips and laughed under his breath. "Joey dates older men." He smirked.

"What do you mean?"

"She's dating her boss."

"Ew. Why?"

"Because he's established and already has money and a house, and she doesn't have to start from nothing like her parents. She's watched so many people come into the shelter, for one reason or another. She fears poverty like the plague. She doesn't have a solid grasp on some things. She's my friend, I love her, but she can be pretty shallow."

I stared for a long time and accepted his hazel gaze. Finally, the battle was over and I laid my forehead to his. He sighed. "She doesn't matter here. We don't have to prove anything to anybody or for anybody. I know that I love you and that's all that…"

It had been hinted at, but never spoken, and it was out now. His face scared me for a split second. Was it regret? Was he regretting it was out there? No, he was just worried that I was. I wrapped my arms around his neck and held on tight. He held me back tightly, but soon began to smooth my back with his hand. "Sweetheart, you're scaring the bejesus out of me."

I laughed against his ear. "I'm sorry."

"You don't have to say anything, certainly not *that*, but don't just sit here and hang on to me like you'll float away if you don't. You really are scaring me." I leaned back to see his face as he continued. "I didn't think it was that big of a secret."

"It wasn't really." I laughed once under my breath. "I think I've known since the day you bought me tires."

He smoothed my cheek with his thumb. "Joey is the only real friend I've ever had, and you're the only girl I've ever been…" he smiled as he brushed his thumb over my lips, "in love with. I'm sorry I don't know how those two things work together. I thought easing you two together would be better, but it seems like I've just pissed you both off."

I sighed at his sweetness. He was trying so hard to make this work. "It's okay." I kissed him, over and over. "I think the fact that you tried and care at all scores you major points."

"Does it?" he growled against my lips and hoisted me higher.

"Yeah," I sighed.

"Good to know," he joked and cupped my cheek as he took my lips softly.

By the time he was done with me, the feral Milo I had seen before was back in full swing, and we were having to rein it in. He groaned as his fingers combed the hair right behind my ear. "All right, all right." He sighed and licked his bottom lip. "All right. Let's go. Your brother probably thinks I kidnapped you and ran away."

I laughed and fixed his collar where I had wrinkled and gripped it. "Thank you."

He took my face in his hands. "I'm sorry I mucked up the night with trying to keep the peace. I should have left things alone. I'm sorry."

"Don't be sorry."

"Thank you, though. You did amazing at helping Joey understand what an addict is. I didn't even really understand until you made me see, so thank you."

"That's my job."

"No, it isn't," he argued and smiled gorgeously as he kissed me once more before letting me slide gently to the floor. "I'm not your job."

"No, you're not." My legs ached when he released me. I gripped his arms to steady me and a little groan escaped. "Yikes."

"Sorry," he said with a smug look on his face. His eyes were so lidded they were barely open at all.

"You don't look very sorry."

He sighed and leaned in. "Okay, I'm not very sorry."

"Milo!" I laughed and pushed his chest.

His forehead pressed against mine for a few seconds while he breathed. When I opened my eyes, he was smiling. "What?"

"I was so envious of Mason," he explained. "He and Emma are so good together." His head lifted, his throat worked through a swallow. "But I didn't need to be envious of him."

I shivered in his warm arms and shook my head. "You think you're this monster, Milo. You think you're not worthy of anything, of forgiveness, of…" I sighed and licked my bottom lip. "But the things that come out of your mouth—you don't give yourself enough credit. I can't imagine many guys say those kinds of things. No other guy has ever said anything like that to me."

He nodded. "Would it be awful if I was happy to hear it?"

"Yes." I grinned.

"Then I'm awful." He tugged me, his hand gripping and linking our fingers into what felt like an unbreakable bond. "Come on, beautiful girl. Let's take Joey home and then you and I can make out somewhere proper."

I laughed into his shoulder as he towed me out where our dinner guests were. They were right where we left them and didn't seem like they even noticed we were gone. Will looked up and nodded his hello before grimacing and fake gagging. "Gross. Will you two just go make future beautiful babies and be blissfully happy somewhere else? For the love of all who are single."

"Shut it, creep," I hissed playfully and picked up his bowl of chocolate ice cream. "Are you eating this?"

"No, Grandma. I'm just looking at it longingly."

I glared at him. "Any idea how many grams of sodium are in this?"

"Maya," he whined and leaned his head back against the wicker chair. "I thought we were supposed to be having fun tonight? It's just ice cream."

"We are, but—"

"Maya," Milo whispered, his thumb rubbing the inside of my wrist.

I looked at him, ready to let him have it, too, but his eyes glanced at Joey and then at Will before back to me. He leaned in to kiss my cheek, and whispered, "Give the guy a break, sweetheart. He's been cooped up in the house for days, and he's out with a pretty girl."

"But…" I tried not to look over at them. I wasn't his mother, but I was the only one there to look out for him.

"We did eat organic," Milo tried again. His eyebrows lifted.

"Fine." I swatted Milo's stomach and he "oophed" for my benefit. I scowled at Will. "But you better thank Milo later for that ice cream."

"I thought you hated being called Milo?" Joey asked, lifting one blond brow high.

"Not when she says it," he answered immediately.

She scoffed, her mouth open. "What the heck? So I can't call you Milo? You make me call you Miles."

He pointed. "You chose to call me Miles when I said I hated the name

Milo. I never said you couldn't call me that. It just rolls off her tongue better."

Joey smirked. "Oh, I bet it does."

I giggled under my breath while Will threw his hands up and said, "I give. I don't know why the three of you are hell-bent on torturing me tonight, but I'm out of here."

"Nu-huh!" Joey called and ran to catch up. "Let's go watch a movie!"

I so did not want to go watch a movie. From the sulking Milo was doing, neither did he, but they looked like they were having fun, and we did make them wait on us. Milo bought everyone's ticket's and we got drinks. By the time the lights went down, the two people in front of us who actually wanted to see the movie were long forgotten, and the guy whose fingers were firmly planted in my hair and behind my knee were all I could concentrate on. It seemed like no time at all had passed and the lights were coming back up. My lips were raw and swollen, but I loved it. I grinned at him as we stood.

"Best. Movie. Ever," Milo growled in my ear from behind me as we made our way out of the rows.

> Some fortune cookies contain no
> fortune.

Milo

I STOPPED by to bring Will some food. Maya and I had a meeting that night, so I told her I would bring him some lunch and at dinner he could warm up for later. And I promised it would be healthy, so I was bringing him some veggies, but he was sluggish answering the door. I was about to get worried when the door opened.

"Hey, man."

"Hey," I said and looked him over. He was extra pale. "Did we keep you out too late last night?" I chuckled, but instantly felt terrible. "You don't look so hot."

"Nah, I'm good. Come on in."

I put his containers of steamed veggies on the counter and watched him walk over. "Are you sure?"

"Yeah." He smiled and rubbed his hair. "Look, don't feel bad. I had a lot of fun last night. This isn't from last night, I promise."

"Okay," I said, not believing a word of it.

He leaned on the counter with his elbows. His breathing was a little louder than usual. "You know what I have, there's no cure for it, right? There's no medicine. There's no way to stop it."

I scowled. "But Maya—"

"Maya believes there's hope, and that's what I want her to believe, but that's just not the truth. Some people can't be saved. I just…" he cleared his throat, "I just want you to know that I'm really glad you came along. She hasn't been this happy since my mom was alive."

Whoa, that was a big statement to fill. "Will, will you stop talking like—"

He started coughing…and kept coughing.

"Will?" I went to his back and patted it a little, hearing him clear his throat. When he fell to the floor and I had to catch him, I knew it was bad. "No, no, no."

I yanked out my cell and called 911, telling them I needed help and the address. Then I dialed the number I dreaded most of all. Her sweet, chipper, playful voice ripped me in two. "Maya, come home, now."

"Milo, what's wrong?"

"Will."

She didn't ask questions. She hung up and I knew she was on her way. Will struggled to breathe so I laid him out flat and tilted his head back to keep his throat open. His eyes were on me. He shook his head. "It's my time," he rasped. "Milo, it's okay."

"No, it's not," I answered.

"Yes," he argued back. "Milo, it's my time."

"No!"

"Thank you for giving me some fun," he whispered and smiled, even as his skin turned pale. "Watch her for me, man."

I didn't argue. I nodded. "Of course."

His eyes were closing and I begged him to say something, anything. "No, stay with me, Will. No." I started to push on his chest, over and over.

Minutes went by and nothing happened. He was so pale and he didn't move.

I heard Maya run in and slam on her knees beside me right before the sirens blared outside in the street. She put Will's head in her lap and started to rock him softly. I didn't think she'd want me to comfort her. I stole her last minutes with her brother, but I had to try. I crawled over behind her and wrapped my arms around her. When she didn't push me away, I sighed. "I'm so sorry, baby."

"Was he already like this when you got here?" she asked and sniffed.

"No. He let me in, but he wasn't acting right. We talked for a little while and then he collapsed. I tried to give him CPR, but he wouldn't come back." She looked at me over her shoulder, her pale face tear-streaked and shaking. "Maya, I'm sorry."

"At least he wasn't alone," she said and closed her eyes. She leaned her forehead against my shoulder. "He wasn't alone."

She cried hard—so hard I checked to make sure she was breathing a few times because her heaves were so long. When they tried to take the body from her, I knew we were about to have a problem. She fought them for a few minutes, saying she needed some more time, why couldn't she just sit with him for a while longer. But after a few minutes turned into more than an hour, they had to take him. I wrapped my arms around her from behind and her shaking made me ache in ways I'd never ached before. The police came because I had called 911, and I gave my statement and name to a nice officer. It was all very quick and straightforward. I tried to get Maya to eat something that night, but she wouldn't. She just sat on the couch and stared at the wall.

When the chaos was over and it was only her and me, I wanted to do anything I could to help her feel an ounce better. I knew that was stupid. Your brother dying wasn't something that could be fixed, but I hated not being able to do anything for her.

I went to the couch and sat beside her. Pulling her into my lap, she surprised me by straddling me instead of sitting sideways like she usually did. She sighed against my lips. "Milo," she begged.

"You want me to fix you some tea or some coffee? Anything, you just tell me and I'll do it for you."

It was dim in the room. All the lights were off but one lamp. Even still, I could still see the look in her eyes as she lifted her gaze to meet mine. "Make me forget."

I froze. "What, baby?"

"Make me forget that my brother died today. Make me forget that I should have been here." She leaned in and slammed her mouth on mine, pressing her entire body, hips to head, against me. The groan that rattled from me was inevitable.

And I felt guilty as hell.

"Baby," I pleaded and pulled back, holding her face like she was the precious thing she was, "you don't really want to do this."

She pulled back and took the hem of my shirt in her hands before yanking it over my head forcefully. Her lidded eyes and forceful hands said she did want to do this, but the tears on her cheeks and the way her breathing hitched every few seconds in her efforts to control her sobs begged to differ.

She was back on my lips before I could say anything else. She pulled me down on top of her and planted me right between her knees. She ran her hands over my head and down my back. My eyes rolled into my head at how good it felt. I gripped her thigh to gain some control, but found myself pulling her hips closer as she dove deeper and deeper into my mouth. She made this cross between a pant and a moan, and it was my undoing. I let all my weight fall onto her, and it seemed to be what she was waiting on. She dug her nails into my back and shoulders as I tugged her closer. She got pretty ferocious after that, seemingly satisfied that she was getting her way, but when I felt something cold and wet on my cheek, I remembered the reason why this was so, so not the time for this.

"Sweetheart," I smoothed under her eye with my thumb, thinking of anything I could say in that moment to make her understand this wasn't rejection, "I can't wait for the day that I can have you under me like this, with that look on your face," I turned my face in her palm, "with your hands on me, doing everything I ever wanted to do to you." I bore my eyes into hers to make sure she knew I was right here with her. That I just wanted to be here with her, for her, and not take advantage. "But not like this, baby. I want to take you when we both *have to* or the world will catch on fire. Not when your heart is breaking. Please don't ask me to do that. Let me hold you. All night, I just want to hold you."

Her eyes begged me. No longer to take her in a rush but for another kind of relief. I slipped my shirt back on quickly and turned us so my back was open to the couch and she was in the cocoon of my arms and the couch cushions. Pulling the blanket from the back of the couch, I felt bad that it was Will's blanket, but she didn't seem to care or mind. I tucked it up to her chin and she nuzzled her face into my neck, her lips slightly parted, and her breaths puffing against my neck as she tried to keep her sobs silent and in check. "Let go, baby."

"No," she said immediately. "I can't."

"If you can't let go with me, then who?"

"I'll…" she hiccupped. "Milo."

I cupped her face. "I'm right here. I've got you." I pressed my lips to her forehead and whispered, "Let go, sweetheart."

Her fingers dug into my side before they slipped into the fabric of my shirt, gripping and twisting. I squinted at the thought of leaving her ever again. I couldn't imagine her here in this apartment by herself. I shook that thought away to think of that another time. The first of many wet tears ran down my neck and my chest shook with hers as she could no longer hold on to her plight.

I wrapped my arms all the way around her and held on tight. It was a long, sleepless night for us both, but that was the burden of love, wasn't it? Only it wasn't a burden at all. There wasn't anywhere else I wanted to be than there with her. I'd never seen a girl so broken in my life. Not even Mamma when Dad left or when her brother died, though I was pretty little then. Maybe it was different because my heart felt different about Maya.

In the morning, there was barely any light coming through the window. I felt exhausted, but somehow looking down and finding Maya asleep with a peaceful look on her face made me feel a million times better.

There was a buzz in my pocket, so I grabbed my cell quickly. A text from Mason said he was almost to my apartment. I chuckled under my breath. I should have known Mason would come when I told him what happened. I sent him Maya's address and told him where the spare key was so I didn't have to get up and wake Maya.

I lay there and listened to Maya's soft breathing for the next twenty minutes while I waited for him to arrive, brushing her hair behind her ear over and over, wiping under her eyes to remove her marred makeup from crying, smoothing her cheeks just because I wanted to.

When I heard the click of the lock, I lifted my head to see Mason with armloads of food and Emma behind him, baby in her arms. I sighed. "Hey."

"Hey." He set everything down on the counter and came to stand behind the sofa, looking down at us. "How's she doing?"

I looked down at my beautiful, broken girl and pressed my lips to her head. "She's the strongest, bravest girl I know."

> No snowflake in an avalanche
> ever feels responsible.

Maya

"SHE'S THE strongest, bravest girl I know."

My breath hitched in my throat, but I let it out slowly. I didn't want them to know I was awake. I wasn't ready to face the day that had already wrapped me tightly in its grip. But strongest? Bravest? I scoffed bitterly in my mind. What girl had he fallen for?

"It's hard," Mason said, his voice was gravelly, "to lose a brother. I'm sure." He cleared his throat.

"I'm sorry, Mase."

"Nah, man. I'm not trying to guilt you. I'm just...relating. Or not, really." He sighed. "You're here. Her brother's not ever coming back." I gritted my teeth, lightning shooting through the back of my eyes. Pain. Nothing but pain.

I felt my hair being touched and then Emma's voice near my head. "Was she able to eat anything last night?"

"No. She bawled all night." His voice sounded as though he was in pain just from saying that. "I've never seen a woman cry so hard. I

171

couldn't do anything except lay here and hold on to her. I've never felt so useless."

"I promise you that's what she needed," Emma told him. "We brought a little of everything. We didn't know what you liked."

"You didn't have to," Milo insisted.

"We wanted to." I could hear the baby grunting. "We're your family."

His head nodded against mine. "Family. God..." he laughed, a little choked noise. "Will was...the funniest guy. He busted my chops at every move, but would turn around and be so totally cool about Maya and me. He told me once he was glad Maya had someone because he knew— " He gripped me tighter and spoke softer. "He knew this was going to be hard and didn't want her to be alone. He asked me if I was in this for the long haul." Milo gave a sharp, breathy laugh. "He said if I wasn't to leave then." I thought back to something Milo had said to me once... *This is what the long haul looks like...* I barely kept my sob under control. "He could come up with these comebacks like you just... He was good to Maya, and she was good to him. They were all they had left."

"She has you," Emma whispered.

"Is that enough?" Milo asked. My heart could have shattered right there on that couch. Even after last night, he still thought he wasn't enough for me? "Will was a saint," Milo said, his voice as low as gravel. "Will was such a great guy. He deserves to be here for her. After all the things this girl has been through, she deserves just one break." I felt his hand cupping my jaw and holding me tighter to him. "She deserves more than me."

Mason's hard-edged voice cut through the tension. "Stop." Milo kissed my forehead and moved his fingertips in circles on my skin, whether or not to ignore Mason, I didn't know. "I've seen you two, and what I saw was my brother in love with a girl who's in love with him. Two people who have had a bad run. I told you once that it took a long time to forgive myself for what I did."

"Mason—"

"And it's something that still creeps up every now and then, but are you really going to let her go because you don't deserve her?"

Milo's throat made a small growl. "I never said anything about letting her go."

"Then what the hell are you talking about?"

"I'm just… Maya did everything she could to keep Will healthy. And Will hated it, but it's health food. Who likes it, you know? Will and I snuck some junk food a few times, and Maya would get so angry. She just wanted to keep him as long as possible. We were friends. He trusted me. He knew I…" He made an angry noise in his throat. "He knew I had pull with Maya. I persuaded her to lay off, let Will live a little, and now look. Look what my meddling did. She'll never forgive me." His whole body was shaking. Mason was trying to say something, calm him down, but Milo kept going. I just held on to his shirt and couldn't believe what I was hearing. "She's going to wake up and hate me. She's going to remember how I told her it wasn't a big deal if he cheated once in a while and she's going to hate me for taking the only person she had left in the world."

No more. "He wasn't."

Milo sucked in a quick breath and tucked his chin in to see my face as I looked up at him. His thumb rubbed across my cheekbone. "This is probably the dumbest question I'll ever ask, but how are you, sweetheart?"

"I'm awful," I answered truthfully. His face fell even further, which I didn't think was possible. "Isn't that how I'm supposed to be? Wouldn't I be a million times worse if you weren't here?"

His eyes looked hopeful. "You would?"

"Will wasn't the only person in the world I had left." The first tear of the day slid from the outside of my eye and I let it go. "You are."

He kissed my forehead and left his lips there. "I'm so sorry. Are you hungry?"

I shook my head. "No."

"You need to eat sometime, sweetheart."

"And I will. I'm going to take a shower, okay?"

He looked unsure. "Uh…okay."

He helped me from the couch and watched me go. I didn't say anything to Emma or Mason, which I know wasn't polite, but I got a pass from the couth police when a family member died, didn't I?

I tossed my clothes on the floor of my bedroom as I went through and let the water beat down on me as I sat on the tiles. I stared at the glass and wondered how a person was supposed to act. I didn't even have family to come to a funeral. Will hadn't had a job in a long time. He barely had friends from school he kept in touch with. I doubted there would be very many people there, and that in itself would break my heart.

I could imagine getting up there to give his eulogy and all I could think about was how there was no way I was doing it sober. I covered my head with my hands, but it was too late. It was in there. It had been a long time since the urge to get drunk outweighed everything else. The pit in my stomach gnawed and begged me to feed it. Just toss something in there to make the pain go away. Anything, everything.

It hadn't felt like very long when I saw Milo's face in front of mine, but in actuality, it could have been forever. "Sweetheart, please talk to me."

"What?"

He sighed. "You've been in here for almost an hour."

I looked around. "Sorry."

"You don't have to be." He swept his thumb over my cheek. "Please don't shut me out. Let me be here for you."

I looked down at myself and realized the water had been turned off and Milo had wrapped a towel around me. A gasp escaped before I could stop it. "What?"

"It's okay," he soothed and took my arms to help me stand. "Come on. You need to eat something."

"Not hungry."

He set me on the bed and went to my dresser to search for clothes.

"At this point, sweetheart, I'm not really giving you a choice." He pulled open all the wrong drawers, but I didn't help him, just let him look and watched him do it. When he opened my underwear drawer, the little hitch in his movements didn't escape my notice. He grabbed the first pair he saw on top, the bra that was next to it, and came to me. His words were spoken so softly, as if he thought I'd break from them. "I'll help you if you want me to."

I stared at his neck in my line of sight. "You've already seen me naked, haven't you? I doubt it matters now."

"I didn't look before," he replied, a little hurt by what I said. He lifted my chin. "I think if I wanted to take advantage of you like that, I could have done it last night."

I felt my bottom lip quiver, no matter how hard I tried to hold it in. "I'm sorry." I gripped his shirt front hard in my fingers. "I'm so sorry."

He cupped my cheeks gently and kissed my lips. "You're allowed to break down, baby."

I reached up on my toes to kiss him again and tasted the tears on my lips. "But I'm not allowed to be a jerk to you when you stayed with me all night."

"If it helps you get through this, you can," he said, serious.

I scoff-laughed. "No." I wiped my eyes. "Okay. I'll get dressed and then come eat something."

He looked like he wanted to stay, but nodded. "Okay." But he didn't leave. He looked at me closely, his hazel eyes on mine as he wiped away the last tear from my eye. "I love you," he said low, just for me.

It was only my second time hearing it, but it felt like I'd been hearing that in my soul my entire life from this boy. "I love you."

"Oh, my gosh," I groaned quietly as I bit into the roll and pork chop Emma had set before me when I emerged from my shower. That was almost half an hour ago, and I hadn't even realized how hungry I was until the first bite of bread and butter hit my tongue. We stood at the counter and ate together. Milo stood behind me, his arms under mine as his palms rested on the counter top. "This is so good, Emma. Thank you."

"I didn't make it." She laughed. "I wish I did." She nuzzled the baby. "But Jackson doesn't let me get anything extra done, do you, buddy? But you're welcome."

"Either way, thank you. You didn't have to come, but I appreciate it." I leaned back into Milo's chest, feeling the safe warmth there. He kissed my neck and I turned my cheek for him to kiss me there, too.

"Of course," Mason answered. "We're family."

That statement may have been an attempt to make me feel better, but it wasn't doing the trick. It actually made me feel as if bile was rising in my throat. I didn't look up at him, just kept eating. I looked over my shoulder at Milo and lifted a bite of cornbread for him. He took a small bite at first and then took my hand, going back for a bigger bite that wiped out half of my piece of cornbread. I couldn't help but let a chuckle slip through.

He laughed, too, and licked the crumbs off his lips, but the sounds of our laughs together…made me feel physically ill. He saw the change come over me, and his arms around me pulled me against him tighter. "It's all right. You can laugh. Will would want you to. It's okay, sweetheart."

I stared at the granite countertop and tried not to break down, because all I wanted to do was snatch the keys I knew were in the little blue bowl by the door, stop at the first store in town, and grab anything with alcohol, just to take the edge off the pain, just to numb the way I felt in this moment.

Emma and Mason were good at the cutting tension. I had to give them that. Every time I pulled an awkward move or silence, they were there to pick up the conversation once again.

Finally, I could take it no longer and decided to take the awkwardness into my own hands and took the baby from Emma. I almost thought she might refuse me. Jackson was only a couple weeks old, and who knew what they thought of my mental state. It was getting dark. We'd sat around my living room and kitchen all day long, eating and cleaning up, eating again and cleaning up, doing anything and everything to keep me busy and not talk about what I was inevitably going to have to talk about tomorrow—Will's funeral.

"Do you mind?" I asked and held my hands out for the baby.

"No." She smiled. "Of course not. I practically owe you this baby anyway." She laughed and stood, setting him into my arms along my chest. "He didn't even want to come until his friend Maya coaxed him out."

It was impossible not to smile down at the baby. I gasped a little at the way he looked so entirely like Mason and Milo. Even more so in the last couple weeks. Mason and Milo sat at the bar opposite each other on the stools, but I saw Milo's eyes on me every few minutes. I tried not to return his gaze, because a part of me wanted to be angry he was so worried. Like I couldn't take care of myself, but that small rational part of me knew that I was breaking down, and she was silently begging him to see me, really see me, and know that I was falling. He said he would catch me, but would he really? When he saw me falling further and further down into myself, being that girl that I used to be, the girl I hated so much but didn't know how to send away…would he still want to catch me? Would he still chase me?

I found his eyes on me once more, but he wasn't worried this time. His eyes were smiling along with his lips as he looked at his nephew in my arms. I watched him and Mason together and could hear some of their conversation as they talked. They were trying to work out their own crap. With everything that had gone on they hadn't had much time to do it. When they started in on old stories, it changed however.

I didn't want to listen to them talk about the things they used to do as kids. When Mason asked Milo if he remembered them making their mom crazy with their rap songs they used to write in middle school, or making four grilled cheese sandwiches each on Saturday mornings, or how they jumped on her bed to wake her up on Christmas morning. But it was when Mason brought up him teaching Milo how to drive—it was too much. My body moved on its own. I was done.

I handed the baby to Emma, placing little Jackson in her arms, and made my way across the living room. I guess it was obvious that the conversation had upset me because I heard Mason's curse from behind me before I shut the bathroom door. Milo was knocking a few seconds later. "Maya, baby, open up."

"I want to be alone," I heard myself say, and even I was frightened by how dead it sounded. "For a little while."

"Maya," he said louder, a little more desperate. "Please."

I steeled myself and knew there was one thing I needed right now. One thing I could get easy as pie. One thing… Just one. I straightened my face and hair and took a deep breath to compose myself. I opened the door and tried to smile. "Sorry. It's just hard to hear those stories, you know?"

His mouth fell open and he backed up to let me out, shocked that it had been that easy. "We weren't even thinking. Sorry-"

"I'm okay, just needed a minute." I took his hand. "Come on. Let's go back before things get even more awkward."

He looked at me closely, but nodded. I tugged him to the couch and immediately waved away Mason's apology. Honestly, I didn't care. It wasn't his fault my brother, who taught me how to drive, died. It wasn't anybody's. They should be able to reminisce with each other.

"So, I thought maybe looking at the photo albums might help," I suggested and beckoned everyone to the couches.

"Really?" Milo asked, concerned. "You don't have to do this now."

"No, I think it'll help." I pulled all the albums I could find from the bookshelf and plopped them on the coffee table. Jackson was in his car seat asleep, so I ticked my head for Emma to see.

"Look at this." I pointed to a picture of me with and my mom. Both of us had highlights and heels on with our Christmas dresses. Milo leaned over my shoulder and whistled. I smiled up at him. "My family used to make a really big deal about Christmas. All the holidays, really." I turned the page, biding my time, hating myself, loathing that girl I was becoming all over again, but wanting nothing more in that moment than just one thing.

I showed them several books, and it broke my heart over and over again to see Will in them. Finally, I felt like Milo had trusted me enough to think I was okay. "There was this one picture of us that… I don't see it here. Hold on, I think it's in the hall."

"Huh, look at *that*," Milo joked wryly as I walked away. I turned, looking over my shoulder for a split second, hating myself so much for ruining this with him. He smiled, holding up a picture of me and my senior prom date in front of the Chinese place he lived above. "Doomed accidental kismet? I think so."

I managed a laugh. "Did you read that in a fortune cookie?"

"Of course." He winked.

And then he turned back to the pile of pictures. Because he was waiting for me. Because he trusted me. Because why wouldn't he? Because he loved me. Because I'd told him I loved him. Because he'd take care of me and wanted to keep doing so. Because he had no reason to believe I'd betray him.

I wiped a tear that raced down my cheek and stepped quietly into my ballet flats by the door. His zip-up jacket was on the hook, so I grabbed that, too, along with my wallet and the keys, as quietly as I could. I stopped and stared at my four year coin at the bottom of the key bowl. It was always in my pocket. It was always with me. Always... I picked it up in my fingers, but immediately set it on the table, unable to look at it. I had to go.

When the door opened without a creak, that little part of me, the piece that wanted to get caught and be rescued, the part that wanted Milo to chase me and find me and stop me before I could get very far, was screaming inside.

The other part, the part that was currently winning, smiled her evil smile that her plan was working and walked down the driveway to the car. I would be down the end of the road before they even realized I was gone, and by then it would be too late.

I pulled into the store and knew I looked like hell, but couldn't and wouldn't care. I grabbed the first frosted, tall bottle I found in the refrigerated section and slammed it on the counter. He jumped and spouted something about ID. I glared and rolled my eyes before pulling out an extra twenty and slipping it to him across the counter. I didn't even look back as I tossed another twenty on the counter to pay for the bottle and left.

My insides warred. All I could see as I climbed the hill was that four-year coin and Milo's face when he realized I was gone. His disappointment, his anger, his worry. He would look for me for a little while. An hour, maybe two, but then he would be angry and know how selfish I was being. He would know how disappointed Will would be in me, too.

He'd remember how I lied and manipulated to get away, how I tried to get him to have sex just to make me forget my pain. I scoffed angrily at myself and tripped over the gravel rocks, scraping my knee and leg. I cried out, but didn't stay down. I needed to get to the top. No, no, not only would Milo be done with me forever for this, he would be better off.

Milo deserved better than me or anything I was or could give him. I slipped through the fence, pushed myself up to sit, and set the bottle in front of me upright. Pulling my knees up to my chest, I stared at the bottle and fisted my fingers so tight. My fingers inched around the rim, needing that one thing. My eyes burned, and the tears wouldn't stop. I hated myself. I hated myself. My crying got louder, but I couldn't stop. I felt crazy, but it had all come to this. My fingers tightened on the cap, turning it, and I begged with everything in me.

Chase me, Milo. Please chase me.

> The intention is not to see
> through people, but rather to see
> people through.

Milo

GLANCING TO the hall, I knew in that instant something was wrong. The knock on the door was too hard to be polite, and this was a small town. Everybody would have heard about Will and would be giving Maya her privacy. I moved to the door quickly and noted Maya wasn't in the hall. I cursed under my breath and prayed to God she was in the bathroom, but knew in my gut that she wasn't. Damn it all to hell. She wasn't going to let me help her with this, was she?

I opened the door, my heart lifting a smidge at the thought that it might have been Joey changing her mind about coming for Will's funeral, but no, it was Maya's friend—her boss—the coffee mug lady. "Hotshot," she muttered with a small smile. "I'm so glad to see you sticking around."

I sighed, seeing my coat and Maya's shoes gone. I leaned in the doorframe, bumping my head against it, probably a little harder than was necessary for dramatics. "Too bad Maya's not."

"Oh, no..."

"Yeah. She's not taking it well."

"Kid, you have to go after her!" she insisted.

I bristled. "I know that, lady." The scoff slipped from my lips before I could stop it. "I just realized that she slipped away from the house. I don't know where she went, but I'll find her. I have to. I love her, and she's hurting so bad, and I don't know why she's pushing me away, but it doesn't matter." I shrugged. "I'll find her and make her come back."

Her eyes watered and she touched my cheek. "Her production has gone down twenty-one percent at work because of you, mister."

I swallowed, knowing she was joking but she was also wasn't. She was telling me something, telling me that Maya loved me, too. "I hope it's enough to make her come back."

"Me, too."

"I've got to go."

She nodded. "I'll drive around, but she'll avoid the obvious places. They usually do."

"They?" I asked while I shoved my feet in my boots.

"Addicts, Milo." She smiled sadly and turned to go.

I felt all the blood drain from my head at once. That hadn't even crossed my mind what she might be doing. I thought she just wanted to get away, but her boss was right. Maya did want to get away, and she was in more trouble than I thought.

"Mason!" I yelled. I told him the gist of what was going on and told him to stay there in case she came back. I was going to my place first and then over to the shelter, to her job where the meetings happen, then to the church. I'd be back.

As soon as I pulled up at my house, relief flooded me at seeing a light on in my kitchen. I bolted up the stairs and opened the door slowly so as not to startle her. I shut the door and rounded the corner near the dining room. "Maya?"

"Not quite," I heard. I stiffened. Turning I found Roz himself. I'd only ever met him a couple of times. I always met with the little people who worked for him. He wasn't alone though. There was another man there in the kitchen at the counter. "Maya and Milo. How does it go? Sitting in a tree?"

"What do you want?" I growled.

"That's no way to treat someone you owe money."

"I was a stupid kid who made even stupider mistakes."

"Not my problem."

"You set us up to fail." He cocked a brow, looking amused. His black leather coat crinkled as he twisted in his chair to laugh.

"Oh, this I have to hear. Please indulge me."

"You only let the runaways work for you. The ones who are most likely to have a problem. The ones most likely to steal from you either because we got addicted ourselves or because we needed the money. Why?"

"Because it's not good to have the same people work for you for too long. This way, you take care of the problem yourself. I barely have to lift a finger to eliminate the problem, and finding another boy to sell my goods is like finding a kid to eat candy."

"You're such a bastard."

"You stole from me," he said evenly.

"I did," I admitted. I swallowed. "I'll pay you back."

"That ship has not only sailed, Milo, but sunk." He waved his finger at the other guy and nodded his head. "Do it. It's been years, and I'm ready to finish this once and for all." He smiled at me. "You might be happy to know that it's never taken me this long to find someone before. You played quite the game of hide-and-seek with my men."

My heart pounded, but it wasn't for me. It was for Maya. No one would know to go look for her, and she would think I would come. She told me to chase her and she'll think I'm not coming. I won't make it in time to save her. I hated him for that alone more than I'd ever hated anyone or anything.

If was going to die anyway, I wasn't going to lie down and take it quietly. I moved to make a run for him when a knock sounded on my door. I froze.

"Milo? Milo Sawyer? It's the police."

Roz's cold smile shined brightly before he stood and ticked his head toward the back door. "Your luck won't keep going, Milo. I'm coming for you. I'll come after your friend's funeral." He smiled. "See? I can be gracius."

I opened my mouth, wondering how he knew about Will, but they were gone. They walked out the back and I answered the door, not understanding what in the hell was going on. Why were the cops at my door? "Officer?"

"We had a call from your neighbor that there was some breaking noises coming from your apartment?" His eyebrow rose.

"Um?" I shook my head. "Nope. My friend ran off. I'm just out looking for her."

"Okay, well." He shrugged like he didn't know what else to say.

"Thanks."

I leaned against the door and breathed deep through my fist. What the hell. What the hell. What the hell. What the hell was I going to do?

The first thing was find Maya. If I had to send her away with Mason or something, so be it, but the first thing was find her and make sure she was okay, make sure she was safe.

I jumped up and ran down the stairs, jumping back in the Jeep. I headed toward her job, where they held the meetings. We had so many talks out there on those steps and in that foyer. I smiled thinking about what a pain in the butt she was when we first met. I hoped beyond hope that's where she was. I hopped out and looked all over, but she was nowhere in sight. I went to the shelter and the church, but right before I climbed out, it hit me how stupid I was. Of course.

I slammed my Jeep into gear and went across town as quickly as I could, without regard to other drivers or stoplights. When I pulled into the convenience store parking lot and saw her old truck there, I felt like I failed her. I should have known she'd come there. What if I was too late? What if she didn't want me there? She had run away after all. The thoughts I remembered this morning, of how I pushed her to let Will live a little, that she could blame me completely for this, came back to my mind.

No. I pushed all that away as I ran up the gravel hill behind the store. Even if she hated me and wanted nothing more to do with me, I owed it to her to make sure she was safe and sound. Ger her through this, get her home, get her with her friend if nothing else, and then I'd leave and she'd never have to see me again. It was probably safer that way anyway.

My heart ached at that thought.

And then there she was. It was freezing outside and she was in shorts with my jacket, her little cute shoes on, her knees pulled to her chest. A big bottle of something that would have put her way out of her misery was staring across the satellite dish at her, and she stared right back.

The bottle was full. The bottle was full…

"Sweetheart…" I said when she didn't seem to notice me approach. Even the clang of fence hitting didn't make her flinch.

She turned and looked at me. Tears streamed down her face and chin. "You came?"

"Of course I did. Are you all right?" Her face crumpled and she cried even harder. "Aw, you're breaking my heart." I knelt down, turning her knees toward me, forcing her to let me be in her space. If this was my last little bit of time with her then I needed to be as close as I could get. "What are you doing out here?" I looked over at the bottle. She did, too. Then she looked down at her palm and opened it to reveal the metal cap. Her palm was cut in a jagged, circular pattern from where she had pressed and gripped it so tightly.

"Sweetheart," I scolded in a whisper. "Why did you do that?"

Wide Open

"I couldn't do it," she finally admitted. Her eyes lifted and her gaze locked onto mine. She wasn't looking at me or through me or to me. She was with me in every way, like she was inside my very soul. I took that gorgeous, tear-streaked face in my hands and begged her silently to tell me. "I couldn't do it," she repeated again. "I opened the bottle and my fingers wouldn't take it. At first, I couldn't do it because I love you." Another tear slid down and over her lips. "I knew you were already so disappointed in me," she hiccupped, but kept going, even when I opened my mouth to stop her, "because I left and was so rude to your family after they came all this way just for me. I'm sorry. I'm so sorry." Her head shook violently. "Milo, I thought I was going to bust…wide open. I thought this was what I needed. I just needed to be numb. I needed to get away. I needed to not think. I needed to not feel. I needed to not be awake. I needed to not be me anymore. I bought it, I came up here, I opened it and I looked at it. This bottle was all I've been able to think about all day long." She had yet to take her eyes from mine. "I thought if I could just get something, anything, in my system it would all go away, at least for today." A fresh round of tears of emerged, but my brave girl pushed through them. "But as soon as I opened the bottle, and I heard the suction it made, I couldn't do it. It made me sick to hear it, to smell it. I couldn't throw all those sober, clean years down the drain, I couldn't stand to let my dad down after he was the one who saved me the first time. I couldn't stand for Will to see me take a nosedive because of this—because of him—and I didn't want you to find me here with that in my stomach, but most of all…" she leaned forward and whispered the last words against my cheek, "drinking one sip or the whole bottle won't bring him back." She sobbed harder. "It won't bring Will back."

I pulled her up and traded places with her, sitting in the dish and putting her in my lap. I could tell how absolutely exhausted she was because her sobbing was more breathy and panting more than it was powerful. She had one hand around my neck, but everything else was limp and she let me hold her there.

She did manage to kick out her leg and knock the bottle off the edge of the dish. It busted against the rocks on the ground. She sighed against my neck and seemed to calm. I kissed her forehead, her eyes, her wet lips, smoothed her hair and rocked her, anything I could think of to soothe her.

"Thank you," she finally whispered when all her hiccups and tremors were done.

"You told me to chase you, didn't you?"

She looked up at my face like I was more than a hero. "You're doing a really good job."

I couldn't help but grin at that. "Your approval is all I could ever want."

I lifted her easily into my arms and made my way slowly, carrying her to her truck. I'd come get my Jeep later. She was exhausted. There was no way she could walk, let alone drive. Besides, I didn't want her away from me. This could very well be my last night with her.

God, help me...I had to talk to Mason and Emma.

I thought about Roz—about what he said he was going to do to me, about what that was going to do to Maya to lose her brother and then me right after that. Maybe that was vain to think so highly of myself, but I just hoped and prayed she survived it. I hoped she could look back on the same reasons she didn't take that drink this time and use them for next time.

I set her in the seat right next to me, keeping my arms around her, and drove the short distance to her apartment. Mason was pacing and Emma's gasp stopped me when I came in carrying a now passed out Maya. "Oh, my gosh, Milo. Is she all right?"

"She's okay," I assured her and kept walking back to Maya's bedroom. "She went to this place she took me to a couple of times. I found her there, but she was okay. She just…"

"You don't have to explain," Mason said. I laid her on the bed and looked over my shoulder at him. "I can imagine what she's going through. We got a hotel for the night. We'll be back in the morning. Do you need anything before we go?"

"Nah, man. I'm OK," I told him, taking her shoes off, but refusing to look at him.

"Milo," he called.

"Hmm?"

"Milo?" he called harder.

"What?" I whispered as I stared at the bed next to her. Before I knew it, he was wrapping his arms around me and pounding his fists on my back.

"I'm so sorry," he said, the sincerity pouring off him. "I'm sorry she lost her brother and you lost your friend, and everyone in both of your lives seems to leave for one reason or another." He leaned back and gripped the back of my neck, putting his head almost to mine as he spoke hard. "But know this—I'm not running out, I'm not leaving, I'm not walking away. I'll be back. Anytime, as fast and as long as you need me. You got me? For you and for Maya." I stared at the face that had been the *only* person to never walk out on me. "I never left, Milo." His cheek jumped as he stared at me. "I never left. I never stopped looking for you."

"I know, Mase."

"I won't ever leave."

"You never did, Mason. I know that." He breathed loudly through his nose and held onto me tightly. "It was me who let you down. I gave up. I was the coward. You held on and I let go. I didn't want to deal with my grief and it was easier to just blame someone. Thank you…for never giving up on me."

"Never," he growled and hugged me hard.

Maya rolled and moaned a little in her sleep. Mason leaned back, but looked me in the eyes. "We'll be back in the morning. She can get the

189

funeral expedited if she wants, up to her, so she doesn't have to just keep waiting for it. That's the part that would kill me, I think. Something to think about."

I nodded. "We'll be here. I, uh…have some things to talk to you about in the morning."

"What's that?"

I almost lied. Almost. "Roz came to see me."

He turned pale as the moonlight coming in from the window. I nodded. There was no point in sugarcoating it. "First, let's just get Maya through this," I told him, "and then…I don't know what'll happen, but promise me you'll take care of—"

"Shut up," he growled and backed away. "Shut up. No, we'll figure something out."

"What? All of us are going to run away and hide out together? Maya and Mom and her nurse, too?" I shook my head. "No, Mason. It's no good. Look, no more talking about it tonight. I just didn't want to lie to you. I wanted you to know he knew where I was."

"How?"

"When Maya's brother…when he… I was pretty upset. I accidentally blurted my old name to the cops when they took my statement. You know Roz has his pocket cops. Didn't take them long to find me."

He sighed, his shoulders sagging. "No…"

"I'm sorry, Mase."

He looked so beaten. "I…"

"Look, go on to the hotel. Get some sleep." I rubbed my face and looked down at Maya. "One day at a time. Tomorrow, I need to help Maya, then I'll worry about me. A cop came to my apartment earlier. That's the only thing that stopped them today. Roz said he'd be back after the funeral."

He blinked. "I can't just go."

"You can. Take Emma and the baby to get some sleep. Go. I'll be fine."

It took some more convincing, but once he was gone, I laid down with my girl and wrapped my arms around her from behind. I tucked her hair behind her ear and pulled her hips to mine, but didn't need to. She nestled in, tucking herself into every place possible. I put my arm under her head and pulled the blanket over us.

Kissing the back of her neck, I sighed into the soft skin there.

"I'll be right here," I promised, but it broke my heart that I would be breaking that promise soon. Not just the promise I made her, but the promise I made to Will as well. I said I would watch over her and not leave her when he was gone, but I didn't know what to do now.

If I left, Roz would just use them, hurt them, to make me come back. If I stayed, he was going to kill me no matter what I did because I was a loose end. The police couldn't help me, just like they couldn't help me back then.

I was going to have to face this alone.

> A chance meeting with someone
> from the past is in store.

Maya

I woke with a cry-headache, which was worse than a hangover if you asked me. The instant balm to my ache was the feel of Milo's arms around me. The events of yesterday and last night crashed down around me and I sagged, the instantaneous guilt almost too much to bear. The forceful sigh pushed from my lips as I remembered how sure I was that all I needed to do was get away and find some pills, but in the end, a bottle was the easiest thing to get, so that's what I had done.

In the end, Milo's love and trust had saved me. If he had never come along, Will would still be dead right now, and I would be drunk somewhere, numb and gone to the world for the rest of my days. I had no doubt of that. Because as much as Milo says I taught him what being an addict meant, he had taught me a lot, too.

I turned in his arms as slowly as I could, so as not to wake him, but when I got on my side, I found his eyes already open watching, gauging me. "Hey," I whispered lamely.

He spoke softly. "Again, I know this is the dumbest question ever, but is it a little better? Is there anything I can do for you today?"

"You're doing it," I told him. I stuck one of my legs between his and put my arms around him. His big warm hand crept up the back of my shirt to settle on the middle of my back. "I'm better than yesterday. That's saying something." I cleared my throat. "Not once last night did you use the *Will wouldn't want you to do this* card." I played with the creases on his shirt. "Why not?"

"Because you taught me that addicts have to do it for themselves. I didn't want you to do it for Will. I didn't want you to do it for me. I wanted you to do it for you."

I nodded, so proud of him for how much he had grown in the short time I'd know him. He didn't think he had, but he had. "I'm so sorry about last night."

He shook his head. "I know why you were angry yesterday and needed to get away from me."

"From you?" I asked. "Why would I be angry with you?"

"I'm sorry, Maya." And he did look sorry. "I'm so sorry. I told you that ice cream and going out into the cold for dinner and all that hell didn't matter; to give him a break." He laughed angrily and turned his head. "I made you feel like you were being too hard on Will. We ganged up on you, and you were right."

I put my hand on his cheek and turned his face to look right at me. "Milo," I whispered and drowned in hazel, bathed in the relief that my brother trusted him and left me in the care of this man. "He had cancer. A bowl of ice cream made no difference. He got to have some fun the last few nights he was alive, and that was thanks to you. If it had been my choice, he would have been cooped up in the house and would have just…" I choked on my words, "died alone while I was at work."

Milo shook his head slowly, not wanting to accept. "Maybe he…"

"Instead, he died with you there. He wasn't alone," I almost yelled to make him *see* as I cupped his neck. "He was with you, his friend. I'll never be able to thank you for that."

His eyes were red as he tried to fight his anger and grief. "All I wanted to do was save him. I tried to save him for you."

"I know and I love you for that, but…he couldn't be saved. I didn't understand that. We have the people in our lives for the time we have them. We can't dwell on the time that we don't." I moved in and kissed him once. "I'll always be thankful that I got to reconcile with my family and spend this time with Will before he left. I could have been too late."

"The fact that you can look at it that way right now, sweetheart, is pretty amazing." He swiped under my eye. "If I could make this better, I would."

"You are. You're here." He made a pained face for a split second, before it was gone, but I saw it. "What?"

"What do you want for breakfast? And don't tell me you're not hungry."

Mason and Emma arrived shortly after, and we ate Milo's scrambled eggs and toast. Marybeth stopped by again, per Milo, but she didn't grill or scold me. She and Milo kept sharing looks and glances, like they had this secret language now. I hated that they worried about me, but couldn't deny I had brought that one down on myself. I made sure to hug her extra hard and try to be honest, not hide anything. If I needed to cry; I cried. If I wanted to talk about Will; I did. If something was funny; I tried my best to laugh.

She kept calling Milo "hotshot" over and over and over. It was pretty funny because it irked him so bad, even though I knew she was only doing it to keep the tension from being tight. A couple other people from work stopped by and brought food, but most of the people I knew would wait until the funeral to pay their respects.

I could tell Mason and Emma had no idea where I'd gone yesterday. I should have known Milo would protect me in that way, too. I almost wanted to tell them, just because being open felt like the theme of the day.

And I would tell them, I knew I would, but first Will's funeral had to be arranged. Mason and Milo took me to the funeral home in town, the only one our little town had, and when the funeral director asked me when I wanted to do it, I said as soon as possible. When the details were too much or I didn't understand something, Milo would let me rest in the refuge of his neck and Mason would work out the rest of the details.

When it came down to choices and colors and cost, I froze.

All the money was gone. We used it all on Will's treatments and the apartment, and keeping some back for his funeral just seemed too morbid, but now would probably have been a good idea. He had said it several times, but eventually let it go, and I never brought it up again.

I looked up at the funeral director, the fresh tears for a completely different reason clinging to my lashes, as I fiddled my fingers around my bracelet embarrassingly. "Um…Mr. Price, how much is all that going to cost?"

I had no idea how much a funeral cost. Maybe it wasn't as bad as I thought. Maybe they worked with a payment plan or something. No, that was stupid.

"What you have chosen as of now is roughly seven thousand five hundred."

I gasped painfully, my eyes no longer brimmed, but spilling over. "Well…um, there's a little problem. Um, is there anything that's not as expensive as that?"

He looked at me curiously. "Well, that includes the burial plot at the church cemetery beside your parents, of course." I sighed. Oh, God help me. What was I going to do? I leaned forward and put my head in my hands.

"Maya," I heard Mason say as Milo's hand rubbed my back, his side pressed against mine. "We can help if you'll let us."

I lifted my head and looked at him like he was crazy. "Mason, I *can't* let you."

Mr. Price cleared his throat. "The funeral arrangements have been paid in full already, up to the amount of ten thousand dollars. Anything that's left over after that is to be refunded back to you, Maya."

We all stared at him silently before my squeak broke it. "What did you say?" When he went to answer, I cut him off. "Who? Who paid it? How? When!"

He smiled, amused by my outburst. "I can't believe you didn't know and I'm the one who has to tell you." His smile was one of sadness and a tinge of happiness. "Will came and paid it, Maya." My heart hurt, my vision blurred. He *didn't* just say Will paid it. "He came months ago. He said his diagnosis was…not good, but you weren't giving up. He wanted to let you have that. He wanted to spend every minute with you with hope that it could be okay, but he knew it wouldn't. So before the money was gone with all the treatments and bills, he came and paid it. He said he was going to tell you eventually."

"He didn't," I heard myself say, but it didn't sound like me. "Will," I scolded him in a whisper, "how could you not tell me?"

"He was your big brother," Mr. Price reasoned. "It's his job to protect you."

"No matter how much I tried to take care of him, he always still managed to be the one doing it, even if he let me think it was me. I was awful at it, and he was so good." I laughed and sniffed. "So typical."

"He loved you." He smiled. "That boy loved his sister."

"I love him." I looked at Milo and remembered what Milo said Will told him. "And Will's still making sure I'm okay."

"Maya, I've known you and Will since you were little. Your father and I actually had a scuffle over your mother when we were in the eighth grade once." I laughed as a tear slid down my cheek. "This doesn't help you feel better, I know, but I hope you know that just because your family is gone doesn't mean you don't have people here who care about you. Think about that."

"I will. Thank you."

"So, do you want to wait a day or two or a few before the funeral? Or do you want to go ahead and get it done?"

So the next day at eleven in the morning, I sat in the front row left side with Milo and we said goodbye to my brother. The church pews were full to the brim, and I was shocked by it. Honestly, most of those people knew our parents, but we pushed those people away by our actions after our parents died. They had been there waiting for us that whole time, and we just thought they abandoned us.

I thought it was going to be torture to listen to the stories of the couple of people who told stories of my brother, but it wasn't. It actually felt like a really big, albeit bulky and uncooperative, band-aid, but a band-aid nonetheless.

That night at the apartment, people came and went, they ate and looked at the photos strung all over the place. I felt I should put them out, let people see them.

Milo had been my silent rock all day. He hadn't tried to coddle me or coax answers out of me with "*Are you okay?*"s every five minutes, for which I was grateful. He stood by me, was polite when I introduced him, cleaned dishes and did whatever needed to be done, and I never felt like I needed to do anything to make him comfortable. That was a relief all by itself.

But I could tell something was up. He was letting me get through the day and then I knew he was going to tell me. He wouldn't lie; I knew it. We were beyond that now. I had no idea what was going on, but I hoped it was something I could survive. Maybe he wanted to move back home to be with his mom and Mason. I didn't know, but as the last few guests were politely shooed away, I knew the time to find out had come.

When our eyes met across the room, he knew it, too. And then I knew he wasn't leaving me. How could he leave? It was obvious he belonged here with me. We practically finished each other's thoughts without even having to say anything.

Mason had taken Emma and the baby back to their hotel a while ago, but was coming back later. He seemed to be in on whatever was going on since he looked really uneasy all day.

"Milo, I know you've had something to tell me. Everyone's gone. Will's in the ground. No more excuses. Please. What the hell's going on?"

He came swiftly and put his hands on my hips, pushing me gently to sit in the chair as he knelt down in front of me. "If I could go back and change it, know that I would do that. I would do anything, pay anything to change it." His eyes were red. He actually looked as if he could cry.

"Baby, you're scaring me."

He leaned up and put his face right up to mine, his palms on my cheeks. "I love you. I love you so much. I don't know how much time we have, but I want to get you out of here. You have to go with Mason when he gets here. Tomorrow morning, you're going to leave with them, get out of town for a while."

"What? Why?"

"Remember when I told you about the night I left home? The night I got beat up and left the hospital? They wanted me to roll over and give up Roz? I ran and changed my name." I nodded. "When I called 911 for Will and the cops came, I accidentally...gave them my old name. They found me." I gasped. "Roz was at my apartment the other night when I went out looking for you."

"No, Milo. No."

"I told you I wouldn't leave you—"

I got it. I got exactly what he meant. "Let's run. Let's just go."

One side of his mouth rose. "I love that you would do that for me, but he'll use Mason and Mamma against me," he explained softly. "Before, he knew I didn't care, but he knows that I do now."

"Why does he want you so badly?"

"Because I used to work for him. I know all his drop-off spots, all his big buyers, the businesses he uses to run his business through. He made a killin'. And I was a loose end."

"So what are you saying?" I asked him, my throat scratching and aching to hold it together. "You're what? Just going to go home and wait for him to come find you?"

"I don't know what to do, Maya. Anything I do, you get hurt and I break my promise." His jaw hardened and twitched. I smoothed it with my finger.

"So, what? That's it? I go with Mason, and you just go home and wait for Roz to come find you? We can't go to the police because they might kill you, too? Nothing? We don't even try?"

He stared. "I won't risk you. Not for a second. You're going with Mason." He stood. "And I'm going to try to talk to Roz. I won't get your hopes up. I know it won't help, but…it's all I can do. I need to face him alone and take this on by myself."

"Milo, no," I groaned and stood.

He made the most pained face I'd ever seen on him. He cupped my face and kissed me so softly. "Do this for me," he said harder and kissed me again. "I love you, Maya. I love you and I want you to know that what you said about not dwelling on the time that we didn't get to spend with someone, but being thankful for the time we did get with them? I'm so thankful I met you and you got to change me so completely." His lips opened my mouth with his and I knew something was coming, but I just couldn't make myself put things together. I hung on to him and sighed against his lips. "I love you, sweetheart. Thank you for the privilege of letting me catch you."

"I love you."

"Promise me you'll do this for me." I hesitated and he asked again. Harder. "Promise."

"Okay," I answered, but I didn't really even know what I was promising.

A sob broke free of my chest just as clapping resounded in my ears. Milo stood, yanking me behind him as I peeked just barely around his shoulder to see two men in my living room. One was tall with a gun pointed at us, one shorter one was clapping and smiling as if something pleased him very much.

"Aw, Milo, don't look so surprised to see me."

"You said you'd wait until after her brother's funeral."

He looked at his watch and raised a sarcastic eyebrow. "It's after."

"Come on," Milo coaxed me forward. He handed me his cell. "Mason's number's in there. Get out of here."

My breath skidded painfully. "Milo."

"You promised," he begged me, his eyes on mine. "Go." He pushed me toward the kitchen, his hand on the small of my back, but I didn't get far.

"The girl doesn't want to go," the short one said with a high-pitched chuckle. "Sounds to me like someone's having a lover's spat."

"Let her go," Milo growled.

"I think it's better this way," he plopped down into the plush club chair and smiled, "seeing as how she's seen my face and all."

Milo tugged me back behind him and tried to soothe me, his thumb running over my pulse point. His voice, however, was anything but calm as he spat his words to the man sitting down. I could only assume that was Roz. "You bastard. You never had any intention of letting her go."

"I guess you'll never know."

Milo jumped right into it, just like he told me he was going to. "I don't care about your business, Roz. I never did. I was a stupid kid you used to do your bidding. I don't care what you do. I have no interest in you. I'm not going to the cops or anybody else with this. All I'd be doing was incriminating myself anyway. You can trust that—"

He laughed. "No loose ends, Milo. That was the number one rule when I hired you, remember?"

Milo's grip tightened. "You hired *me*, not her. I was the screw-up who ruined his life, not her. She didn't screw you over, I did. I stole from you and used your goods, not her. Don't punish her because of what I did." He was shaking. "You want me to beg, I will. Please don't do this to her. Take me, do whatever you want to me, but let her go."

"No," Roz answered immediately. The gunman at the kitchen counter snickered at that. Milo glared at him, and I knew if he a gun hadn't been pointed at me, this whole situation would be very different. I tried not to cry, not to shake. I tried to be brave for Milo since he was being so brave for me.

"Sweetheart," Roz drawled and I knew he was mocking the way Milo said it to me. "Why don't you scoot to the kitchen and make us some tea?"

"Don't you—" Milo barked, but I gripped his arm to stop him. I shook my head, just barely. I leaned up and kissed his bottom lip, not knowing what I could do, but knowing that Roz obviously thought little ol' me wasn't a threat or he wouldn't have sent me into the knife-filled kitchen to get his tea. I glanced at Roz and didn't see a gun on him, but that didn't mean he didn't have one.

I turned up the shakes and tremors to give him an even bigger reason to doubt I was a threat as I made my way to the kitchen. I shook so badly that I dropped the spoon to the floor loudly and left it there, grabbing another one as I rattled it against the cup and started the kettle on the stove.

When I neared the knives, I heard a grunt. The gunman slung the knife block across the room, throwing knives and splinters of wood and wall chunks everywhere as I screamed and crouched down.

"Wouldn't want you to get any ideas," he drawled. I looked up to see his gun pointed right at Milo's chest. Milo's face was so red, his fist so tight. When I filled the kettle with water from the tap, it rattled against the metal from my exaggerated shaking, but I had to admit some of it was real.

Roz chuckled and went back to surveying Milo, which was exactly what I had wanted. Distraction. The gunman still had his back to me, leaning on the counter facing Milo. I quickly pulled out Milo's phone and searched for Mason's number, sending a quick text.

This is Maya. Roz is at my house with a guy w gun. I'm in kitchen. Will stall long as can. Frying pan to head of gunman. Bring what you can for Roz. Hurry. As soon as I see you, I start swinging.

I would have rolled my eyes at myself, but would save that for later. I turned off the ringer in case Mason texted me back.

I turned the kettle to medium so it wouldn't boil too quickly and hoped that Roz was trying to drag this out for Milo's torture. I brought the sugar and teabags from the cabinet and then spilled sugar on the counter for good measure. I looked up at Milo to find him watching me with an agonized expression as Roz blabbered on about his operation's code of ethics. I didn't know if this would work or not. We may all be dead in a few minutes, but I hated that Milo thought I was this scared. I couldn't do anything about that, though.

Roz's creepy smile found me and I stared back. "What?" I asked.

"I take mine with lots of sugar, sweetheart."

I gritted my teeth.

Milo made a growly noise. "Will you just do something if you're going to do it and leave her the hell alone? Come on. I'm right here." He pounded his chest with his fist. "Get it over with."

Just wait it out, Milo… Just wait. Mason's coming. Mason's coming… Mason's coming…

Mason hadn't answered my text though, and it had been more than seven minutes. I turned so they wouldn't see the defeat washing over me. The kettle whistled and I took it from the hot stove. I stood there, gripping the handle, so mad I couldn't move even if I wanted to. I wasn't angry with Mason. It wasn't his fault.

I could hear Roz talking to Milo behind me. He was saying something about life not giving you anything and taking what you want is the only way that you survive.

I was just angry that I would never get to live out my happily ever after. I heard the smallest of taps. I lifted only my eyes and looked over to the window above the sink, and there he was. Mason was surveying the room, me, and the kettle in my hand. Mason was a handsome, kind, tall, and sweet man, but I hadn't seen this side of him yet. He was beyond livid and past the point of pissed.

He pointed to my back door and himself, letting me know that's where he was coming in. I barely nodded once before picking up a hand towel off the counter and wrapping it as discreetly as I could around my wrist. As soon as I turned and saw Mason, I wasn't using this metal pot for tea anymore. I was hoping it wouldn't burn too bad, but as long as I got Milo out safe, I didn't care about anything else.

I turned, trying to keep my face straight and sad as it had been before. Roz was still speaking, but I wasn't even listening anymore, it was just sounds. I poured one cup on autopilot, spilling half of it on the counter.

My lips parted when I paid attention and started to hear the words.

No, we were too late. Mason wasn't going to make it. I lifted my face and looked at the back of the gunman to see his raised arm toward Milo. Milo's face as he looked at me was one of determination. He was trying to tell me something. I wasn't having it. I reared back, just as Milo yelled for me to run and started to plow toward the guy, I bashed the guy's head as hard as I could. The sound was unlike anything I'd ever heard—sickeningly thick and solid, crunching as he slammed to the counter and then the floor—but the pain in my hand was actually something I hadn't expected. I dropped the kettle and moaned, cradling my hand. As Milo reached me, I looked up just in time to see Roz lift a gun from the back of his pants and fire the handgun, his face a blaze of anger at things not going as he planned for a second time.

It wasn't in real-time. I couldn't act fast enough. It was Milo who swung himself in front of me to catch the bullet with his body.

Almost as soon as Roz's gun fired, Mason had turned the corner and slammed the back of Roz's neck with something large, but I didn't see what it was. I didn't see anything but the growing puddle of red that was growing on Milo's shirt as he panted and tried not to fall over as I gently placed him on the couch. "Oh, God, please," I begged.

He touched my chin. "Are you all right? Did he hurt you?"

"Me?" I said hysterically. "Did he hurt *me*?" The tears were pouring from me as I ran to the kitchen and grabbed a handful of kitchen towels and came back to look for the wound. "You don't worry about me. He shot *you*." I pulled out the cell, but my fingers were shaking so badly. "Mason!" I sniffed and panted. "Mason, call 911."

He was already right beside me. "Maya," he said soothingly. "It's okay."

"No, it's not okay. He's been shot."

"I already called them. They're coming."

"Oh." I finally looked up at Milo's face, unable to avoid it any longer. He was watching me with this smug little pained smile. I felt my mouth pop open. "What the hell are you smiling about?"

He licked his lip. "Come here, sweetheart."

"No, I'll hurt you. I'll—"

"Come. Here. Sweetheart."

I broke down like a flooded dam. I climbed into his lap sideways gently where he beckoned me and held on to him like I never wanted him to let go again. Because I didn't.

"It's just my arm," he explained into my hair. "I'm okay."

"There's so much blood."

"There are arteries in your arms. Hold on, Milo," Mason said as he yanked tight one of the towels I'd brought on Milo's arm. Milo groaned and panted for a few seconds until it passed. I hissed in sympathy for him.

He put his good arm around my waist and pulled me tightly against him. He sighed into my hair. "I could spank you for what you did." He glared over at Mason. "And you. What are you doing here?"

"I texted him," I confessed.

His face changed. "You what?" I told him everything about my plan. To say he was pissed was an understatement. "I told you I didn't want you to get hurt because of the stupid mistakes I made. If you had taken that bullet instead of me just now..." He shook his head. "You promised me you would stay safe. You—"

"I promised I would go with Mason and let you handle it, but things didn't work out that way." He closed his eyes. "I had to do something. The world losing every person who's ever been good to me just didn't seem right," I explained.

"If I had lost you, I would never have forgiven myself."

"Good thing you don't have to worry about that then, huh?" I ignored his glare and moved in slowly so as not to hurt his arm. I kissed his lips and his chin, his cheeks, his neck. Finally, I gripped his neck and held on because he was there, he was alive, and that was all that mattered, even if he was angry with me. The tears came again, but I didn't want him to see them. He could be mad all he wanted as long as he was here.

"Don't ever, ever do something like that again," he growled in my ear. "Ever. Do you hear me?" I lifted my head and he sighed. His mouth opened a few seconds before his words came. "Ah, baby. I'm sorry. I've just never been so scared in my entire life as I was when I saw Roz's gun pointed at you and there was nothing between you two. I didn't think I was going to make it in time."

I smiled sadly and whispered, "I would have taken a bullet for you, too, you know."

"I know," he whispered gruffly and lifted my chin, "and that pisses me off and turns me on at the same time."

He pulled my mouth up to his roughly. When I felt his warm tongue flick out to lick at the seam of my lips, I gripped his neck to turn his head, sort of loving the control this gave me, and sucked his lip into my mouth. He groaned, and I didn't know if it was pain or something else so I pulled back to question it. He shook his head. "Come here."

Wrapping his hand around the back of my neck so he could go in deeper, I could tell he was hurting, but he didn't let me go. His panting against my lips was harsh and I pushed back again. "Does it hurt bad?" I touched his face.

"Nothing hurt worse than thinking you were going to take that bullet," he told me, his eyes lidded with pain as he stared, but his mouth smiled. "Kissing you makes it better though."

He brushed his mouth against mine, but Mason chuckled, reminding me this whole situation was pretty ridiculous. "All right, hero. Can we try to remember you just got shot?"

But Milo wasn't listening. I was drowning. Drowning in Milo before sirens brought us back to ourselves. He huffed a frustrated breath against my lips when the paramedics came through the door.

They fussed over him and it was then I realized how pale he was. I opened my mouth to say the words when they said something about him needing a transfusion waiting for them at the hospital. "What's your blood type?" they asked him.

Mason butted in. "We have the same blood type. I'll give him whatever he needs when we get there." Mason gripped Milo's hand, their thumbs overlaying as they stared at each other.

"Thanks, man," Milo whispered. It frightened me that it was all he could do.

I had scooted back to give them room when they came in, and now I hugged myself and watched as the room was filled with people. The cops came in and began to ask questions left and right. All the while my eyes kept searching Milo as they patched him up, and his eyes were always on me. When the cops moved on to Mason, since I told them he was the one who had snuck in the back door and saved the day, Milo beckoned me to him. They were about to take him away as soon as they got his IV in, they said, so he took my hand and pulled me down into his lap on the gurney.

I huffed. "Are you insane?" I hissed through a laugh.

"Apparently."

"Sir," the paramedic complained and went to grab my arm, "she can't sit—"

"I wouldn't do that," Milo told him, and even in his state I felt awfully sorry for that guy. I pressed my lips together to stop from laughing. The guy quirked an amused brow and put up his hands in surrender. Milo pulled me down to lay sideways on his chest and sighed as if that one action made him feel better as he stroked my hair.

I didn't know what was going to happen. I didn't know what any of this meant or what would become of this day. But Milo was here, he was safe, and so was our family. We were together and no matter what this life threw at us, I planned to stay that way.

With my face pressed into his neck, I knew my life would be filled with happiness—wherever we were. We would find a way to be together, someway, somehow. All of these things didn't add up to this one day for nothing. They meant something.

And we would chase each other to the end of every day and fall with arms wide open, knowing that we were safe. My heart was safe with him because not only would he—and did he—take a bullet for me, but he saw me for my possibilities and my future, not for all the things I used to be. And he trusted me with his future, too.

Even now as I listened to the rumble in his chest as Milo barked orders for the paramedic to check the miniscule scratch on my chin, I was falling further and harder for him.

But I was no longer afraid.

> You will be hungry again in one hour.

EPILOGUE
Milo

HER FINGERS always ran over the scar absentmindedly, as if she couldn't help but think about it. And then she would swallow, as if it was all too painful to remember. Her eyes would lift to mine and she'd know she was caught. She'd would smile coyly, roll her eyes sometimes, but always reach over and press her lips to the mark before whispering, "Thank you."

"You can stop thanking me," I whispered back and kissed her forehead.

She smiled up at me and handed me a glass of juice. "How was your run?"

I chugged it down before answering and placing it in the sink. "Good. I think the neighbors are finally warming up to me."

She laughed. "Well, now I know you're lying."

She scooped the bacon she fried while I was gone and put it on my plate along with some eggs, and then got some for herself, setting them at the bar stools for us. I pulled some silverware from the drawer and poured coffee for her.

She leaned her head on my shoulder and told me about the neighbor lady coming over and saying how I get her dogs too worked up when I run in the mornings. They think I'm a criminal because I look like one with no shirt on, and they'd appreciate if I'd run elsewhere. She giggled as she took her bites of eggs and told me how she had to keep a straight face.

My arm had been in a sling for a few weeks. No pain meds were given, but I wouldn't have taken them anyway. Addicts didn't get pain medication. Maya had hurt her hand whacking that guy in the head with that kettle, but it hadn't been too bad. Just a sprain and she wore a wrap for a few days. But me? She was the best nurse to me. All I could take was over the counter Ibuprofen and I kept bumping into things. Sleeping was a disaster, running wasn't fun at all, working was near impossible, but Maya fussing over me? Her always square in my lap when we made out because I couldn't hold myself over her? Her playing my little nurse when she re-bandaged me? It almost made it worth it to go through it all over again.

The federal bureau had come to the hospital that day after everything happened and said they'd been trying to catch Roz for years—yada, yada. I'd known all that already. That's why I ran from the hospital the first time. I knew they'd want me to talk, and I knew I couldn't do that because he'd kill me.

Even though he was no longer an issue, all the people in his pocket were still out there. The feds didn't think we'd have any problems with anyone. If anything, people would probably be grateful to be rid of Roz, but they thought getting out of town, out of state, would be a good idea, however I couldn't leave Mamma again. If I honestly thought there was a threat I would have been on the first train out of there, but I was a small fish in that pond. I was a nobody. The only reason Roz ever cared about me at all was because I had dirt on him. He was gone. None of his cronies and buyers would give two craps about me now. I'd been silent for two years already. Why would I start talking now?

So we stayed.

Now, eight months later, we lived in a small apartment that was the perfect size for the two of us. It was about fifteen minutes from Mamma's house and we'd already found our new favorite Chinese place.

We woke up next to each other every day in our small crappy double bed. It was home and I loved it. I wouldn't have lived anywhere else. Waking in those cheap white Target sheets in the morning with Maya's legs wrapped around mine, her in my boxers and t-shirts, because that little fad stuck—to my never ending enjoyment—was the highlight of my life. Sometimes I couldn't believe it was real. I'd reach over and think it was a dream, or a nightmare even, and I was back to being that punk kid and this wasn't my Maya, but some girl I didn't even know the name of.

But I'd run my hands over her, behind her knees, her behind, her back, her arms. It was her—my broken angel who just wanted to put other people back together again.

Moving back home was something we debated for a while. Maya's whole life was back in the town we met—her job, her friends, but she insisted she wanted to start over, start fresh and with my family who had done so much for her just a couple hours down the road, it just made sense for that to be the place to do it. She said everywhere she looked, she saw her brother in that little town.

In no time, she found a job at the center here as a counselor. She said she didn't want to do anything else. That even though it was a rough job, it reminded her every day why being sober and clean was so important. We went to meetings there at least once a month, but seemed to be there more than that. Just like the other center, she showed a lot of support for the people there, helped them more than she helped herself. She was good at it because she didn't see it as a job. It was her life.

And me, I actually started working at the center, too. No more greasy work for me. Which worked out great because the more time we spent at the center, the better.

Mamma seemed to be doing as great as she could be. We saw them all the time. My nephew was growing faster than they could clothe him, and Mason was already trying to get Emma to have another one.

The knock on the door sounded, but before either of us could get up, the door opened and a loud squeal rang out. "Oh, my. Oh, my. Yes," I heard Emma soothe him. "Yes, I get it. You're happy to be here."

I got up laughing and put our plates and cups in the sink as Maya took Jackson from Emma, who handed me his bag without looking at me and searched in her purse for something. "Uh, he's been teething, so I'm sorry if he's a little cranky, but if he starts crying, just give him this and let him suck on—"

I took her shoulders and made her face me. "Em." She looked up at me, her big eyes bright. "It's all right. We've got him. He'll be fine. We'll be fine. You just go take your test and all will be well."

Emma grinned up at me and sighed. "All right. Okay." I hugged her to me and kissed her forehead. She pulled back and pushed at my chest. "Eww. Put a shirt on, McBeefy." She waved as she hurried out the door. "I'll be back!"

Maya laughed as I shook my head and made my way to my nephew. Emma had finals today and Mason had some kind of convention. Who better to watch the kid on a Saturday morning than the responsible uncle and aunt? I rubbed his chubby little cheek and chin with my finger. He latched on and then grabbed a handful of Maya's hair.

He was the cutest little mess I'd ever seen. A Wright boy to the core. I changed my name back to Wright recently. It only seemed fitting with the future plans I had in store.

I looked down at my future with dark hair and big eyes, watching her as she flipped Jackson's lip up and down, him chortling so loud. It didn't seem like very long ago, but it had actually been months since I'd done my NA meeting *coming out* speech, as I called it, not too long after Will's funeral and Roz and the move and…all of it. I still had my sling on, in fact. Maya had given me that two-year coin and I held it in my palm, crushing it as I faced all my demons and told a room full of strangers and my family every sin and transgression I'd ever done—every ugly detail, every awful thing, every way that I had been too weak to control myself.

But my eyes stayed on my Maya and she never once let me fall. She knew it was hard for me, the first time was always the hardest, but she was my rock. Afterwards, we all went out to the Chinese place for dinner, then that night Mason and I went out for the first time in years, just the two of us. In truth, I wanted him to come with me because I was picking up Maya's ring. I say *picking up* rather than *picking out* because I knew that I'd find one. It wasn't a matter of finding one. Maya wasn't one of those girls who needed some big rock. It was just a matter of finding something that didn't cost a fortune and I could imagine it sitting on her finger. I wanted Mason to come with me and didn't tell him what I was doing, but when we reached the store, he knew. After a few minutes of looking, I glanced over before looking back at the glass and spoke without looking at him.

"Aren't brothers supposed to talk you out of it? Tell you it's a mistake? Getting married is a one-way ticket to hell and all that other bull?" I grinned, unable to help it.

He chuckled as he came behind me to my other side. "That one." He pointed to a small one that was so simple, so pretty and beautiful and it kind of amazed me how he could get her so easily. "And no, I'm not going to talk you out of it."

I turned my head. He was smiling, but my brother, the sap that he had always been, the only father figure I'd ever known, looked like he could burst at any moment. "Thanks for letting me come, letting me do this with you."

I nodded. "There's no one else I would want to bring." I looked at the guy who had been hawk-eyeing us from the side since we came in and gave him a nod. "Can I see this one?"

He pulled the one Mason pointed to. I slipped it on my pinkie and gave Mason a side glance. He shrugged. "You don't have to go with that one, but…"

"It's perfect." It didn't even fit over my knuckle, but I knew it would fit her. Her other ring wouldn't fit over my pinkie knuckle either. That may have been a stupid way to gauge it, but I just felt it in my bones that it would fit. This was the ring. The stone was almost a light yellowish color.

"It's a canary stone," the clerk informed. "Very popular this year."

I scoffed under my breath. He was barking up the wrong tree with the "popular" approach.

I looked at the price and it was little more than I had expected to pay, but I wanted it for her. It was her ring. I took out the only credit card I had to my name and smiled as I gave it to him, making my very first purchase on it. "I'll take it."

He nodded. "Excellent choice. What color engagement box and wrapping would you like? We have maroon and black-"

"Don't need one," I told him, "but thanks."

I was doing this simple. After that, with the ring in my pocket, I was infatuated with the feel of it against my leg in my jeans. I showed Mason the coin I'd gotten her, the five-year sobriety coin and told him how I was going to propose to her with both of them together because from now on they went hand-in-hand—us, together, being clean.

Once again, Mason would never really know what it was like to be an addict, but the way he was so open to understanding, the way he was so supportive and didn't pull the I *understand what you're going through* speech was awesome. He was just *there*. That's all I needed him to be.

After that, we got coffee and donuts for everyone and went back to spend the rest of the night, our last night at my old apartment, with my family. Maya seemed peaceful in a way that was different than before. When I asked her what was up, she said that she was proud of me, and she knew starting over was going to be one of the best things she'd ever done for herself.

She hadn't been wrong. Every day, it got easier for her. Every day, her smile got brighter. Eventually, she wasn't sad anymore and I felt like she was finally my happy girl again. Will was proud of her, I knew. There was no way he could look at the girl she was, all she'd been through, and not be.

Now, Jackson entertained us for hours before Emma came and got him. Maya made this weird bubble noise that would get his giggle going, and it was the most hilarious thing. It made me think about kids of our own one day. Yes, we wanted kids. We figured we'd wait a long, long while. We were in no rush. We had my brother and his wife—the baby makers—who were apparently on a roll anyway.

After Emma picked him up, telling us that she'd see us later on tonight, Maya was in our room getting ready as I picked up the rest of the toys in the den. I found her leaning over the dresser trying to fasten a necklace. Her hands were shaking a little. I knew she was nervous about tonight and pressed my back to her front, taking the ends from her and putting my lips to her ear.

"Need some help?" I whispered soothingly.

"Mmhm," she hummed her acceptance and leaned back into me.

"Don't be nervous, sweetheart." I fastened it and kept my hands on her shoulders, kissing the place where her neck met her shoulder. "You look beautiful, number one. Number two, everyone who loves you will be there. Number three, Will will be there, too, and he'll be watching and thinking how proud of you he is." Her hair was up in some twisty knot, exposing her long neck. I leaned in and kissed her skin in several spots. "Are you ready to go?"

She turned in my arms and looked up at me, her face glowing in a way I hadn't noticed before. "I don't think I've really told you how happy I am here."

"You are?" I asked, a million pounds lighter. That's what a man wants is to make his girl happy. I wanted to do that, but honestly didn't know if I was truly succeeding. She seemed happy, but I didn't know if she was just trying to be happy because she knew I was.

"Yes. Very." She wrapped her arms around my neck. "Your family loves me the way mine used to." Her smile was widening the more she spoke. "It made me feel guilty at first, like I was replacing them, but I'm not. They would want me to be happy." She reached up on her tiptoes, but she didn't have to reach far, and right then I knew she was wearing some nice little high heels. I swallowed. "You make me happy," she said with certainty. "You make me feel the most normal I've felt since before my mom died. I didn't think I was ever going to get that back. I love you so much for coming into the meeting and being the one who tried to creep out halfway through." She smiled and bit her lip. "You changed my life that day."

I shook my head. She was ruining my plans. If she didn't stop being so sweet, I was going to get on one knee right here, right now. "You changed *my* life that day. If you hadn't been there to stop me from walking out, I'm not sure I would have come back."

She nodded with certainty. "You would have."

"I love you." I lifted her chin and kissed her, just once so as not to ruin all the work she'd done to make herself so beautiful. "Still nervous?"

"A little," she admitted honestly. We were always honest with each other. "But you make everything better."

I couldn't help but sigh down to my core at that. I took her shawl off the bed and wrapped it around her shoulders. It was a shame to cover her bare shoulders and the black dress she was wearing. I took her arm and placed it in mine.

"All right, it's time."

As we walked, I grabbed the keys and my wallet on the way out the door. We borrowed Emma's mom's SUV so we all could ride together. Some of Maya's friends from her old job were coming, but mostly it was a small affair.

When Maya learned that Will had paid for the funeral, she started to wonder about how she had missed that amount of money. She knew the treatments cost a lot, so she called his doctors and the cancer center and finally, she got some answers. On one of the more middle visits, they told Will he was welcome to do treatments, but there was basically no chance of coming through. The cancer had spread too much, and it was best for him to spend the rest of his time living his life instead of being sick from the treatments.

He never told Maya that.

So, from the timeline of things we put together and what the cancer center told us, after that, instead of paying for the treatments, he paid for the funeral, and then when Maya thought he was going in for his treatments, because no one was allowed back with him, like the time I had taken him myself, he was actually going and hanging out with the older guys who were getting treatments or going and reading to the kids in the children's ward.

Maya had been hysterical. With good reason. It was the second time in our life together that I stood there, looked at her, and knew that there was nothing else in her mind or thoughts but getting a drink, but getting something in her system, but finding somebody with some pills and getting some from them, anything. It hurt so bad to watch, but this was what it was to be an addict. My strong, brave Maya once again came out on the other side victorious with her four-year coin intact.

She didn't even run away this time, and she didn't push me away, though I could tell she wanted to. That's what a relationship was. Push and pull, progress and moving forward together. The day would come again when I would want to run like I did on her that day at that meeting, and I knew in my soul that she'd be there for me.

That was the best feeling in the world—knowing that no matter what happened, no matter how hard or how far we fell, the one we love would be there to make sure we got back up.

So, there we were, Mason, Emma, baby Jackson, Mamma, and the nurse, all piled in the car to head to the section of the library that they were dedicating to Will. When they found out what he had done and why he was at the hospital all the time, not just to spend time there, but to give his sister hope to the very end, they said they wanted to do it.

At the dedication, they wanted some of the kids to read the last book Will was reading to them in turns at the dedication. Maya said she was going to lose it and bawl like a crazy person. That was probably true, but I told her people expected her to lose it, and it was going to be okay.

Maya played with Jackson almost the entire way there and I knew she was distracting herself. So I did my bubbles and made him giggle extra hard for her. She looked at me gratefully and mouthed, 'I love you.'

'I love you more,' I mouthed back.

"And then the llama jumped up and down and said, 'If you can do it, I can do it, too!' The end."

Maya wiped her eyes and clapped, but I couldn't take my hands from around her to do so. I stood behind her and held on to her so she'd know that she wasn't ever going to be alone again. I got to keep my promise to Will. And Will was here, too. He was everywhere. He was in the kids' smiles, the patients he came and cut the fool with, played cards with. You would think cancer patients would be sad or bitter, but no. Most of them seemed to be like Will—thankful to have had the life they had at all.

Nine kids got up and read nine chapters of the last book that Will went around to read to them on his last trip to the hospital. My and Will's trip. The fast food trip, my and Maya's first fight. I felt kind of like I cheated her out of that last trip, but she said she was glad I got to spend time with him.

That trip changed things in some ways.

Afterward the reading, she talked to some of the kids and a few of the older guys, but mostly spent her time trying not to cry.

When the time came for her to go up on stage for the dedication, I gripped her hand and lifted her chin. She was shaking so badly. "Sweetheart, look at me."

"Will didn't trust me not to stay clean. That's why he didn't tell me the treatments wouldn't work," she whispered, her voice low, her eyes still cast down.

"Look at me," I said more forcefully. She did reluctantly. "He didn't tell you because he loved you." Her chest shook once. "He wanted you two to spend the last little bit of time you had together just being happy, being hopeful. He knew you, baby. He knew you loved him and he knew how sad you'd be. He just wanted to protect you from that for as long as he could."

"He could have told me."

"Big brothers protect their little sisters."

"Didn't he think it would be harder for me when the treatments didn't work?"

"Was it?" I asked honestly. "Was it better to have tried and for him to have lost than to have not tried at all? He did some of the treatments. The doctor told you he did do several rounds before they told him it wasn't working. He tried *for you*. And instead of just giving up and being sad, he kept coming here and tried to give a little hope to others because he knew what it was like to hope." I moved my hands up to her cheeks that were now wet, but she didn't seem so sad now. "He knew you'd be okay."

"Because of you," she murmured.

"What?"

"He knew I'd be okay because of you." I squinted. "I heard you telling Mason what Will told you. That Will made you promise."

My lips parted. She heard that? She leaned up and kissed my cheek. "It's okay." She smiled. "If my brother approved of you, who am I to argue?"

She took a deep breath and wiped her face with the side of her hand. I pulled the white hanky I brought for this out of my inside pocket. She looked like she could swoon on the spot as she took it. "I came prepared," I told her.

"Thanks," she whispered and dabbed at her eyes at an attempt to keep her makeup intact. When she was satisfied, she gave me one final look before making her way up front. There were about forty people there total, but that was enough to make my girl nervous. The fact that her eyes kept drifting back to find me—as if I were her anchor in the world—was a privilege I didn't even know how to be grateful for. But God, thank you, I'd take it.

I'd even gotten Joey to come by threatening to de-friend her. I wasn't serious, but sometimes my shallow, self absorbed friend who went so out of her way to help me way back when, forgot how to be a friend to others.

She and her boss-slash-boyfriend who was way too old for her, stood next to me and we listened as Maya thanked everyone for coming, the kids for reading the story, the guys for telling us how much her brother helped them through their rough patches. There were parts she barely got through, but the point was she *got through them.*

And she would continue to get through things, and hopefully, she would want me around with her.

The two items were burning a hole in my pocket. Mason and Emma started the dancing off as Mamma held Jackson. Everybody thought it was some kind of little miracle that no matter what, Mamma never remembered Jackson—his name or why she was holding him or whose son he was—but always held him and kept right on playing with him like he was precious and asked questions later.

They had been worried about the baby and Mamma in the beginning, with good reason. With Mamma's memory loss, she might unintentionally hurt the baby if she became frightened, but when they saw how she was with him, Mason decided to test it out. After several of her memory lapses, the baby was still on her lap and she was still confused, but it actually made her confusion a sort of happy one instead of sad. She would ask the baby who he was and coo to him and play. She never cried when she was told about the accident as long as she was holding that baby.

Emma and Mason danced and basically kept everyone's attention on them for me like they promised, and I took Maya's hand and towed her away from everyone to our own little corner near Will's picture. I jingled the two items together in my pocket and gulped.

I prayed that this was the right place, the right time, the right everything. She was so overwhelmed that I was starting to second guess my decision.

She looked at Will's face and I waited, gauging her reaction. She smiled at him and shook her head.

"He sure did make an impression, huh?"

I nodded. "So you're happy?"

She squinted and turned her head. "What kind of question is that?" She leaned in and put her hands on the inside of my suit jacket on my shirt. "Of course I'm happy. I'm…a mix of wanting him here really badly and really happy at seeing all the awesome, sweet things he did. But mostly, happy. It was good to hear all those people talk about him." She grinned and bit the corner of her lip. "And it got you into a suit. I must say, bravo."

I chuckled. "Thanks, baby." I reached into my pocket to make sure I was grabbing the right one. "I got you something."

"You did?" I held it in my fist and kissed her cheek before opening my fingers and letting her see what was sitting in my palm. Her breathing pattern got funny pretty fast. "You remembered my sobriety anniversary?"

"Of course. I plan to remember every year from now on." Hint number one. I read the coin. "Five-year coin." I smiled. "One day I'm going to have one of those."

"Yes, you are," she promised me and reached up to kiss my bottom lip.

"And you're going to be there to make sure that happens, right?" Hint number two.

"Of course," she said, slightly offended. "Why wouldn't I be?"

"You will be," I assured.

"Is there something going on?"

"Just trying to keep my promise to your brother is all." Hint number three.

"Gracious, he was such a butthead, wasn't he?" she scoffed. "Even now he has to have the last word."

I laughed, putting my back to the crowd of people, boxing her in to the wall. "Baby, I'm not sure where you're going with that, but—"

"Where are you going with it?"

I smiled. "I have something else for you. And honestly," I looked up, "no offense, Will, but this had nothing to do with you." I looked back at my girl. My beautiful, scarred, broken, brave, girl. "This has everything to do with you." I pulled the ring from my pocket and held it between my thumb and forefinger." She looked at it. Stared. "I wanted to do this tonight, which may seem strange to some people, but you—this is your bravest night. You faced a roomful of people who loved your brother, you faced five years of sobriety, and now I want you to face me." I leaned in and pressed my lips to her forehead, speaking my words of love right against her so she'd not only hear, but feel them for what they were. "I love you so much. I want to spend every day trying to make all of your cheesy little Chinese fortunes come true. I want to chase you for the rest of my life. Marry me, sweetheart."

Her eyes lifted and they spilled over with tears as her lips parted with her gasp, as if she were just now understanding what the ring was for. My body took a hit like a physical blow.

God help me…she didn't want to.

"*Good night*," I groaned and licked my lips as I leaned back a little to give her some room. "I'm sorry. I shouldn't have done this here—"

My feisty little girl yanked me down to her just like that very first time and proceeded to suck the tongue right out of my head. Little did we know that the party had basically stopped behind us and were now very privy to our not-so-private-very-public proposal. The claps in our ears made her gasp into my mouth and we both turned to find a roomful of happy people. Mason mouthed for me to put the ring on her finger.

I realized I hadn't even done that; we'd just jumped right into our favorite part. "Sweetheart?" I whispered.

"Yes," she laughed and I saw the tears on her cheeks. "I can't believe you even have to wait for the answer. Yes."

Maya joked from that day on about Will's last word. He wanted her taken care of—well, he definitely got that.

We wasted no time. Three weeks later, we got married in a very small ceremony. It was a hard day for her, I knew. It was another reason to keep it small and not make a big monstrosity out of it. Her brother, Dad, and mom weren't there for the big day, and I actually felt pretty guilty for asking her when it came down to it because of that, but she said she would get through it and she did. Emma and Mason helped a lot. And baby Jackson of course. No one could be sad with Jackson around.

We got a little cabin in the mountains for a week for our honeymoon from Mason and Emma as our wedding present and it was the perfect thing. To be away from everything and everyone, to just get lost in each other and fall, over and over and over again.

I chased Maya all over that cabin, and the sounds of her giggles and laughs and many of her *other* sounds would follow me forever into our life together. All I really wanted was someone I could love who would love me for who I was and not expect me to be someone else. Someone I could fall completely for and know that no matter what, she'd always be there when I needed her. And I promised to be that for Maya every day, every second. I was hers—body, soul, and every future Chinese fortune cookie. And she was mine.

Because when you fall, all you really want is for somebody to catch you.

THE VERY END

PLAYLIST

Hide : House of Heroes

Pompeii : Bastille

Fall Asleep : Jars of Clay

Just Like Heaven : The Cure

Between The Raindrops : Lighthouse, Natasha Bedingfield

Stubborn Love : The Lumineers

Wants What It Wants : Andrew Belle

Centered On You : Atlas Genius

Wild : Parade of Lights

Things Ain't Like They Used To Be : The Black Keys

The World I Know : Collective Soul

Dust To Dust : The Civil Wars

Let Her Go : Passeger

Run : Shorelines End

Welcome Home, Son : Radical Face

Let It Be Me : Ray LaMontagne

Say Something : A Great Big World

This Is What It Feels Like : Armin Van Buuren

Falling Slowly : Glen Hansard

THANK YOU:

God, thank you that I'm still here. Thank you for everything.

Thank you so much to my family!
My three guys are always there for me and I'll always love you to pieces for it.

Thank you to my street team, Sweet Street!
You're awesome. I appreciate you. I see the ones who are always sharing. You may not think I see it, but I do. I see J

To the HELLCATS, thank you for ALL you've done for my sanity this year—not just for this book, but for them all. When I have a problem or a good thing, you're the first people I want to run and tell. You always know the right thing to say. You're the best advisers, the best friends, the best authors, the best people I know. Personal, professional, and otherwise. I love you girls. You know how hard I heart you all! Massively!

To the book bloggers and readers, you rock my socks off as always. I do this for you. Even with all the craziness with my health and personal stuff going on, you've all been so awesome. I appreciate all the well wishes! More books to come.

And thank you, Mom. No one out there knows that my mom has Leukemia, on top of lots of other health issues. With my health stuff plus her health stuff, I usually avoid books that deal with cancer and illness and such because they hurt to read. So the fact that this book sprung itself on me was as much as surprise to me as anyone. When I got to the second chapter and Maya is fixing Will's drinks for him, thinking about how all she wanted was for him to get better, I almost scratched the whole project right there. Honest to God. But, I put the book aside for a few days and came back to it. My mom deals with her illness much like Will, and her illness is diagnosed much like Will's. It is what it is and there is no medicine for the type of Leukemia she has. In a way, I guess this book helped me to understand the way she copes and handles her illness better. This book was healing and therapy in more ways than one for me, not just for my own health issues and my mother's, but also for the fact that I grew up around alcoholics and drug addicts. Both the kind that were in denial and the kind that wanted help so badly, like Milo.

If nothing else, I hope this book could be just a little bit of therapy for you, too. Best wishes, and happy endings.

Shelly Crane

Shelly is a *New York Times* & *USA Today* bestselling author from a small town in Georgia and loves everything about the south. She is wife to a fantastical husband and stay at home mom to two boisterous and mischievous boys who keep her on her toes. They currently reside in scorching North Florida. She loves to spend time with her family, binge on candy corn, go out to eat at new restaurants, buy paperbacks at little bookstores, sightsee in the new areas they travel to, listen to new music everywhere, and LOVES to read.

Her own books happen by accident and she revels in the writing and imagination process. She doesn't go anywhere without her notepad for fear of an idea creeping up and not being able to write it down immediately, even in the middle of the night, when her best ideas are born.

Shelly's website:
www.shellycrane.blogspot.com

Other Books by Shelly Crane

Significance Series
Collide Series
Wide Awake Series
Devour Series
Smash Into You

Book by Shelby Fallon
Stealing Grace Series

Now, turn the page for a sneak peek of

Shelly's other novel

Smash Into You

One

It was a case of mistaken identity.

The worst kind.

The kind that ended with appalled, parted lips and evil glares.

The girl was cute enough. Cute wasn't the problem nor the solution for me. I needed to blend and be invisible in the most plain-as-day way and girls like this, girls who just walked up to guys because they had hope somewhere deep inside them that I would fall for that pretty face, were the opposite of plain-as-day. Those kinds of girls got guys killed. At least the kind that were on the run.

She had mistaken me for a normal guy.

And this girl who approached, who could see that I was already surrounded by two, which was more girls than I knew what to do with, must've thought I had a hankering for something sweet. Because when she spoke, her words were soft and almost made me want to get to know her instead of send her packing. But I couldn't stay in this town. It was better to hurt her now when she wasn't invested than it would be to leave one day without a trace.

The girls who were currently soaking up my attention - that they thought they had - they'd move on to their next prey and forget I ever existed. But sweet girls got attached and asked questions.

Don't stop running...

I swallowed and stared bored at her as she finally made her way to me from across the hall. She tucked her hair behind her ear gently and smiled a little. "Hi, uh, can I just-"

Showtime. "Honey, that's real sweet, but I'm not interested." I slid my arm around one of my groupies. I didn't even know her name, but they were always within arm's reach. "As you can see I have my hands full already, but thanks for offering."

She scoffed and looked completely shocked. I took her in, head to foot. She *was* cute. She had a great little body on her and her face was almond shaped. He lips looked…sweet. She was not the kind I wanted within ten feet of me. She was still standing there. I had to send her packing.

I grinned as evilly as I could muster and felt a small twinge of guilt at the vulnerable look of her. I looked away quickly. I didn't even want to remember her face. "Run along, sweetheart. Go find a tuba player, I'm sure he's more your speed. Like I said, I'm not interested."

She didn't glare, and that was a first. Most of the girls who approached a guy were confident, I mean that was the reason they thought they had a chance, right? But she looked a little…destroyed. When her lips parted, it was in shock, it was to catch her breath. I continued my bored stance, though at this point, it pained me in my chest.

But I was doing the best thing for this and any other girl. People who got involved with me were collateral damage when Biloxi came around. He was a ruthless bastard and if he found me and knew someone cared about me, or worse, that I cared about someone, he'd be all over them.

So when she turned without a word and swiftly made her way down the hall, I was thankful. I probably saved her life, though she had no idea. She thought I was an ass, but I was really looking out for her. That's what I told myself as I watched her go. That I had hurt her feelings for a reason, and that she'd get over it.

A slender hand crawled over my collar.

"What's this from?" she asked in a purr and slid her thumb over the long scar from my ear all the way to my chin. "Mmm, it's so sexy."

It followed my jaw line and it was not sexy. Unfortunately, it wasn't the first time some girl had said as much and it pissed me off to no end that they thought that, let alone said it out loud.

It was my reminder of what happened when I let my guard down and it was anything but sexy.

I bit down on my retort and sent her a small smile that showed her I was listening, but she had to work for my attention. "Is that right?"

"Mmhmm," she said and kissed my jaw. "I have a little scar, too." She pointed to the place between her breasts. "Right here. Wanna see it?"

I managed a chuckle. "Is there really a scar there?"

"Pick me up tonight and you can find out," she purred, making her friend giggle.

"Don't think so. Busy."

"Ahhh, boo." She pouted and let her other hand hook a finger into my waistband. "Well here's something to keep you company tonight."

And then she pulled me down by my collar and kissed me. I tried not to cringe away, but her lip gloss was sticky and sweet. When she tried to open my mouth with her tongue I pushed her away gently with my hands wrapped around her bony arms.

"Let's keep this PG, honey. Settle down."

She giggled. I knew she would.

It was the last week of school. It was my last week to pretend that I was still *in* high school. The next time I made a move to evade Biloxi, I'd enroll in college because I was getting too old to be a high-schooler. I didn't know where I was going. I would have graduated from high school years ago, but at the rate I was going, I didn't know if I would have *actually* graduated or not. School was not a place of learning for me, it was a cover, a place to blend in and be normal until Biloxi found me and then I'd be gone to the next place.

This was my life. No time or want for girls, no parties, no movies, no parents.

This was my life, but it wasn't a life at all.

Two

Six months and one lonely birthday later…

College sucked.

The big one.

I had only been going to class for a couple of days and was already dreading the long classes. It was part of my cover. I practically chanted those words in my mind as I trudged everywhere I went. But one thing remained the same. Desperate girls ran rampant and I still wasn't interested. Every once in a while, they were good for a distraction if need be, but mostly…not interested. There was this one chick, Kate, who would not take no for a answer. She'd 'found' me over the summer when I was apartment hunting and hadn't 'lost' me yet, no matter how hard I tried. To get her to go away one time, I'd even given her my phone number. I was going to ditch it in a couple weeks anyway when I undoubtedly had to move again, so it didn't matter, right?

Wrong.

The girl was as annoying as a Chihuahua all hopped up 'cause there's a knock at the door. The texting and come-hithers in text code were nonstop.

And now, as I stared out into the dark rain to see a POS car sideways in the road, I knew the world hated me, had to, because someone had just smashed her car into my truck.

I got out and braced myself. It wasn't easy to pay cash for new cars every time I needed to skip town. It was hard living when you couldn't be who you really were. Finding people to pay you under the table was almost impossible these days.

I groaned and glared at the beauty standing at the end of my truck. "Look at that!"

"I'm so sorry," she began. I could tell she really was, but I was beyond pissed. "I'll call my insurance company right now."

That stopped me. "No!" I shouted and she jolted at the verbal assault. "No insurance."

"Well," she pondered, "what do you mean? I have good insurance."

"But I don't."

She turned her head a bit in thought and then her mouth fell open as she realized what I was saying. "You don't have *any* insurance, do you?"

"No," I answered. "Look. Whatever, we'll just call this even-steven, because you did hit *me*."

"Even-steven my butt!" she yelled and scurried to jump in front of me, blocking my way.

"And what a cute butt it is."

Even through the noise of water hitting metal, I heard her intake of breath. The rain pelted us in the dark. I hoped no one came around the corner. It would be hard for them to see us here in the middle of the road. She might get hurt. Then I wondered why I cared.

"Look, buddy," she replied and crossed her arms. It drew my eyes to her shirt. My eyes bulged 'cause that shirt…well, it was see-through now. She caught on and jerked her crossed arms higher. "How dare you! You're on a roll in the jerkface department, you know that!"

"My specialty," I said and saluted as I climbed in my truck. "Get your pretty butt in your car and let's pretend this never happened, shall we?"

Because if cops and insurance were brought into this, I'd be on the run sooner than I thought.

She huffed. "Excuse me-"

"Darlin'. Car. Now." She glared. "Like right now."

She threw her hands up in the air and yelled, "I knew chivalry was dead!" before climbing in her car and driving away. She didn't know it, but I was being as chivalrous as they come. I made sure she got out of the rain and back into her car, even though she didn't like the way I did it, and I got her as far away from me as I could.

In my book, I deserved a freaking medal for being so chivalrous, because people that stuck with me didn't live long.

Just ask my mom.

Oh, wait, you can't. She died long, long years ago saving my life. I refused to bring anyone onto this sinking ship with me. If it finally did go down, I was going down alone.

Available now through all formats and sites

This paperback interior was designed and formatted by

www.emtippettsbookdesigns.blogspot.com

Artisan interiors for discerning authors and publishers.

Made in the USA
San Bernardino, CA
09 May 2014